THREE HOUSES ON A HILL

NICHOLAS HOLLOWAY

THREE HOUSES ON A HILL

NICHOLAS HOLLOWAY

JPM
PUBLISHING CO

ALSO BY NICHOLAS HOLLOWAY

The Loop

© 2020 Nicholas Holloway

All rights reserved. This book or any portion thereof may not be reproduced or used in any manner whatsoever without the express permission of the publisher or author except for the use of brief quotations in a book review.

Published in Austin, Texas, by JPM Publishing Co. Publisher can be reached via the contact form at www.jpmpublishingco.com.

Ordering Information:
Quantity sales. Special discounts are available on quantity purchases by corporations, associations, and others. For details, contact the publisher at the address above.

Any references to historical events, real people, or real places are used fictitiously. Other names, characters, places and events are products of the author's imagination, and any resemblances to actual events or places or persons, living or dead, is entirely coincidental.

ISBN: 978-1-7332291-7-3 (Paperback)
ISBN: 978-1-7332291-8-0 (Ebook)

Library of Congress Control Number: 2020925090

Printed in the United States of America

JPM Publishing Co.
www.jpmpublishingco.com

To my lovely wife,
for always putting up with my procrastination.

To Michelle & JP,
for taking a chance on me.

And to Harvey,
for being such a good sport.

1

IF YOU ARE READING THIS

By the time you read these pages, I will be bones in the earth.

I have thought of you every single moment since the night I lost you. As I lie here dying, I think of you still.

I have cried an ocean of tears in the hope that I will see your cornflower blue eyes again, though I know it can never be. I wonder where you will end up in this hurricane that has become your life. Much of it is my fault, for I am the man responsible for whatever has happened to you.

Recently, I have taken up a new habit of praying for your health. I sit and talk to the ugly wallpaper of this prison where I will meet my end. I beg the wallpaper to grant you a long, happy, healthy, successful, and fulfilled existence. I pray that you have found tropical waters, for the warmth in your soul never belonged in Alaska.

I pray to no one in particular. Certainly not God, for how can there exist such a being when so much chaos has led to so much death and destruction? I tried for years to seek Him out, to find His working in my life, but here I am, with no answer to His existence.

You came so close to death yourself, but by now you'll have no recollection of the events leading to your rebirth… and to my demise.

As I type this manuscript while the biting snow and winter winds billow outside my window, I silently pray to the wallpaper that one day, you will forgive me.

You do not know me, and you never will. Not entirely. You only know what others have said about me.

This is the knife in my heart.

If you are reading this, then you recently received a package from an anonymous sender. This sender is a friend of mine, a person with whom I have entrusted my story. If I know this person as well as I think I do, you will have ripped open an old potato sack and found this dusty stack of pages. Far be it from my friend to surprise you with shiny wrapping paper.

You've doubtless had thousands of questions over the years…

Where did I come from?

Where is my mother?

Who exactly is my father? And did he really kill that woman?

My purpose in writing these pages is to enlighten you. This is the story of who you are. Who you *really* are.

I will give you a moment…

If you are still reading this, you've surely wanted these questions answered. If you are reading this, then you are clearly old enough to make your own decisions. And if you finish reading these pages and decide that my story is fiction, you have the right to continue thinking of me as a liar and as a murderer. But please, if only for just the amount of time it takes to read these pages, take a moment to process this possibility:

I did not kill anyone.

This is as much my story as it is yours.

I have spent the last two weeks on this icy earth, turning over the details of that blackest of nights in my mind. I share these details with my friend who has agreed to deliver these pages to you. My friend sits in silence, all shoulders and shadows, and watches with sorrow as I type the details of the months leading up to that tragic Christmas night.

My friend remembers some, but not all, of the events of that night and has agreed that I possess something of a photographic memory. Whether this is a blessing or a curse, I have yet to decide. I have replayed the details in my mind far too many times, and I will die thinking of them.

Growing up, I was an athlete, not a scholar. Even now, lying here coughing up my lungs, I would run to you if I could. Kick aside anyone and everyone that got in my way. I'll admit, I've always hated writing. But considering I can't even stand or speak anymore, I've decided to pick up the pen (in this case, an old laptop) and attempt to win you back with my words.

To be as accurate as possible in the retelling of this story, please note that the events documented in this manuscript contain a sort of grit. There is anger. There are a few choice words. There is blood. There is death.

If you are reading this, you are old enough to know the details of your early years in full. I will not hold back.

The events of our story unfold in a small Alaskan town, a place dripping with deceit and soaked in secrets. The inhabitants of this town are of a peculiar sort. They despise the biting cold of winter, but they embrace it as a familiar warmth. They are rich in oil, but they choose poverty over privilege. They drink to celebrate, but they binge to forget.

Why?

Well, who the hell knows?

Perhaps living in shadow is easier than coming to the light. Perhaps silence is louder than truth. Perhaps living in simplicity is more complex than we will ever understand.

Just outside of this little town is a blue, frozen lake. Skirting along its southern shore is a large, horseshoe-shaped hill. Atop this hill stand three very different houses – a Cabin of logs, a Mansion of bricks, and a Shack in shambles. And in each of these houses, our story will unfold.

I suppose the first gift I ought to give you, other than these pages I arranged to be dropped on your doorstep, is my name.

Please don't laugh.

Then again, I wouldn't blame you if you did.

My first name is Lazalier. Pronounced *Laz-uh-leer*. Those who knew me best called me Laz. Not a very cool name. Not a Chuck or a Brad or a Todd. Just Laz. My first name is my mother's maiden name. She was a wonderful woman, my mother, a happy woman who gave herself to an angry and brutal man.

My last name is Brady. Growing up on the outskirts of Ketchikan, my parents and I were known, quite literally, as the Brady Bunch. We weren't, however, quite as happy-go-lucky as our television counterparts. Quite the opposite, in fact.

But I digress.

If you are reading this, you are giving me the voice I never possessed after that dark December night. You are giving me a chance to redeem myself. You are giving me a chance to expose your mother's true killer.

Should you wish to learn more, simply turn the page and read on.

Let's begin.

2

ANCHORAGE AND ANCHORS

O f all the days to see a ghost, I suppose it only makes sense it had to fall on Halloween.

I awoke slowly that morning with a slight buzz in my brain, leaving me to wonder if, just for a moment, I was still asleep. But alas, the sudden and dull throb of a whiskey headache made me recognize that, sadly, I was indeed awake.

And there he was.

He stood at the end of my bed, watching me with those milky, lifeless, and blackened eyeballs as I calmly rubbed the sleep from my own.

One side of his face was completely seared, flaps of meat dripping from his cheeks like melted candle wax. His firefighter's turnout gear, routinely tidy and pressed to impress, was instead scorched with much of the Kevlar fused to his crimson flesh. His hair had been burned clean to the scalp, exposing the blackened bone of his broken skull. Lodged in the fragmented hole in his head was the pick-end of

6

a firefighter's axe.

He stood silent and stoic, charred lips stuck in an eerie grin. It wasn't unlike the playful smirk I'd grown fond of over the years, but now it exuded the shadowy guise of a man caught in a malevolent enigma.

He raised a finger to his lips, willing me to keep our little secret...

I closed my eyes.

I lowered my right hand over the side of my bed until my fingertips grazed a soft head of black hair. I scratched the small head and felt the warm and comforting lick of a dog's tongue. The gentle lick was my morning ritual, a way of reminding me that I was still alive.

When I opened my eyes, ol' Smitty was gone.

It wasn't his first visit, and I knew it wouldn't be his last.

In his place sat my lonely, haggard reflection staring back from my bedroom mirror. Five days of stubble darkened my crooked jaw. My eyes were bloodshot, as they were most of the time these days. My brown hair stuck up on one side and was patched with premature gray. I was only thirty-one, but my hair seemed to believe I was well into my forties. My shoulders, once broad, were slender and bony. As I opened my mouth to yawn, my nose turned upward at the sudden stench of my unbrushed maw.

Slowly but surely, I was falling apart.

And I couldn't care less.

I listened to the faint *clink-clink* of metal dog tags as Harvey scratched his ear. After the separation, my adopted mutt was the only thing reminding me that I wasn't entirely alone.

"Mornin', Harv," I croaked.

As he did every morning, Harvey bounded his front paws on the edge of the bed, big honey-brown eyes glistening. His mouth hung open, large bubblegum tongue lolling in oblivious glee. And as I did every morning, I became mildly jealous of Harvey's zeal for a new day.

"What are you so pumped about?" I asked.

He cocked his head to the side and continued to smile at me. The happy idiot. But hell, I loved him. He never blasted my ass about needing to sweep the floor. He never told me I needed to change my attitude. He never screamed at me for leaving the toilet seat up.

God, how I missed her.

"You're a good lookin' boy, Harv," I reminded him.

I set my feet on the floor, noticed immediately that the hardwood was damn near freezing, and sighed. Three months of neglecting to pay the utility bills had finally caught up with me. I cocooned myself in my old, tattered blanket. My breath billowed and coiled in the frigid air as I let Harvey out onto the balcony to do his business on a small rug of AstroTurf.

To the east, bathed in early morning sunlight, the buildings (you could hardly call them skyscrapers) of downtown Anchorage were dwarfed by the Chugach Mountains, a towering spine of sharp and jagged peaks "dusted with powdered sugar," as my mother would have said.

Though it was only fall, the snow was already falling in torrents. The air was colder this October than it had been in years. The cloud cover hardly ever let up. Part of my semi-depression, if you want to call it that, I attributed to the weather.

8

The rest, however, I attributed to ol' Smitty.

To what I had done to him.

Harvey followed me into the kitchen. I noticed the digital clocks on the oven and microwave had gone out. No electricity then, either.

Great.

I poured myself a mug of cold, stale coffee that had been sitting in the pot for four or five days and choked it down for the caffeine buzz. I pressed the Home button on my phone, and there you were:

Your cornflower blue eyes squinted up at me. Your hair, a brown mess of ringlets, had finally grown back after chemo. Your goofy grin sported small, crooked teeth behind the clear plastic of an oxygen mask. So happy, even when the first two years of your life had been so cruel.

She's a fighter, the doctor had said.

I stared at the screen, hoping that I would be able to see you soon. Hoping that your mother would come back. Hoping that one day, I would find my way out of this funk.

I choked back the sudden golf ball in my throat, but only just.

Noticing that the battery on my phone was almost dead, I scrolled through my apps and went through my morning routine.

I checked my emails.

Nothing.

I checked my texts.

Nothing.

I checked my bank account.

Mega nothing.

And then I heard it. The simplest of sounds. A sound I had been

9

dreading for weeks. The telltale knock on my front door, followed by a soft *whoosh*. An envelope slid under the door, skirting across the frozen floor before it touched my toes.

Great.

I picked it up, opened it, and all at once, I was homeless.

EVICTION NOTICE

That's all I read. It's all I needed to read.

I knew exactly why this letter had come. Even if you're in good with the apartment manager, as I had been with Mrs. Newbury, eventually a person's patience runs thin. Excuses run out. Funds run dry.

I could try to fight it, but what was the point? The tarnish to my name had already grown black. I had no job. I had no savings. I had no idea where my wife had taken my daughter. I had no plan.

But I *did* have Harvey.

Sensing my melancholy, the handsome little turd lapped his tongue against my knuckles, staring up at me with those soft mocha pools.

"Thanks, Harv," I said. I crumpled up the eviction notice and headed for the toilet, Harvey hot on my heels.

***

The inferno of newfound enthusiasm that Harvey's licks had sparked within me were quickly doused when I met with Anchorage Fire Chief Gerald Whitehorse.

"You know I can't hire you back on," Whitehorse mumbled

behind the billowing bristles of his walrus mustache.

"Chief, I – "

"You were good, Brady. I ain't sayin' you weren't. But Smitty's family – well, his wife. It's just, I ain't got time for a lawsuit. We settled with her, y'know, and your job was one of the terms."

"Please, sir, I have to – "

"I can't."

"I'll take a pay cut. I'll wash the engines. I'll do all the grunt work. Just please – "

"No more," Whitehorse said.

And while I wanted to continue to beg, the steel in his eyes said that this conversation was over. I stared at him a moment longer, willing him to reconsider, but the remorse behind those old eyes had long since evaporated. I hung my head and walked to the door.

"Juneau," I heard him say.

"Chief?"

"I know the Fire Chief in Juneau. I'll make a call. No doubt he's heard about what happened with you and Smitty, but I'll do my best to see if he can – "

"No, thanks," I said.

"I wouldn't do it for just anyone, Brady, so take the fuckin' charity offer."

"Anchorage is my home. Not Juneau."

"I ain't goin' to offer again, Brady. It's better than nothin'."

"It's Anchorage or bust, boss," I said.

"Swallow your goddamn pride," he barked, flecks of spittle glistening in his mustache.

"Pride's all I've got left," I told him, then walked out the door.

When I stepped outside, Jack Frost slapped me across the cheek.

I followed 4th Avenue to E Street, and by the time I made it to Town Square Park, my chapped lips were cracked, and my nose was dripping. Graffiti webbed across the concrete plaza. Trees stood dormant and stripped of their leaves. The lawn was peppered with homeless men and women, wrapped up in frayed blankets like wet burritos. They slept and shivered beneath tents of discarded cardboard.

All at once, I saw myself among them. I saw myself, normally cropped stubble grown into a chest-length beard. Hair down to my shoulders, greasy and matted. Back hunched, a discarded Big Gulp cup in my hands jingling with spare nickels.

This is where I was going to end up, fighting with a toothless vagrant over a stolen shopping cart.

It was time to get my life together.

My almost-dead phone buzzed in my pocket. I pulled it out, and there, on the screen, was quite possibly the answer to my prayers: a text from my best friend, Tom Clark.

Tom Clark, Anchorage's district attorney.

Tom Clark, Anchorage's most eligible bachelor.

Tom Clark, the modern sellout I never wanted to become.

The text read, *Stopped by your place. Your apartment manager was banging on the door. I want to help you, bud. Meet at Anchors at 6. Beers on me.*

I read the text a couple of times, sighed, and texted back, *See you then.*

And then, I sent a follow-up.

Bring a phone charger.

***

Anchors had been Tom's and my favorite pub since our freshman year at UAA. As I walked in at a quarter to six, the cold of the impending evening was washed away by the familiar smoky warmth of the hundred-year-old tavern. Though whaling had been outlawed for a century, the place still burned with the fishy odor of whale oil.

Inuksuk, the notorious proprietor of Anchors, visited Barrow every spring to indulge in the ancient whale hunt, a tradition of the Inupiat Eskimos that was regulated and permitted by the federal government and the International Whaling Commission.

"As if we need permission," Inuksuk always said.

I looked around for Tom Clark through small cliques of patrons dressed in Halloween costumes. A pirate here, a vampire there, a very convincing Donald Trump mask pursing its lips in the corner. I checked my phone to see if Tom texted me back, but the battery had been sucked completely dry.

Hopefully he hadn't forgotten to meet me. As much as I hated to admit it, I needed him.

The floorboards plunked as I made my way to the bar. A group of bearded fishermen, mid-gulp, watched me with suspicious eyes.

I took the stool closest to a large Inuit *qulliq*, an elliptical soapstone basin. The *qulliq* held within it the oil of a bowhead whale – Inuksuk's favorite. The wick was a long strip that stretched from one end of the basin to the other, a thin sheet of flame dancing on its edge, tendrils of black smoke swirling in front of my face.

I allowed the smoke to flood my senses. I watched it swirl. I smelled its musk. I passed my fingertips through the fire, listened to the occasional pops of the wick, tasted smoke on the roof of my mouth.

As always, I became hypnotized.

And there, through the sheet of flame and smoke, warped by the heat, ol' Smitty stared at me from across the bar. Those blackened, lifeless eyes were unmistakable. He raised a finger to his lips.

Shushing me.

I closed my eyes. Counted to ten. And when I opened them, he was gone.

In his place sat a woman. Chestnut hair fell in tumbles over the shoulder pads of an olive-green pea coat. High cheekbones descended into an exquisitely pointed chin. Manicured fingertips pushed aside an empty glass before flipping through a stack of papers, diligent in her efforts to jot a note here, make a scribble there. It was her lips that caught my attention, plump and supple, yet pursed in focus.

And when she looked up, large, brilliant green eyes pierced my soul.

I'd been caught staring.

Through the refraction of the fire, a familiar giant suddenly blocked my view of Chestnut.

"Ain't seen your skinny ass in 'ere in months," Inuksuk chortled.

"Been a while, Inny," I replied. I leaned on my stool in an effort to see around his beer belly, to no avail.

"Still locked up in 'at old apartment o' yours?" he asked, fat brown fingers stroking a scraggly beard of salt and pepper.

"Most days," I replied.

"Tom done said you's been havin' some issues since… well, it ain't my place to stain your dirty laundry."

And hell, was he right.

"You heard from 'er?"

"Not once," I said. On instinct, my left thumb rubbed the tan line on the inside of my ring finger.

"'S not right, what she did," he continued. "Takin' the kid and all that."

"Inny, please."

"Sorry, Laz," he sighed. "You want the usual?"

"I don't have any cash on me." *Or at all.*

"'S on me," he offered, then grabbed a bottle of Malamute Alaskan Whiskey and poured me three fingers. "You need a big'n, looks like."

"Thanks, Inny. Do me a favor and add one more thing to my tab. Another of whatever the lady is drinking."

Where this newfound confidence stemmed from, I had no idea. Perhaps the realization that I needed to get my life together had branched into a new desire to start the mating rituals again. It had been a year since the separation, and I was only getting older.

"You got it," Inny replied with a toothless grin.

I sipped the aged Alaskan whiskey with a satisfied grunt and watched as Inuksuk poured a glass of ice water. He set it in front of the woman still absorbed in her paperwork.

"It's on him," Inny told her with a laugh, pointing a thumb over his shoulder in my direction.

Blood rushed into my cheeks. My ears burned. My palms became sweaty. I wasn't very good at this. Hell, I never had to be. I had been with your mother since we were 17. She had pretty much jumped into my life and clung on until something better came along.

Chestnut looked at the ice water, then at Inny, then at me. She stood up. Red-bottomed high heels clicked on the floorboards as she walked around the circular bar, straight toward me.

And to my surprise, she smiled.

"I'm going to need something stronger," she said. She picked up my glass of Malamute and swallowed a finger for herself.

"You must be pretty important," I replied, nodding at her stack of pages. "That's a lot of paper."

"Nothing important. Just finishing some discovery," she answered.

"So, you're a lawyer?"

"Prosecutor."

"Putting away all the bad guys."

"Guilty as charged."

I considered dropping Tom Clark's name, but we were suddenly interrupted by the real thing. Phone charger in hand and dressed in his best Armani suit, my best friend pushed through a group of UAA sorority girls dressed up as sultry kittens, sexy ghosts, and one very busty Sarah Palin.

"Oh, good! You've met," Tom boomed. He clapped both hands on my shoulders and, to my dismay, leaned over and planted a kiss on Chestnut's lips.

"Not formally," I said. I wiped her lipstick off the rim of my glass and downed the rest of the Malamute.

16

"Soph, this is the guy I was telling you about," Tom said, draping an arm over her shoulders. "My best friend and drinking buddy, and the best damn firefighter in Anchorage, Lazalier Brady."

"Ex-firefighter," I corrected him – Chief Whitehorse made sure of that. I held out my hand and she shook it.

"Sophie Dilbrook," she said. "Tom informs me you're in a bit of a career pickle."

My ears grew hotter. I suddenly wanted to slug Tom right in his perfectly rugged jaw. No man wants to be seen as less-than.

"I don't need any charity."

"Just hear her out, Laz," Tom said. He waved at Inny, who brought over three fresh glasses of Malamute. And in his best Don Corleone, he told me, "She'll give you an offer you can't refuse."

I rolled my eyes, then swallowed my second whiskey and the remainder of my pride.

"Okay," I conceded. "Shoot."

Sophie Dilbrook reached into the inner pocket of her pea coat, withdrew a business card, and handed it to me. The watermark was an ornate, serpentine **M** interwoven around a shiny copper anchor.

It read:

MAINSTAY OIL & ENERGY FIELDS
DILBROOK ENTERPRISES
UKIPPA, AK

"You want me to work on a pipeline?" I asked.

"Not quite," Sophie said. "My father is Don Dilbrook, President and CEO of Mainstay. The oil field is one of the richest in the interior. If you've filled up your truck recently, our fuel is likely in your gas tank, and – "

"Had to sell the truck," I interrupted. Over her olive-green shoulder, I watched Tom clap an exasperated hand to his forehead.

"My father has stage four multiple myeloma," she continued. "Terminal blood cancer."

I watched Tom place a hand on her shoulder as wetness glistened on the edges of those big green eyes. She was much too beautiful for her own good.

For *my* own good.

"Mainstay's shareholders are taking care of the company," she continued. "But Mom needs some extra help with Dad and the house. With your background, you'll likely have had lots of experience with first aid and – "

"I'm not a nurse," I said. "I'm sorry."

"It's not a nurse we need," she replied. "Between Mom and the live-in nurse, Dad is well taken care of. But it never hurts to have an extra set of hands. The house is falling apart. It's far too big for two people, but Mom insists on keeping him in Ukippa until – "

Her voice broke.

"All they need is a little help," Tom said. "I told Sophie how you used to be in construction before you got into fire. That, plus the fact you're quick on your feet and know how to handle yourself and others in an emergency, if there ever is one."

"I'm not sure if – "

Tom leaned forward and whispered, "You can't deny you need

the money."

"I promise you my mother will pay you well," Sophie insisted. "I'll pay the expenses for a rental car until you have enough to purchase one in Ukippa. There's a used car lot on the edge of town, and Slim will give you a deal. You'll live in the guest cabin which, in itself, is far bigger and nicer than anything you'll find in Anchorage."

"Well, that there is the biggest issue I have," I said. "I'd have to leave Anchorage. I can't. I have to stay."

My thumb rubbed against the tan line on my ring finger once again, and this time, Tom noticed. He took his hand off of Sophie's shoulder and, instead, placed it on mine.

"She's not coming back," he said.

***

At half past eleven, I stumbled out of Anchors feeling more downtrodden than I had all day. The world spun and my senses were numbed, thanks in large part to Tom's generous wallet and Inuksuk's even more generous pour.

Tom shrugged off my incessant objections and bought me a ride home. As I rode away in the back of the Uber, I couldn't help my drunken eyes from straying out the back window. I watched as Tom wrapped his arms around Sophie and planted a hungry kiss upon those perfectly pouty lips.

After my fifth Malamute, when Tom had excused himself to head to the john, I half-considered advising Sophie to tread carefully. To not get her hopes up. She wasn't the first of Tom's girlfriends I had met that year, and I doubted she would be the last. Out of respect for my best friend, however, I held my tongue.

His eyes may have had a habit of wandering, but nobody on God's green earth had a better heart than Tom Clark. Tom, you see, was the closest thing to a brother I've ever had. He'd been with me when Dad went off the rails, when Mom passed, when I had nothing and nobody except your mother. And when your mother chose thin white lines over our marriage, when she stole you away into the night, Tom swore to me that he would do anything he could to make sure you ended up back in my life. He had a bit of an angry side, as most of us do, and when he saw me in pain, he did anything in his power to make me feel whole again. "You're better off without her," he would say. "Hell, the world would be better off without her."

Without you, though, Tom Clark's words were as dry as the bitter winter winds.

My cab rounded the corner of 8th and Stolt, and Tom and Sophie were gone. I sat back, closed my eyes, slipped my hands in my pockets to warm up, and felt Sophie's business card press into my palm. Part of me knew I ought to have accepted her more-than-generous offer. As Tom had said, I needed to accept that my days with the Anchorage Fire Department were caput. I couldn't, however (and much to Tom's chagrin), give up the hope that one day, Vanessa would return.

And with her, *you*.

I don't remember much of the ride home after that. I recall staggering up to the apartment. Fumbling with my keys. Shining the light of my newly charged phone (thanks, Tom) to navigate through the kitchen, sans electricity.

I fed Harvey a bowl of stale Cheerios, stubbed my toe on

something hard that hadn't been there that morning…

And then, I heard the familiar cry of a toddler.

Drunk as I was, the memory is more vivid than any memory I've had before and any I've had since.

I shined the light at my pulsing toe and noticed I had stubbed it on a small oxygen tank. Five others stood beside it. Next to the tanks was a cheap, plastic crib. And there inside the crib, staring up at me with big, cornflower blue eyes, was you.

My little Ellie-bear.

I was dreaming. I had to be.

But then, I reached inside and, careful not to disturb the oxygen cannula in your tiny nostrils, I picked you up. You simply stared at me, reached out, touched my unkempt stubble, and giggled.

I pulled you close to me, held you tight, and cried.

I dropped my phone into the crib, and noticed the light shining on a crinkled envelope. Wiping my eyes, I cradled you in one arm and ripped it open.

Vanessa's key to the apartment slipped out and clattered to the floor. I pulled out the letter inside, unfolded it, and read nine simple words that made me love and hate your mother all at once.

Laz,
I can't do it anymore. She's yours.
-Ness

***

At midnight, while I watched you sleep, I decided that

homelessness was no longer an option. I'd been given a second chance with you, and I was ready to finally make the right choice.

I loved Anchorage, but I loved you more.

I pulled Sophie Dilbrook's business card out of my pocket. Then and there, I made the call that would alter the course of our lives forever.

Until my dying breath, I will eternally regret making that call.

3

AT THE GATES OF THE ARCTIC

As promised, Sophie Dilbrook set me up with a truck rental agency the next morning. The balding man behind the counter stared at me with a cocked, bushy eyebrow.

"You're nuts, you know that?" he said.

"I've been told," I replied. I bent over to sign my name and handed him my debit card, which was now linked to the charitable thousand dollars that Sophie had given me as an advance.

("Not a gift," she'd said.)

"They're predictin' twelve inches in Fairbanks tonight," Walter (or so his nametag read) told me. "S'posed to be icier'n a snowman's nuts."

"That's pretty icy," I mused.

He handed me the keys and pointed to a neon orange '96 Ford Bronco sitting in the lot like an old, discarded traffic cone.

"That's Betty. In case y'all get lost in the flurry, she won't be difficult to spot," Walter assured me. "Third gear sticks a little bit, so you'll need to wriggle her like an old girlfriend to get her up into fourth."

"If it were that easy, I'd still be married."

Walter laughed at that.

"Ms. Dilbrook said you'd be purchasin' something of your own while you're up in God's armpit. Don't know anyone in Ukippa, but my buddy owns a garage in Bettles, 'bout an hour east. Little used truck lot called Sitka Slim's. Tell him Wally sent ya, and he'll give you a helluva deal."

Walter scratched his bald spot, brushed a few flakes off his pate, and nodded toward the blazing Bronco.

"Better yet, just show him ol' Betty. He's the one who fixed 'er up."

"Sitka Slim's," I repeated. "Got it."

Walter's gaze wandered to the corner of the office, where you sat playing with an old abacus. Your pudgy little fingers jammed the painted wooden pegs along the rusted metal rungs, blue eyes alight with reckless abandon. Your oxygen tank gave a small *pffffft* as you breathed through the cannula fastened around your ears.

"When y'all get settled in something of your own, just leave ol' Betty with Slim and he'll make sure she gets back to me. I'll bill Ms. Dilbrook with however much you go over. The Dilbrooks are a good family to be friendly with, they really are."

"I reckon so," I said. "I promise to take good care of Betty. Thanks for your help, Walter."

"Call me Wally," he said, and shook my hand. He nodded at you and smiled as you furrowed your eyebrows, clacking the abacus pegs together in a perfectly imperfect rhythm. "You take care of that one, y'hear?"

I watched him for a moment, and noticed wetness collecting in the corners of his crow's feet.

"Children should never go before their parents," he stammered.

I didn't press the matter, but I knew then that Wally and I both had children who had touched death's doorknob.

His child, it seemed, had stepped over the threshold.

***

We swung Betty by the apartment (where, with your bouncing little body and one of your travel-sized oxygen cannisters pressed to my chest, we snuck underneath the window of Mrs. Newbury's office) and collected Harvey. I left a note for Mrs. Newbury, thanking her for all she'd done for me the past eight years, that I was sorry about all of the missed payments, and that one day, I would find a way to pay her back.

I took one last, long look at the apartment.

There was the faux marble countertop, where (I apologize for telling you this, but as I said, no secrets) you were conceived. The old and scratched stainless steel refrigerator, where your mother hung your ultrasound and where we would stand, staring at it and smiling long into the early hours of the morning. The faded hardwood floor, where your mother had collapsed, bleeding profusely, when her water broke two months too early. The large dent in the wall, where she had attempted to throw the coffee maker at me.

Eight years of memories. Some good. Most bad. All locked away in my mind.

I left the key on the counter and locked the door from the inside. With you in my left arm and Harvey's leash wrapped up in my right, I said a final goodbye to the apartment.

Time moved slowly after that. My feet stuck to molasses sidewalks as Anchorage tugged at me, beckoning me to stay. I drank in everything, taking mental photographs and storing them in an old chest in the deepest cupboard of my mind. (It is from this particular chest that these vivid memories now flow down my arms, through my fingertips, and into this manuscript.)

A sluggish thirty minutes later found us driving along AK-1, you fast asleep and dreaming in the newly purchased car seat behind me. I watched you through the rearview mirror, my gaze often wandering farther beyond, to the shrinking buildings and the lofty, snow dusted Chugachs in the rear horizon line of my life. To my left, the swirling, splashing white caps of the Knik Arm sloshed under a gray and stormy sky. To my right, Harvey rode shotgun with his overly large bubblegum tongue bobbing out the side of his mouth. And ahead, I saw nothing but an empty highway and a looming fear of the unknown.

We drove ever onward over the Matanuska River (in the summer, a spectacular cerulean, now a silty and rain-washed battleship gray). As we passed through Wasilla, I watched through the rearview as you giggled and pressed your forehead to the window.

"Dawggy! Dawggy!" you jabbered, pointing excitedly at a billboard showcasing a team of huskies bolting through wakes of snow. The huskies dragged a dog sled behind them and within it, a driver cocooned in elk skin.

IDITAROD TRAIL SLED DOG MUSEUM,
NEXT RIGHT

"Next time, Ellie-bear," I said. "I promise."

Lying here now, I realize I never got the chance to keep that promise.

***

Betty's windshield wipers needed replacing. They scratched loudly across the windshield, leaving streaks of icy white upon the glass. My vision got so bad that twice, I had to pull over and use the ice scraper I'd found under the seat to clear a porthole in the frost.

My plan had been to drive straight through, beyond the Gates of the Arctic to Ukippa. The weather, however, had other plans for us.

By four o'clock, we were forced to stop in Fairbanks. The Alaskan winter sky had darkened to a gloomy steel, patches of indigo occasionally breaking through the clouds. As promised, the flurry that Walter the rental man warned me about was in full swing. The roads leading out of Fairbanks would be closed until snowplows could get through to lay salt.

And so, we shacked up for the night.

The Muckrock Motel was a shabby collection of black and white cabins standing like a rookery of penguins huddled against the cold. The front office was a rusted shipping container with a rectangular hole cut in the steel, affixed with an equally rusty door. Small squares had been carved out, and where glass should have been, instead were windows of clear vinyl that whipped and popped against the whistling wind.

An intimidating Inuit woman with broad shoulders presented me with the key to Cabin 13.

"Thirteen. Just my luck," I said with a smile.

She glared at me behind coke bottle glasses, unamused.

"There's a space heater in the bathroom closet. Toilet's on the fritz, so you'll have to use the outhouse."

"It's ten degrees out there."

"Just your luck," she reminded me.

Cabin 13 smelled like stale cigarettes and urine.

I sat down on the edge of a musty bed. A plume of dust billowed around me as the old springs groaned their discontent. It was obvious that this room hadn't seen a human in months.

I pressed my face into my palms and pushed filthy fingernails through my graying hair. The room cost me forty-seven dollars for the night, and while this would have been chump change last November, I was beginning to feel that all-too-familiar itch in my bones.

Stress. Fear. Angst.

Whatever you want to call it, money troubles were something I'd never had to deal with.

Forty-seven dollars felt like a fortune.

I took a deep breath and held it. Considered holding it until my heart slowed. Until the backs of my eyeballs swelled. Until I ceased to exist. And I might have, had you not been there with me.

I breathed out, in, and then out again. Deep and slow until the itch subsided, and my pulse evened out. I opened my eyes, peered through my fingers, and watched you.

Harvey chewed lazily on a flap of neon green fur he'd ripped from his muddy tennis ball. His long black tail swished back and forth along the vomit-stained carpet (*or was it blood?*), and you tried to grab it. Over and over, you reached, and he swished it away. At first, you grunted in disapproval, but after the fourth unsuccessful attempt, you laughed.

And as I watched, I began to smile.

For months, I felt like my lowest self, a piece of filth that had no money, no wife, no child, no home of my own. But now here we were, with a little less than a thousand dollars. You were laughing, and I was smiling.

We didn't have a lot. But we had each other.

And Harvey, of course.

Your stubby little fingers grazed his black fur, and finally, you caught his tail. He released the tennis ball and planted a wet, slobbery kiss on your lips, your cheeks, your forehead. You giggled profusely, and I laughed.

The two of you, a dog and a sick toddler, seemed completely at peace. There was a roof over our heads. The space heater kept us warm. I had two cans of Campbell's Chicken Noodle Soup in my bag.

We were halfway to our new home, I realized, and I wiped a tear from my cheek. I hadn't failed you.

At least, not yet.

Later that night, Shania Twain trilled about how she felt like a woman from the speakers of my phone as we devoured cold soup. I fed you an entire can with a plastic spoon before I sucked mine down directly from the aluminum rim. Harvey munched on the cheap dog food I'd purchased at Wally World that afternoon.

A feast fit for kings.

After dinner, you nodded off, drool running from the corner of your pouty little lips. I had no intention of wrapping you in the sheets left on the bed, fearing you'd contract some new disease. Instead, I wrapped you in my jacket, zipped you up, placed your oxygen tank beside the bed, and made sure the cannula was fastened securely around your ears and into your nostrils.

Harvey jumped on the bed and curled up beside you, honey-brown eyes fixed on me. And while I normally never allowed him on the bed, the newfound kinship between the two of you had softened my stubborn heart.

"Only for tonight," I told him, and then scratched him between his floppy ears. My head hit the pillow, and in seconds, I was out.

***

Thick, acrid smoke enveloped my senses. My eyes stung with ash. I choked on scorching heat, sucked clean of oxygen. Funnels of white-hot flame roared up the walls, holding me hostage in a fiery hell. I tried to scream his name, but my voice held no tone against the raging inferno.

I have to find him.

Slabs of flaming roof crashed down onto the floor, spitting embers into my face. The place was coming down, and fast.

I have to find him.

I brushed the ashes out of my eyes, held my breath, and bolted down a scorched and blackened corridor. My legs felt like lead, my turnout gear heavier than I'd ever known it to be. Exhaustion was settling in, and with it, tunnel vision began to cloud my senses. I was going to pass out. I was going to die.

I have to find him. He gave me his helmet, after all.

Again, I yelled his name into the flames. There was no response.

I swerved around a corner and narrowly avoided a flaming beam as it struck the floor at my feet. I shielded my face as a sheet of fire rose in front of me. Without thinking, I jumped through the wall of flame, and there, at the end of the corridor, I saw a doorway.

And in the doorway, I saw his boots.

"Smitty!" I screamed a third time. His boots didn't move.

I sprinted the length of the corridor, fell to my knees by his side, and felt my heart stop. His face had partially melted. His skin was black with soot. The whites of his eyes swiveled behind flickering lids. And there, protruding from the top of his skull and embedded into his brain, was the pick of a fireman's axe.

My axe.

What have I done?

He wheezed as the life drained out of him. The flames rose higher around us, pressing in. But I felt nothing. I saw nothing. All I could do was listen to the ragged wheezing of his lungs. Louder and louder it became, until the roar of the flames was but a whisper. My eardrums pounded with the sound of his wheezing...

And then, all went black.

***

I awoke in Cabin 13 of the Muckrock Motel, drenched in sweat.

But still, I heard wheezing. I looked down, and just as it had in my dream, my heart stopped.

The cannula was still properly affixed to your nose, but you were blue in the face. Lips purple. Tiny lungs begging for oxygen.

Panic spread through my body.

I weighed the large oxygen tank in my hands. It was heavy and mostly full. I tried twisting the valve. It was still on. I checked the pressure gauge. All was normal.

Instincts kicking in, I tugged the cannula out of your nose, pinched your nostrils together, and passed my breath into your lungs. I checked your pulse, and it was racing as fast as mine. You wheezed once more against my lips, and then, you stopped breathing altogether.

"Come on, Ellie, breathe," I yelled. I exhaled into your lungs again, but you began to fade.

Harvey awoke and licked your cold face.

"Get out of the way!" I screamed at him. Brown eyes wide, he bolted to the corner of the room with his tail between his legs. And then I heard it.

Not a wheeze, but a soft *hisssss*.

I trailed shaky fingertips along the cannula tube until they met cold, wet, green fur. The middle of the tube rested against Harvey's tennis ball. Having grown bored of the damn thing, he had found something new to chew on.

I wrapped my right hand around the holes in the tube, tight enough to stop the leak but loose enough to allow oxygen to pass through. I pushed the cannula back into your nose, pushed another breath into your lungs, and then I waited.

"Come on, Ellie-bear," I muttered. "Come on, baby girl."

But still, you were blue. I checked your pulse, and it was weak.

"Breathe, Ellie, breathe!"

I gave you one more breath. And then, I did something I hadn't done in ten years. I closed my eyes and whispered three small, simple words.

"Please, God. Please."

***

At 4:47 a.m., the glass doors of the Fairbanks Walmart opened.

Dry, freezing wind stung my cheeks as I held you, fast asleep against my left shoulder. Your tiny chest rose and fell, cheeks glowing their usual fat, rosy red. The wheels of your oxygen tank clunked on the asphalt behind me as the newly purchased cannula did its work.

The moon glowed high overhead, and while the air was a biting four degrees, the snowfall had at least stopped. This far north, the sun wouldn't rise for another five hours.

Having left the sordid memory of the Muckrock Motel behind us, Betty's chained-up tires rolled mile after mile along the newly plowed and salted highway. And though we were both breathing easier now, I couldn't help watching you sleep through the rearview every few seconds.

It had been far too close a call.

I began to recognize just how fragile you actually were. How lucky I had been, there in unlucky Cabin 13, when you finally took a breath. And another. And another. Lymphoma had taken its toll on your lungs for too long. I realized then that even though you were in remission, you weren't out of the woods. Not by a long shot. Your mother had left you in my care with enough oxygen to last two, maybe three weeks. But what would I do then, when you had sucked those tanks dry? I didn't have insurance, after all.

This was my reality now. Our reality. The severity of it was finally settling in.

As the star-studded blackness slowly became a lilac sky, Harvey yawned from the passenger seat. He looked at me with saddened eyes. Somewhere in the depths of those big eyes, he knew he had done something wrong.

"You're a good boy, Harv," I reassured him.

I felt bad for yelling at him, reminding myself that at two years old, he was still a puppy. A big puppy, but a puppy, nonetheless. Clueless, carefree, and curious.

"Stick to the tennis ball from now on, bud."

I scratched him between the ears, and he perked up.

Lilac became pink, and then periwinkle. And when the sun finally traipsed over the mountains, we arrived at the Gates of the Arctic.

4

THREE HOUSES ON A HILL

I should have seen that last snowstorm for what it really was:

A warning.

A sign alerting me to kiss Fairbanks goodbye, swerve Betty around, and turn tail back to Anchorage. Beg Chief Whitehorse for his recommendation. Do my damnedest to ensure that I land a position with the Juneau Fire Department, and with it, the best insurance I could afford to maintain your welfare. Any smart, sane, desperate man would have done just that.

I was smart. I was sane. And I was beyond desperate. Why, then, had I chosen the icy wilderness over the bustling Alaskan capital?

Well, one reason was that Smitty was back.

I had gone two months without seeing him, two months that I had successfully forced his memory, his ghost, deep into the forbidden trunk of my mind. A year of sleepless nights had finally given way to two months of dreamless slumber. Countless bottles of Malamute had proven the only effective sleep-aid against the spectral memory

35

haunting my dreams.

The red-rimmed eyes of the insomniac had become the red-rimmed eyes of the closet alcoholic. But even so, I slept.

Why, then, had he come back?

This I asked myself at least a dozen times since leaving Anchorage, and at least a dozen times I had no answer. He'd visited me on Halloween morning, and again last night. And his visits, like they always did, only solidified within me one simple truth:

I would never... *could* never fight fire again.

The other reason for choosing Ukippa was the mystery of the unknown.

I was born in a trailer in Ketchikan. Spent my childhood tossing a baseball to a hard-knuckled, God-fearing, sharp-shooting mother in the suburbs of Juneau. Was forced to pay monthly visits to my stiff and sour deadbeat father in Skagway. Wrecked my first truck in Wasilla. Went to college and through the academy in Anchorage, then met your mother and had you.

I was, in every shape and form, a Southie. And on top of that, I was a city boy. And look where it had landed me.

Here was my opportunity for a fresh start. Perhaps the life, the security, the purpose I'd dreamt of for so long was waiting for me, for *us*, in the north. In the bush. In Ukippa.

And if I'm being entirely honest, I must confess I had one more reason for accepting Sophie Dilbrook's job offer.

And that reason *was* Sophie Dilbrook.

I was excited to get to Ukippa, if only for a chance to see her again.

***

My first impression of Ukippa was one of quiet trepidation.

The first few houses on the outskirts of town (if you want to call them houses) resembled hovels built from corrugated iron, discarded sheet metal, and driftwood, each distanced about two miles apart from the next. Lonely, gray islands casting long shadows on a vapid sea of white snow and black ice.

It was noon when we drove past. The pale November sun was low on a twilit horizon, providing no warmth to ease the chill in my bones. A chill brought on by more than just the subzero temperature.

Through the windows of one hovel, I noticed the soft, gentle flicker of firelight. A lone, elderly silhouette looked up from her careful dishwashing and stared with milky eyes as we drove past. At another hovel, an Inuit man ushered his two young daughters inside, watching me while he cocked an old shotgun. Further still, one hovel boasted a steel sign tattered with bullet holes and a simple greeting in red paint (or what I sincerely hoped was red paint):

SOUTHIES WILL BE SHOT

Clearly, we weren't welcome here.

Harvey sat with his nose pressed to the passenger side window, breath fogging up the glass. He growled at a herd of caribou, watching as they hoofed at the snow to graze on tufts of dead grass. You sat silently in your car seat, glassy eyes fixated on the mountains as they grew larger and began pressing in around us, encircling us on all sides like towering, snowy vultures.

The township itself was less intimidating than the unfriendly

37

shacks we passed on the outskirts. Off the main road were three intersecting lanes, each ending in a cul-de-sac complete with a collection of small, wooden homes. Twenty in all, perhaps. This was a census designated area.

Small and isolated. Neat and compact.

The main road led to what appeared to be a town square with a Village Peace Office (a sort of minuscule equivalent of a police station), a humble general store, and the town's only watering hole, a dive bar called Galoshes.

What anyone did for fun here was entirely beyond me. I'd heard that bush folk maintained a constant buzz to combat both boredom and bitter cold, and I assumed that's why Galoshes was able to stay open for business.

It was here that I had arranged to meet my new employer.

She stood on the porch of Galoshes, waiting for me with a simple smile and a wave. She possessed the same lovely features as her daughter, albeit a bit grainier, with high cheek bones and a rosy, snow-baked tan. It was in her face that I could picture Sophie in thirty years. She wore no makeup to cover the dark circles and laughter lines crowding her confident eyes. Her hickory hair was streaked with gray, falling long and thick to her lower back, longer than any I'd ever seen on a woman her age. It suited her.

I parked, kept the heater on and the engine running.

"You must be Lazalier."

"Laz," I replied and held out my hand. She took it in her own, boasting a firm, calloused grip that bespoke decades of manual labor. She exuded a warmth I had only ever known in two other people: my own mother, and you, Ellie-bear.

"Gloria Dilbrook," she said. "Welcome to Ukippa. It ain't the prettiest place on earth, I know, but it's done our family very well."

"I like it," I lied.

"Sophie's told me a lot about you."

"That can't be good."

"Hush," she said, offering a smile. "Hard times keep us human."

"Then human I surely am."

"I hope you don't mind driving me back up the hill. I had Lizanne drop me off on her way out."

I had no idea who Lizanne was, and I didn't ask.

"No problem," I said.

"I'll give you the ol' tour." Gloria's gaze drifted over my shoulder at Betty. "I'm surprised you risked the drive at all. Shows a lot of balls braving the snow this far north. Most people take the air taxi." She cocked an eyebrow and shrugged. "Not that anyone ever visits anymore."

I didn't bother asking if she meant Sophie.

"Probably for the best that you did drive. Will help with the work," she added. "We have a spare Silverado that Don can't drive anymore, but the damn thing is shiftier than a kid with his hand in a cookie jar. That one will do you just fine."

I found her inherent charm and her adoration of the township slowly altering my skewed disposition towards Ukippa.

"Care for a drink before we head out?"

"Rain check," I replied. "Got a couple stowaways."

Gloria squinted her eyes and noticed Harvey through the

window, happily oblivious with his tongue pressed to the windshield. She noticed you, too, because her normally brash eyes became soft.

In them, I saw sadness, and I saw understanding.

"She's beautiful."

"Yes, she is," I replied.

"Like I said, you've got balls." She looked at me, and her eyes became hard once again. "Keep a *very* close eye on her."

Gloria wriggled her fingers into a pair of old, insulated mittens. She clapped her hands twice, then brushed past me, feet crunching on the snowpack.

"Onward!"

***

She led me out of town and to an old service road, one that snaked a few miles through an ascending valley. Within ten minutes, a break in the mountains gave way to a sharp right turn, and suddenly, we followed the icy road through a thickening wood of spruce and hemlock.

More than once, Betty's back tires fishtailed on an invisible patch of black ice, sending my stomach into my throat before she regained tread on the slushy asphalt. I released my breath, and Gloria laughed.

"Are we even in Ukippa anymore?" I asked.

"Technically, yes. This is Horseshoe Bend, the closest road south of the Gates of the Arctic. You'd need a plane to go any further north. You'll take this road through the woods for about three miles, then you'll hit... well, I'll let you see for yourself when we get there."

I chewed the inside of my cheek and glanced nervously in the rearview, at you.

"She'll be fine. I promise," Gloria said. She placed a hand on my arm as I drove, then turned and glanced into the backseat, where Harvey snoozed with his head in your lap. Dusk began to settle, and you began to doze.

"Can I ask what happened to her?" she asked.

"You just did," I replied.

"If you'd rather we didn't talk about—"

"Her mother had an accident," I told her, my hands gripping tighter to the steering wheel. I didn't mention the overdose. "Ellie was born two months early. Three pounds, nine ounces. Her lungs hadn't fully developed. They kept her in the hospital for four months, until her lungs started to inflate on their own. But once they did, we discovered another problem."

I coughed to disguise my frailty.

"We don't have to—"

"High-grade B-cell pulmonary lymphoma." I'd relayed the information enough times in my life, to my parents, to Vanessa's parents, to friends, to Tom Clark. It was a phrase I knew too well, one I wished would never have to leave my lips. I focused on the frozen snowbank, green and white trees whizzing past my periphery.

"Lung cancer," I heard her say. It wasn't a question.

"How do you – "

"In another life, I was a nurse," Gloria said.

"No shit."

She reached behind her seat and stroked soft fingertips along your plump little forearm. "Too much shit," she confessed with a sigh. "Most people get it from smoking. But kids… that's different. A complication of immune suppression. Given her prematurity, it makes sense."

"What sort of medicine were you in?"

"Pediatric oncology at Ecclesiastes in Fairbanks."

"Well, what are the chances?" I said with a smile.

"Sophie," she deduced. "Nothing gets past that girl. Clearly, she didn't send you here just to fix fences."

In my drunken stupor at Anchors, I'd mentioned you, Ellie. You and your condition. I now remembered all of it, confessing my worries to Sophie while Tom had gone to the bathroom. Remembered her running her fingers through my hair. Remembered her wiping the tears from my scratchy cheeks.

"She's in remission, though" I added hopefully, now keen to discuss matters of importance with someone who actually knew what I was talking about. "That's the last I heard."

"The last you heard?" she asked, cocking a tussock eyebrow.

The new light in my eyes vanished.

"Her mother got bored of me. Of us. Met a guy she tended bar with. Next thing I knew, she and Ellie were gone."

"Bitch."

"Yes, she was."

I reached into my jacket, pulled out the note Vanessa left in your crib, and handed it to Gloria. She unfolded it and gave it a once-over, then clicked the inside of her cheek and handed it back to me.

"Some women aren't meant to be mothers."

We drove in silence for a few minutes. The trees thinned out as we rounded a sharp bend, and immediately, the breath was ripped from my chest.

A vast lake dominated the mountainous bowl, a miniature sea of cerulean blue and foaming white caps that stretched all the way to a tall, snowy peak towering over the northern bank.

"Jesus," I whispered, my eyes glassy as I drank in the view.

"Welcome to Lake Adamant," she said. "This is why we stay."

I guided Betty along the road that hugged the icy shores of Lake Adamant. I noticed that the northern edge of the lake, shaded by the watchful gaze of Mount Poe, Ukippa's highest peak, had already frozen over. The temperature was well below freezing and six weeks of endless darkness would soon be upon us. I deduced that in the impending night of the coming weeks, the rest of Lake Adamant's choppy waters would become still and solid.

Out on the ice stood a single shanty, a fishing house for those brave enough to hunker in, drill a hole, and cast a line. As we drove further on, I couldn't help pitching my gaze through the rearview.

Call it intuition if you want, but something about that little shanty caused goosebumps to rise along my arms and neck.

"There she is," I heard Gloria say.

I shifted my eyes forward as snow began to fall on the windshield. I flipped the lever, and as the windshield wipers did their work, I observed a large hill forming a crescent along the southern shore of Lake Adamant.

"Horseshoe Hill," Gloria proclaimed.

She pointed a finger, and there atop the eastern ridge stood a massive house silhouetted against the trees, all turrets and towers.

"Home, sweet home," she whispered.

She led me to an ornate iron gate at the base of the hill, which had lost its sheen to countless winters and now sported a rusty veneer. She got out, and as she crunched along the hard-packed snow to unlock the gate, I looked over my shoulder and watched you continue to doze, and then I ruffled Harvey's ears.

Gloria yanked the gate along its swiveled radius carved in the snow and beckoned me through before closing the gate and climbing back inside the warmth of the cab. We slowly ascended a steep road, chained tires shifting on the ice. With your safety at the forefront of my skull, I drove slowly upward, following the countless dizzying switchbacks.

Stars began to glitter across a velveteen sky and along the blackening ripples of Lake Adamant below. The first night of our new life had come. As we drove ever upward, evening succumbed to nightfall, and nightfall surrendered to darkness.

"This must be a big change from Anchorage," Gloria said.

"Bigger than most."

The tires crunched on an abrupt gravelly grade, and as we turned the final rise through a scattering of trees, I set my eyes upon the Dilbrook Mansion.

The front yard was an acre of sloping white, peppered with tall black spruces covered in snow, giving the appearance of yuletide trees. I imagined I could smell Christmas.

The house itself was constructed of log and river rock, four stories rising high in the middle while the eastern and southern wings stretched with endless windows and concluded in cylindrical turrets.

Cupolas atop the turrets possessed panoramic windows, yellow light blazing through the frosted glass like strange, arctic lighthouses. Through the darkness, I could just make out twin weathervanes depicting howling wolves. I didn't realize it at the time, but I was so affixed to the spectacle that I stopped the car, my jaw hanging slack. I'd never seen a more beautiful home.

A prickle of bitter envy was enough to convince me to look away.

"I know what you must be thinking," Gloria spoke softly beside me. "How can two people live so excessively while their neighbors sleep in squalor?"

She sent her gaze first at the estate, and then at the moon.

"Before I met Don, I would've asked myself the same thing. I would've raised hell. Broken windows. Thrown eggs." She then looked at me and squeezed my shoulder in a motherly sort of manner. "But this is my life. I can't apologize for it. He's done so well. Given me so much. Me, and Sophie, and S—"

She stopped. I noticed moonlit hurt glittering in her eyes.

"Anyway," she said, and coughed to clear her throat.

"Can I meet him?" I asked. "Don?"

"Not tonight, I'm afraid," she said, then looked back at you and smiled. "You and I have something in common. We're both in love with, and tending to, very sick people. Lizanne will have given him his meds, and he'll be out for the count. But I promise, I'll give you the full tour tomorrow," she said.

Gloria pointed toward a break in the trees, where the gravel road disappeared around another bend.

"For now, let's get your little one to bed."

Around the bend and half a mile later, my spirits rose to new heights.

I'd grown up in modest, two-bedroom trailers. Spent all of my twenties scrounging money to afford rent in tiny one-bedroom apartments. Two days ago, I'd been momentarily homeless. But here and now, Gloria Dilbrook presented me with a home. A *real* home.

The Cabin, as she'd modestly named it, was anything but.

A steady, stone foundation boasted a first-floor garage that, in itself, was twice as large as the Anchorage apartment we'd fled. Harvey's first plan of attack was to sniff every inch of the vast snowy yard, leaving his own slushy yellow marks here and there, where I assumed countless wild animals had done their business before him. I held you tightly in my arms, listening to you giggling happily as my boots crunched up a steep flight of snowy steps.

I followed Gloria onto the wide exterior deck that wrapped around the entirety of the log building. She unlocked the large oak front door, handed me the key and together, we stepped into the foyer. Wide, glorious windows glowed from within. A chandelier, worth far more than our lives, hung over a large oak dining table.

"Sorry if it smells a bit musty," she told me with a shrug.

"It's perfect," I remember whispering in awe.

"Been a while since anyone's lived here. We initially built it as a guest house, but I suppose we'd actually need guests to call it that."

I carried you into a massive kitchen adorned with new, stainless steel appliances that barely looked used. I set you down, careful to make sure your cannula didn't tangle as you tugged open a cabinet and began pulling out old Tupperware, banging the plastic containers playfully on the marble floor.

"You'll probably want to do a bit of sweeping," Gloria said, leaning a shoulder against the wall. "Our last groundskeeper was a bit of a slob before he left."

"Why would anyone want to leave?"

"A story for another time."

She showed me around the rest of the Cabin, including an enormous master bedroom with a four-poster California king bed, another large room that Gloria herself had painted periwinkle blue (for you, Ellie, complete with a crib and ten tanks of oxygen), a makeshift office with a brand new touchscreen desktop computer, and a den with a basalt fireplace and a 70-inch curved plasma screen TV.

"Call us yuppy, but we like to stay current," Gloria confessed, pulling on her mittens and parka. "Anyway, y'all need your sleep. Come by the house in the morning and we'll get you situated with little jobs to start you off."

I let out a sharp whistle. Harvey bolted out of the trees, up the steps, shook the snow off his midnight coat, then trotted into the Cabin.

"Thank you," was all I could manage.

"Thank *you*," she responded.

"Can I give you a ride back?"

"I'll be fine. I enjoy the walk."

I followed her out onto the snowy deck, and was surprised when she gave me a firm, warm hug.

"You really have no idea how much of a help you're going to be."

And with that, she walked down the steps.

As I watched her go, I suddenly noticed a single light glowing faint on Horseshoe Hill's western ridge. I squinted my eyes and could just make out the outline of a tiny, wooden shack.

"Who lives there?"

"Sorry?"

"That third house," I said. "Is it another one of yours?"

I watched as, even in the warmth of the Cabin's doorway, Gloria's face became white. Her smile fell slack. Her cheery eyes became hard.

"Do me a favor, Laz," she said.

"Of course."

"Don't you go near that house."

"Why not?"

"Because," she sighed. "A devil lives there."

5

THE GIRL IN THE SNOW

Don Dilbrook sat at the window in the Mansion's front parlor, staring out into the snow. He looked healthier than any cancer victim I'd ever seen. His skin was taut and firm. His peroxide white hair was messy and balding, but not unkempt. The pungent and sour smell of impending death I'd long associated with oncology wards was missing, replaced instead by expensive cologne.

Apparently, money *did* stop the spread of decay.

But there was something definitely wrong with him, that much was evident.

Drool dripped down the side of his left jowl, one eye fixed on the frosted glass while the other swung upward at a lazy angle. An oxygen mask was fixed to his face, fogging with each weakened breath he took. He couldn't move on his own; each time he began to tilt to the edge of his chair, Gloria gripped his thin shoulders and propped him back up like an old and unused puppet.

From what Gloria told me when I arrived (and from what

I conjured up on the web courtesy of the touchscreen desktop the Dilbrooks had so generously left in the Cabin), Don Dilbrook was the only reason his clients signed on to any oil contract. He had the uncanny ability of knowing which stretches of the interior had potential to produce the most oil. Growing from just two oil wells to an impressive fifty-five in the first four years of business, Dilbrook Enterprises was renamed Mainstay Oil & Energy Fields. Wildcatters came to him for both business advice and family advice. And after decades in the industry, his name spread from a flicker of candlelight into an oil-soaked inferno. He was an impressive man, Gloria made sure I understood. And in addition to his work, she said, he did the best he could for his wife and children.

Children…

Sophie had a sibling. A sibling Gloria didn't like to talk about.

I didn't press it. At least, not yet.

***

"How long does he have?" I asked.

"Who knows? They told us he had six months, three years ago. He's nowhere near in remission, but he isn't getting any worse. Kind of a twisted cancer limbo. Typical Don, though, fighting like the old stubborn ass he is."

Gloria handed me the long handle of a paint roller and poured liquid sage from a can and into a tray. I dipped the spongey roller into the paint and, with a reassuring nod from Gloria, I rolled a wide smear up the wall. The smear left a new warmth, and with a satisfied grunt, Gloria dipped her roller and followed suit on the adjoining wall.

My first job, the east library.

The high, arched ceiling sported dark maple tresses that formed a vaulting web overhead. A clerestory of colorful, stained-glass windows stretched around the room, each depicting a different species of flower, from Alaska's own Alpine forget-me-not and electric blue scorpion grass to vivid fireweed that seemed to blaze with the weak winter sun shining through its core. In all, the library was reminiscent of a wooden cathedral. Bookshelves towered high along the walls. Thousands of colorful leather-bound volumes slept collecting dust, titles sweeping from the epics of Homer to the horrors of Poe to the adventures of a famous boy wizard.

"Quite the collection," I remarked, rolling streaks of sage green over slate gray.

"Ain't a book up there he hasn't read," Gloria replied. She blew a stray strand of hair out of her eyes and scratched her forehead with the back of her hand, leaving a smudge of paint on her weathered face. "Not much else to do this far north."

"I can imagine."

I turned my head and smiled. You sat on the floor in a far corner, sipping your oxygen, muttering sweet-nothings to yourself, and scribbling with crayons on a pad of paper Gloria had provided.

"He was a writer, actually, before all this." She swept her arm around the room and sighed. To this day, I'm not entirely certain that Gloria Dilbrook gave one shit about the excessive estate.

"Books on business?" I asked.

"Creative writing, believe it or not. He wanted to write novels for a living. Was going to be the Alaskan Hemingway, he always said."

"What happened?"

"His father."

Gloria set down her roller and moved to open a window. Though I'd always rather enjoyed the resinous chemical perfume and slight head-change from fresh paint fumes, the sudden blast of cold air cleared my senses.

"Old Joe Dilbrook told Don his writing was shit," she continued. "That he'd do better in the family oil trade. He wasn't wrong about the oil bit, obviously, but he couldn't have been more wrong about Don's writing."

"Is he published?"

"He tried. God, for years, he tried. A couple agencies in New York were interested, but nobody ever took the bait. He called, and he begged. He revised, and he rewrote. But he never caught his big break."

She chewed her cheek and went back to painting.

"That kind of failure for so many years, it crushed his spirit. He tried to write another book, but the words never came. Then we found out I was pregnant, and he called his dad the next morning. Never looked back on what could have been. Never mentioned the book again. Just worked hard to keep us above the waves."

"And now you're sailing on top of them."

"And now we're sailing on top of them," she agreed. "The writer in him never fully left, so he coped with reading. When he wasn't working, he read. God, how he read. Nose buried in a new book every three or four days." Gloria offered me a sad smile and continued. "The kids came, the money grew, the books piled up, and now here we are with a huge, lonely house and a library we don't even use."

"The cancer?" I asked.

"The cancer," she confirmed. "He hasn't added a new book to the shelves in three years. No more books for Don, and there never will be."

***

We finished up in the library around suppertime, both of us streaked with sage green paint. I carried in a sloshing bucket of hot water from the kitchen. Gloria plunged the paint rollers into their steaming bath, and then clapped her rugged hands together.

"How about a beer before the chili?" she asked.

"Make it two," I said with a smile. Something about a long day's work sparked something familiar inside me, something I hadn't felt since before Smitty.

"Do me a favor and fold up the drop cloths," she said.

"Yes, ma'am."

I watched her hobble away into the abyss of the Mansion, and then I took a moment to relish the silence, to flood my nostrils with the soothing sharpness of drying paint and old oak. I looked around the cavernous room stretching high and wide. Three days ago, the walls of a miniscule apartment pressed in on me. Now, I stood in the vastness of money and power.

I gave you a kiss on the head, adjusted the flow on your oxygen tank. And then, I set to work.

It took twenty minutes to make my way from the western

53

entrance of the cosmic library to a large writing desk set against a vast wall of books. My arms were stuffed with folded drop cloths, the plastic sheets crumpled and tarnished with dried paint and faded shoe prints. Unsure where Gloria would want them, I folded the last one and set them on the desk.

The desk itself was enormous, a hearty and weathered slab cut from thick white marble. But for all its vastness, its surface was completely bare, save for a single leather-bound book. Atop the book sat a black, onyx paperweight carved into the shape of a large diamond, white streaks running through the black stone. My curiosity piqued, I gripped the diamond paperweight, finding it heavier than I expected, then lifted it off the book to read the golden title.

THE GIRL IN THE SNOW
by D. J. Dilbrook

"Pretty, huh?"

I jumped. The paperweight slipped out of my sweaty fingers and thumped loudly on the floor.

"Jesus – "

"Twitchy, ain't ya?" Gloria set a six-pack of Coors on Don's desk, ripped two from the plastic yokes and tossed one at my chest. "I've gotten good at sneaking around this old house."

I picked up the paperweight, made sure the onyx wasn't fractured or chipped, then set it back on the book where it belonged. I cracked open my beer and took a much-needed slug.

"I thought you said he wasn't published."

"He isn't," she said. "This here is the only copy. I had it printed, wrapped in caribou leather, embossed in gold, and left it here on his desk. Sort of a memento of the man he was before all of this."

Gloria caressed her rugged fingertips along the book's spine. And there, in her wizened eyes, I saw a familiar sadness.

"Maybe," she said. "After he's good and dead, his daughter will finally read it."

***

As luck would have it, I found a bottle of Malamute in the Cabin, alone in an empty cupboard above the refrigerator. Whether the Dilbrooks left it for me, or whether the previous groundskeeper had forgotten it, I didn't bother phoning up to the Mansion to find out.

Instead, I poured myself three healthy fingers, then added a fourth for good measure.

After changing your oxygen tank and tucking you into bed, I bundled myself up in one of the extra jackets I found in the hall closet, grabbed my icy glass of firewater (as well as the bottle), and opened the sliding glass door leading out onto the Cabin's vast rear deck. Hot on my heels, Harvey trundled past me down the back steps, leaving pawprints in the newly fallen snow. He quickly thought better of his decision and curled up instead under one of the low hanging eaves.

I brushed fresh flakes off an old porch chair, downed my glass of Malamute, then topped it off with another.

And then, something amazing happened.

Emeraldine ribbons of auroral light shimmered across the star-studded sky. With no city lights to pollute the polar phenomenon, I was able to finally admire the aurora borealis for the first time in twenty-six years. The first and last time I'd watched the northern lights, I was five years old, sitting on my dad's lap on the porch of our trailer in Ketchikan while he drank from a bottle similar to the one I was holding now.

I became hypnotized by the prismatic dance of the midnight sky. My eyelids became heavy. I closed them for just a moment's rest. And then, I succumbed to the warm whiskey in my veins.

I awoke to a growl.

Shaken by the sudden realization that I had fallen asleep and momentarily unable to remember where I was, I noticed that my toes and fingers were numb. A light snow fell around me, peppering my face in cold flakes.

Harvey stood at the edge of the deck, staring out into the woods.

"What is it, bud?"

His growls grew louder. The hair on his back stood on end.

The northern lights had long since extinguished, and I was left squinting through the intense darkness of the trees. And for a brief moment, I thought I saw the source of Harvey's panic between two gnarled spruces –

A face.

I rubbed the snow and sleep from my eyes. When I looked again, there was only brush. A trick of the darkness.

"Come on, Harv. Back inside," I said.

He didn't budge.

"Inside," I repeated.

Somewhere beyond the tree line, a twig suddenly snapped.

Harvey sprinted down the steps, across the snowy yard, and disappeared into the trees.

"Harvey!"

Without thinking, I grabbed his leash and bolted after him. Cold powder whipped at my ankles as I sprinted over the yard and into the woods.

I dodged spruce trunks, following the soft crunch of Harvey's paws in the snow. I heard his barks growing fainter and fainter in the distance. My only hope was to keep following his pawprints. I whistled after him, hoping to rouse his senses, but whatever he'd seen – whatever we both had seen – had stolen his concentration and wasn't giving it back.

The trees engulfed me.

I looked over my shoulder as I ran, and I cursed myself. The light from the back porch had vanished, leaving me stranded in the belly of the unfamiliar woods and brush. I rounded too many tree trunks, tumbled over too many frozen creek beds, tripped over too many hidden rocks.

I stopped and looked around, and I suddenly realized I had lost Harvey's pawprints. I saw nothing but black, gnarled trees and fresh, untouched powder shimmering under faint silvery moonlight seeping through the canopy. Only one set of prints were visible anymore, and they were my own.

I let out another loud, sharp whistle. Silence pressed in on me. I waited, willing Harvey to come bounding out of the trees, pink tongue lolling, a fixed smile stretched across his maw. Imagined us making our way out of the woods, up the porch, and back inside…

Icy panic spread through my bones as I realized you were still fast asleep in your crib. All alone in the Cabin.

How had I not thought about you when I bolted into the woods? How had I forgotten you were still inside? What kind of father was I?

I called out to Harvey one last time, as loud as I possibly could. My voice echoed through the trees and I wondered if, this deep in the woods behind the Dilbrook Mansion and the Cabin, Gloria could hear me.

Gloria.

I pulled out my phone in an attempt to reach her. To beg her to go down to the Cabin and check on you. I pressed the home button, but the screen was dark. I held the power button. Banged it against my hand. Tried again.

But still, nothing.

The cold had killed my phone.

I was forced to make a tough choice, then. A choice between my dog and my daughter. It should have been an easy choice, but I must confess my struggle.

Your mother stole you away for far too long, and so Harvey had always come first. He'd always been there. Always woke me up with a nuzzle of his cold, wet nose. Licked the salty tears from my cheeks when the good times with your mother became too few and far between to remember clearly.

He was my best friend, but under the moonlight on that cold night, I chose you.

I could only hope that Harvey would survive the night. Survive the cold. Survive the wolves.

The snow began to fall again, and I knew if I waited around for too long, my footprints would disappear, the trees would forever claim my icy body, and Gloria would find you alone in the Cabin. Abandoned by your mother. Abandoned by your father. Left to social services and with no memory of your rotten parents.

"Stay strong, Harv," I whispered.

I began to retrace my own footprints and realized that, in my haste to catch up to Harvey, I ran at least a full mile into the woods. Nothing looked familiar out here, but the further I followed my snowy prints, the trees began to thin. The moon became brighter through the receding canopy. I re-discovered the soft golden glow of the porchlight through the trees, and relief began to warm my fingertips.

And then I saw her.

Fifty yards to my left stood a woman. She was young, maybe late into her twenties, wearing a large bushy parka that hugged her hourglass frame. The mocha tinge of her face glowed softly under the moonlight. Her dark, almond eyes were fixed on mine. She appeared hesitant, and I had the distinct feeling I had discovered her when she meant to stay hidden.

Hers was the face I had seen in the trees.

"Hello?" I called out.

She remained silent.

"Are you all right?" I asked. I took a step toward her.

She turned and walked calmly back into the trees. I gave chase, but as quickly as she had appeared, she was gone.

Curious as I was, I was tempted to seek her out. To find her. To ask her if she knew where my dog had run off to. This had been Harvey's target, after all.

The girl in the snow, a shadow in the night.

Who was she? What was she doing out here? Where did she come from? Questions swirled in my head as I followed the glow of the porchlight out of the trees. Harvey's leash hung from my fist, and my head hung on my chest. I walked up the steps and across the deck, grabbed the half-empty bottle of Malamute, kicked off my wet boots, and walked inside.

From the warmth of the kitchen, I stared at the woods through the icy glass of the sliding door. I waited for the girl in the snow to reappear, but she never did. The trees had swallowed her up, just as they had swallowed Harvey.

As I had done a few nights earlier, I sent up a little prayer, this time for Harv. I kept the porchlight on, locked the doors, and took a final gulp of whiskey. Muscles aching from the cold, I turned up the heat and walked upstairs.

I opened your bedroom door. I saw the shadow of your crib and watched the lumpy blankets. The gentle rise and fall of your chest was missing. The blankets lay still.

Something was wrong.

I flipped on the lights, and my world shattered.

Your crib was empty.

6

A DEVIL IN THE TREES

First my dog, and now my daughter.

The idea that you had simply lifted yourself over the edge of the crib, climbed down the railing, and waddled to a distant room of the Cabin was instantly dashed by the fact that your oxygen tank was gone. You hadn't just wandered off...

You had been taken.

I threw open the closet doors to find nothing but your collection of hand-me-down onesies that were three sizes too small and shoplifted from the Salvation Army's Anchorage branch your mother so often perused. My room, opposite yours, sported only the four-poster California king and yesterday's dirty clothes on the floor. My closet was empty. The master bathroom was as large and luxurious as I had left it, but it was cold and completely devoid of your presence. I bolted downstairs, threw open the various hall closets, and found nothing but a black snow jacket, boots, and a ski mask owned by the previous tenant (or so I assumed).

It was only when I had scoured the dining room with its massive oak table and overly opulent opal chandelier that I noticed them…

Snowy boot prints led from the foot of the stairs to the front door.

Careful not to tread on the evidence, I switched on the front porchlight, opened the front door, peered through the blooming blizzard, and noticed the boot prints descending the front steps. The marks entrenched in snow by the boots' treading and outsoles were filling in with powder.

Time wasn't on my side.

The first thing I noticed was that the boot prints were small. I deduced that whoever had taken you was most definitely a female. Sure, a man could have small feet, but with my experience in discerning arsonists' footprints in ash, I knew that a man's feet (even if they were small) were still wide. These feet were narrow. They definitely belonged to a woman.

I thought of the girl in the snow. Had she broken into the Cabin to steal you while I dozed on the back deck, drunk under the aurora?

The second thing I noticed was that the boot prints ended suddenly, and where the next prints should have been, there were large tire tracks. And by the look of the kickback deeply compressed into the snow, these tires had supported a heavy vehicle, most likely a truck. The tire tracks led away from the Cabin and down the switchback that led down to Lake Adamant.

The panic really began to set in.

I was forced to deal with the fact that someone, a strange woman (most likely the girl from the woods) snuck into the Cabin, took you, and stole you away to Ukippa.

But why?

Under a bleached moon, I fell to my knees. You were gone, and whoever had stolen you possessed the power to keep you. How on earth would I ever find you in a place as large, as wild, and as unforgiving as this?

I didn't know, but I wouldn't rest until I did.

I stood up, and then I was blinded by pure and violent white. Brakes screeched. Sleet and mud sprayed my face. I threw my hands up out of instinct, and my palms touched a hot grill.

"Jesus, Laz," I heard someone yell.

I shielded my eyes from the blare of twin headlamps. I heard a truck door open and then slam shut. Boots crunched on the snow. And then, I felt a pair of small and strong arms wrap around my neck.

"Did I hit you?"

"Gloria?" And then, it hit me. The boots. The truck.

"For fuck's sake, are you okay?"

"Ellie?"

"What?"

"Where the fuck is Ellie?" It came out automatically, and for the first time in my life, I recognized the panic and the anger of a frightened father.

"I took her," Gloria said, and pulled away. "I just – "

But before she had time to explain, my fingers gripped tightly around her throat. Fire burning in my veins, I forced her spine against the grill of her husband's Silverado. I strangled her openly and without restraint, my mind intent on freeing you from the woman who had

63

taken you from me. It was instinctual, to say the least, and hell, I never want to feel that way again.

Recognizing my error all too quickly, I released Gloria's neck. I cursed myself as she coughed and hacked and slowly regained her composure.

"She's in the truck," she gasped.

I rushed to the old Silverado and threw open the passenger door. There you were, strapped in, holding crayons and an old notepad. All smiles and scribbles. I picked you up and pulled you into my chest as panic gave way to relief. I turned to Gloria and watched her rub her neck.

I knew I had crossed a line. I wanted to fall to my knees and grovel. To beg her to forgive me for grabbing her.

"Gloria, I'm so sorry – "

She cleared her throat and watched me for a moment, assessing whether or not I was still a threat.

"Please, I just – " I begged her to understand. "That wasn't me."

Gloria took a deep breath and stepped toward me. I prepared myself for a punch in the nose. A slap across my cheek. Silently begged for it. Begged for her to even the score.

Instead, she put a hand on my shoulder and searched my eyes.

"You're a father," she said. "A father who found his daughter's bed empty." She squeezed my shoulder and offered a gentle smile. A smile that hurt worse than the bloody nose I wished she had given me instead.

"Instincts," she said. "That's all it is. I'd be concerned if you hadn't tried to strangle me."

"I'm sorry," I repeated.

"Don't be," she said. "I heard yelling, so I went out to the balcony and noticed the Cabin's lights on. Went down to make sure everything was okay, but you were gone. I waited around for a while, but after about an hour, I figured you'd gone out into the woods and got lost. I hopped in the truck to go look for you. Took Ellie with me, just in case. Is everything all right, Laz?"

"Harvey's gone," I said. "There was someone in the trees, Harvey bolted, and – "

"Who was it?" she interrupted.

"I don't know."

I watched her eyes flash to the west, following her gaze to the old Shack atop the opposite ridge of Horseshoe Hill. Soft light flickered from the windows. Her face hardened, and she let her eyes bore into mine.

"Did you see this person?"

"Yes."

"A man?"

"No. A girl."

"A girl?" she asked. She looked confused. "Was it Lizanne?"

"Who?"

"Our nurse, Lizanne."

"I don't know. I haven't met Lizanne."

"Tall. Odd, jittery Inuit woman. Short, pinkish hair."

"I don't think so," I said. "She was young. On the shorter side. Dark skin. She had her hood up, so I couldn't see her hair."

I watched her eyes flitter back and forth, searching both sides of her brain for a possible identity of the stranger.

"I don't know," she finally said. "Could it have been a hiker?"

"Are there many hikers up here?"

"This far north, you never know," she said. "Sometimes, they come out of the Gates of the Arctic and wind up down here, but it's far too cold this time of year."

"She wasn't dressed like a hiker." We stood in silence for a moment, all three of us staring at the shadowy tree line stretching behind the Cabin.

"And you're absolutely sure you saw someone?" Gloria asked. "It wasn't an animal, or maybe a trick of the light?"

"I'm sure."

"Well, whoever she was, she's going to freeze before morning. In any case, lock the doors and keep the porchlights on. There's a '75 Browning in the garage. Reach behind the gun safe and you'll feel a sticky note. The code to the safe is written on it."

"Do you think that's necessary?"

"Up here, there ain't no big city lawman. It never hurts to have a gun handy." We watched the trees a while longer, and then you shivered in my arms. "Go on now. Get that little blubber-nugget back to bed."

"We'll see you in the morning," I said.

"Looking forward to it. The shed needs mending. Hope you find your dog." She clapped a hand on my shoulder once more, then she turned to leave.

"Gloria," I said. "I'm sorry. Again."

"Hush," she replied. "No more talk of it."

And though she had been quick to forgive me, something in Gloria's voice said otherwise. She looked at you huddled in my arms. She watched you yawn, your eyes glimmering with innocence and fatigue. She crunched her small, narrow boots over the Silverado's snowy tire path. She climbed up into the driver seat and unrolled the window, then shot another fiery glance at the Shack across the hill.

"Keep an eye on her," she reminded me. She rubbed her throat, and I felt another pang of guilt twist my guts into knots.

"Gloria, I swear that wasn't me."

Gloria revved the engine, kicked the clutch, and inched alongside us. Before heading up the steep, snowy path that led to the Mansion, she leaned out the window and fixed me with a shadowy stare.

"There's a monster in all of us, Laz."

***

The swing of a hammer and the thud of wooden pegs was long overdue.

For four long hours, icy sunbeams struggled to break through the clouds as I ripped rotten planks of wood from an old shed Don Dilbrook built back in 1979. A legion of carpenter ants had recently infiltrated the eastern flank of the Dilbrooks' property and took a particular interest in the old, decrepit shed.

To reach it, I first had to squeeze through a thatch of overgrown devil's club. The plot of angry bushes possessed long, sharp thorns (dozens of which I'd already plucked out of my hands), its gnarled and knotted limbs twisting like an old woman's necklace collection. The ferocious foliage backed up against the woods where Harvey disappeared the night before.

Even though the air was below freezing, beads of sweat trickled down my neck as I hammered the shed's new frame into place. A familiar twinge stretched along the base of my spine. I stood up, dropped the hammer, and pressed my hands firmly into my lower back. I pushed my shoulders this way and that, and the sharp pain became a dull pressure.

It felt good to be sore.

A sudden rustle in the leaves roused my attention. I turned and peered through the twisted, dried-up thicket of the devil's club, and the rustling became louder. Careful not to make a sound, I lowered to my haunches and wrapped my fingers around the hammer.

"Harvey," I cooed softly through the thorns.

I heard a final crunch of frozen foliage, and then all I heard was the whistle of the wind. And then, silence. I licked my lips and let out three short, sharp whistles.

The rustle of the leaves returned. I stood up to greet Harvey, but it wasn't a black dog that answered.

A giant wrapped in cracked leather emerged through a clearing in the trees, crunching massive, moose-hide boots over the frosty forest floor. A thick beard hung like Spanish moss over the stranger's trunk of a torso. Thick and wiry black hair sat in greasy tangles across shoulders as broad as Don Dilbrook's writing desk. And draped over those shoulders was the immense, bloody carcass of an adolescent caribou. But what frightened me most was neither his inhuman size, nor the dead animal he carried.

It was his face.

Webs of purple, keloid scars contorted what remained of his sun-worn, pockmarked mug. A particularly nasty scar made its descent from his hairline through a milky-white left eyeball, then down and around the back of his ear. His right eye was black as fresh oil, with no dividing line between iris and pupil.

The black marble and the white marble stared at me, and I was rooted to the spot, too terrified to look away. We stood there for what seemed like an hour, though it couldn't have been more than a couple of seconds. Not speaking. Not moving.

And then, he did something that made my blood ice over.

Cracked, bleeding lips parted and stretched from cheek to cheek. A wicked, eerie leer revealed the remnants of black, rotten teeth. It was not a display of welcome, but one of warning.

He disappeared into the trees, and only then did I finally breathe.

***

"His name is Moose."

Gloria ran her hand along the vertical posts of the shed's new frame. She tried to shake it, and the foundation held steady. Having brought me a beer while I finished up the new shed's wooden skeleton, she found me a little unsettled, glancing over my shoulder and into the trees. She could tell the appearance of the grizzled giant had shaken me, and for a moment, I wished my own foundation had been as steady as the shed's.

"He lives in the Shack on the other side of the hill," she said.

"Is he dangerous?" I asked, point-blank.

Gloria ignored me, trying her luck at shaking another post, but the shed held firm. "You did a great job, Laz."

"Gloria," I pressed.

"I'm sorry. What did you ask?" She appeared a little shaken herself, eyes not meeting my own.

"I need to know if my daughter is safe here. Is he dangerous?"

"Oh, all right," she muttered. "It's just, we lost the last groundskeeper because of Moose. We really don't want to lose the two of you."

I considered this for a moment and decided that bedridden Don Dilbrook probably didn't give a lick either way.

It was Gloria who didn't want to lose us.

"What do you want to know?" she asked.

"The other night, you called him a devil," I said. "Why?"

"Moose and Don go way back," she said. "They were very close for a long, long time. Like brothers, actually. When Don inherited his father's oil wells, he hired on Moose to help out at the oil processing plant a few miles from here."

She turned and pointed toward the western sky, where a waning, pink sun pathetically skirted the horizon line. And there, thick plumes of gray, vertical clouds ascended into the impending twilight.

"He did all right for the first few months, but then, something happened."

"What happened?"

She was silent for a moment, and I could see in her eyes that she really, truly did not want to relive whatever Moose had done.

"A woman, one of the admin workers, disappeared from the plant," Gloria finally said. "All they found was some of her blood and brains on top of her desk."

My blood ran cold.

"Did Moose kill her?"

"Nobody really knows what happened to her. The only thing Don told me is that Moose liked this woman. Watched her. Wanted her. But she didn't want him."

Her eyes moved to the Shack across the hill, lost in the sordid memory.

"Don had his lawyers on the case. He didn't think Moose killed her, and they were able to get him cleared. Lack of evidence. Lack of a body. But there was always a lingering suspicion after that."

"Where did the scars on his face come from?" I wondered.

"Mauled by a bear," she said. "At least, that's what he wants people to think."

"What do you mean?"

"I know the truth," Gloria said. "I didn't learn about it until a few years back. It's the reason Moose and Don had a falling out."

She sighed, took a long guzzle of her beer, and continued.

"Adam Kelsey, our last groundskeeper, wanted to know more about Moose. Call it curiosity. Call it idiocy. Whatever it was, Moose didn't like that Kelsey worked for us. Kelsey would try to talk with him, Moose would threaten to shoot him. That went on for a while. Moose doesn't have much, so Kelsey would take the money we paid him and buy Moose a week's worth of potatoes and some whiskey and just leave it on his doorstep.

"Eventually, Kelsey bugged him enough times and coaxed him with enough bottles of Malamute and potatoes that he finally formed a sort of dialogue with Moose. Just *heys* and *how are yas* for the first few months. Then, Kelsey started having him over to the Cabin for beers and stew."

Simply hearing that Moose had been inside the Cabin made me shiver.

"And then, one day, Kelsey came to me. He was terrified. I asked him what Moose had done or said, but Kelsey didn't want to say. Eventually, I got him to write it down on a slip of paper."

"What did it say?"

"That Moose had murdered someone. A woman. And that's where the scars on his face had come from. He wanted her and tried to take her. She fought back, took one of his eyes with her. So, he killed her."

Gloria took the beer bottle from my hand and drained the rest of it. She obviously needed it more than I did.

"I told Don what Kelsey said, but he didn't want to do anything about it. Said he still didn't think Moose killed that woman. Said it was best to just to leave it alone."

She sighed.

"Kelsey earned Moose's trust, and then he broke it."

Lost in her thoughts, Gloria shook the frame of the shed one last time. Still solid as a rock. She turned and began to walk back toward the Mansion, and I followed.

"Did Kelsey quit after that?" I asked.

She stopped on the steps leading up to the back porch, then turned and looked me right in the face.

"No, he didn't quit," she said. "Adam Kelsey went missing."

7

THE NURSE

During our short time at the Dilbrook Mansion, I watched you thrive.

Where most Alaskans saw the incessant snow as either a nuisance, a cause for complaint, or just another cog in life's machine, you saw the potential for play and magical make-believe. Those first few days, I watched you while I worked, giggling and throwing snowballs at Gloria. She'd given me one of Don's smaller oxygen tanks and fashioned a sort of fanny pack out of old sweaters she'd found in the closet.

You were no longer constrained by the weight of your sickness. Gloria had found a way to let you live. And for that, I will be eternally grateful.

Even after everything that followed.

This particular morning, I watched you from the windows of the third-floor hallway, a corridor that ended at an arched, viridian door. I watched you giggling in the snow, waving little arms and legs that looked like Vienna sausages under the padded sleeves of your coat and pants. Gloria was beside you, both making angels in the snow, one big and one small.

I sat on my haunches, replacing the baseboards. My back was hunched and aching, and it was the best I'd felt in months. The sore ache of my muscles gave me a sense of purpose, of being needed and useful.

As I ripped out a particularly troublesome baseboard crumbling with rot, I heard a deep voice groaning from behind the door at the end of the hall. The Mansion was a labyrinth of hallways and staircases, but as turned around as I was, I deduced this was the door to Don Dilbrook's bedroom. The noise was soft at first, and then the groans became louder and more erratic.

Gloria was outside with you, so I assumed Don was all alone, groaning in desperation.

My reaction was instinctual.

I dropped the decayed baseboard and sprinted down the corridor. I reached the door and jiggled the knob, but it was locked. I pressed my ear to the wood and listened as the hoarse groans reached a crescendo.

I stepped back and launched my leg forward. The doorjamb cracked under the weight of my foot. The door swung open.

And instantly, I regretted it.

Don Dilbrook lie half-catatonic in his large four-poster bed, eyes glazed over and drool running from the corner of his mouth. A tall Inuit woman with short pink hair stood in front of his bed, seductively swinging her hips to the gentle croon of a Johnny Cash record. She was halfway to lifting off her shirt when she suddenly noticed my presence, screamed, and pulled her shirt back down.

Unsure of what I'd just walked in on, I raised my hands and made to leave the enormous bedroom, but her voice stopped me.

"What the hell are you doing in here?" she snapped.

"I could ask you the same thing," I said.

"His blood pressure was spiking."

"And you think that's the best way to bring it back down?" I laughed. "If it were that easy, I'd have started eating more salt years ago."

"Pig."

Convinced I no longer posed a threat, the nurse grabbed a wet towel and dabbed droplets of sweat from the old man's forehead.

"You must be Lizanne," I concluded. "You do realize his wife's out in the yard?"

"She's the one who prescribed it. I'm *supposed* to dance for him!" Lizanne barked. "Now get out!"

And all too willingly, I obliged.

***

"I'm sorry you had to see that," Gloria sighed over a cup of earl gray, the steam swirling lazily around her face. She stood over me as I ripped out the third-floor hallway's final baseboard.

"Looks like woodlice," I said, eager to ignore the conversation.

"You shouldn't have gone in there."

"Yep. Definitely woodlice."

"Laz – "

"Look, Gloria, you don't have to explain anything to me," I said.

"I know it seems odd…"

"Nothing odd about an old man getting his rocks off. I've just never known a hospice nurse to dance like that."

"It's the only thing that seems to help," Gloria replied with a shrug. "It's a little crude, I know, but she's the only one willing to come this far north."

"It's none of my business," I said. "But why her? I mean, you're his wife. Why don't you dance for him?"

Gloria fixed me with a cold, hard stare.

"You're right. It's none of your business," she grumbled.

I nodded, stood up, brushed the rotten wood chips off my jeans, and decided it was time to get back to work.

"I need to grab the sander from the Cabin," I said. I turned to go, but Gloria placed a hand on my shoulder.

"I'm sorry, Laz. I know you came to me in concern. Don and I – well, we have a complicated marriage. When I hired Lizanne, I told her that the position included making Don's final years on this earth a pleasant experience."

"Pleasant in how many ways?" I asked, cocking an eyebrow.

"Don is a powerful man," she said. "Even in his current state, he's a powerful man. He's always been the type of man who gets what he wants, when he wants it." She looked away, unhappy memories clouding her vision. "At least, he used to."

"Including other women?" I asked.

"Including other women," she confirmed. "Thank you for coming to me like you did. But nothing is out of place."

In my head, I disagreed. I considered myself at Don's age,

bedridden and essentially braindead. I considered how Vanessa would feel about my hospice nurse bringing me the only ecstasy I had left.

And then I considered that it didn't matter, that Vanessa was gone and was never coming back. So, my opinion was moot.

"I have a daughter," I said. "She wanders around this house like she owns the place."

"Yes, she does," Gloria agreed. "Feels good to have little feet skittering around here again."

"I don't want her walking in on something like that," I said, holding her gaze and, for the first time, planting my foot as a concerned father.

"Of course."

I finished up the last of the day's work, gathered up the planks of rotten wood, and set off down the hall.

"To be fair," I heard Gloria say behind me. "The door was locked."

***

Returning to the Cabin that evening to find our fridge fully stocked (thanks to Gloria's recent venture into Ukippa), I cooked us up a hearty stew of elk meat and potatoes. Technically, I cooked myself up a hearty stew of elk meat and potatoes. You were quite complacent with a box of Kraft macaroni and cheese. And I was quite complacent to steal a bite – or three.

I turned on the most recent Pixar flick for you and set up a coloring station in the living room, watching with a proud smile as you carefully chose the crayons you intended to create with.

So focused. So intent on your grand, scribbled design.

My daughter, the artist.

And while you colored, I locked you inside the Cabin and ventured out into the woods. After a half hour, my lips were cracked and bleeding from whistling Harvey's favorite tune. My throat was cold and dry from calling out his name. My cheeks were scratched from too-close encounters with brambles and leafless branches. The evening darkened into night. The trees beckoned me deeper.

But you beckoned me home.

I put you to bed, grinning from ear to ear as you sang the babbling rendition of a rather annoying Disney theme song. Coming from you, however, it was the flawless forte of an entrancing aria.

My daughter, the singer.

Gloria supplied us with a few extra oxygen tanks that Don currently wasn't using. I switched out your depleted tank, connected the receiving end of the supply tube, and heard the soothing, familiar hiss of your lifeline. I stroked your hair, now nearly fully grown back after a year without chemo. Your eyes glazed over, your lids grew heavy, and you drifted off to the land of whimsy and wonder.

My daughter, the dreamer.

I was falling in love with you all over again.

I found it ironic that proficient though I was at building fires, and conversely, of putting them out, all the Cabin's fireplace required was the flip of a switch. Flames instantly burst upward from between cubes of multi-colored glass, the crackles and pops of traditional firewood replaced by the steady silence of natural gas.

Giving the fire a minute to warm the living room, I made my

way onto the back deck. As I had done multiple times since Harvey's disappearance, I stared out at those darkened branches. I imagined him bounding out of the woods, black fur plowing through white snow, droopy ears swinging and floppy tongue lolling about.

I whistled for him again, I called his name, and the trees responded with silence. I was forced to consider the possibility that he wasn't coming back. That the woods had swallowed him whole. That the cold had overtaken him, or worse, a wild animal had snatched him up. I hung my head, unable to shake the guilt of having screamed at him only days prior, screamed at him for simply being a puppy.

I poured myself a shot of Malamute, sucked it down, and chased it with another. I thought about tucking the bottle back into the cupboard, thought better of it, and then carried it into the living room.

For the first time in five years, I opened a Tom Clancy novel. There beside the fire, feet propped up on the coffee table, I read until my eyes hurt. Until the whiskey made it hard to focus on dense political secrets and espionage. Until it became a struggle to simply turn another page.

Until I noticed the ghosts watching me from the doorway.

They stood there silently, four in all. One man. Three women. All silent. All staring. All sooty and singed.

I inspected the man first. His name was Mr. Guthrie. He watched me with lifeless, milky eyes, corneas glowing with hemorrhaged capillaries that had burst from a lack of oxygen, from the intense pressure within his brain. His wrinkled and weather-beaten face was streaked with soot, lips and hanging jowls purple with hypoxia. Blue and green capillaries stretched and tangled around his eye sockets like spiderwebs. He had died first, I knew, based on the coroner's report I'd been forced to read a year before. Died of asphyxiation. Soot in the lungs, lungs that were already decrepit from decades of inhaling pipe tobacco. Mr. Guthrie watched as I lowered the Clancy novel to my lap, tilting his silvery head to the side as if waiting for me to respond to a question he never got the chance to ask.

Standing beside Mr. Guthrie were two elderly women that made my guts constrict. I called them the Twins. They stared at me from the doorway, skeletons with blackened sinew and wrinkled skin dangling from their blackened bones. Having died holding one another in a desperate embrace as they had grown together in the womb eighty-five years prior, the Twins' flesh had fused together amid the scorching heat of the flames. Thin strands of hair were all that remained hanging from scalps burned away to reveal charred skull. The Twins didn't appear angry with me, just watched me with curious eyes, wondering why I never got the chance to save them.

The last woman's name was Joy Jones, and she had been Mr. Guthrie's nurse. Her lifeless stare was the singular stare that made me internally collapse. I sat there, numb, drinking in the visage of her blackened flesh and saddened eyes. She was five decades younger than the others when she died, and it was her spectral visit that hit me hardest. Not simply because she was younger than I was when she was burned alive. Not because I had taken her out for coffee a week before the inferno. And not because I saw in her the peace and gentle grace that my ex-wife had never possessed. Seeing Joy here and now knocked me down because she had been the one who lifted me up. She was the one who gave me comfort and solace when I cried about having lost you. She was the one who offered solutions to the financial, physical, and mental struggles your disease had inflicted upon me. She had been there when nobody else was.

Joy was simply that, a joy I'd never known before or since the tragic fire of Turnagain Home. The once-joyful specter hung her head, her eyes locked on mine. It would have been beautiful, that sad and melancholy stare, had it not been for the fact that she never blinked.

"I'm sorry," I whispered.

And then, I watched as the ghost of Joy Jones lifted a scorched arm and pointed at the Cabin's front door.

I stood up and staggered, my equilibrium shot to shit courtesy of the bottle of Malamute I'd polished off in record time. I walked past the four shadowy figures and felt their opaque hues on my back as I made my way down the front hall and to the door. The glass panes were white with humid fog, but as I wiped it away, I saw her.

The other nurse. The living one.

Beneath a blizzard of falling white, Lizanne emerged from the front door of the Mansion. She trudged quickly through the snow, creating her own trail down the front lawn. Through the tiny windowpane, I quickly lost sight of her. I moved instead to the dining room window and pulled the curtain open just enough to catch sight of her once more.

Lizanne stopped at the edge of the tree line, her tall profile dimly illuminated by shards of moonlight breaking through the clouds. From my vantage point, I watched as she stared into the woods. She looked over her shoulder at the Dilbrook Mansion. The lights were off, and by now, I knew the Dilbrooks were asleep. She turned her attention back to the snow-covered branches, and then, her lips began to move.

The nurse spoke to the trees, and she spoke with vigor.

My whiskey-warmed nose was pressed to the cold glass, my eyes squinting through the unyielding blizzard. I watched as she took something out of her coat pocket and held it aloft to the branches.

A gloved hand reached out of the shadows and took the offering.

Lizanne looked at the Mansion, pointed a finger at the stained-glass windows of the east library, and mouthed a few words. And then, my stomach dropped as her gaze shifted to the Cabin. To the window. To my peeping eyes. I yanked the curtain closed over the glass, hoping she didn't see me.

What had I just witnessed?

Suddenly, I felt an all-too-familiar chill run down my spine. I heard a soft, slow, and quiet rasp in my left ear.

I closed my eyes. I didn't have to look.

I knew he was there, standing behind me. Watching me like the others – Nurse Joy, the Twins, and Mr. Guthrie – had watched me.

He had followed me all the way from Anchorage.

Ol' Smitty had returned.

8

SOPHIE

It would go down as the second most memorable Saturday of my life. I say 'second' because, of course, the Saturday you were born takes full precedence.

Sophie Dilbrook flew into Ukippa in a Cessna.

I was there to greet her when the tires touched down on snow-scraped and salted asphalt. The door swung down and for a moment, or for eternity (I wasn't quite sure which), time flowed like molasses in winter. Red-bottomed high heels descended each step, lovely ankles exposed to the cold and stretching into legs hugged in a professional (but flattering) pencil skirt. Adorned in that familiar pea coat that matched her eyes in my favorite shade of olive, she appeared poised and ready to take all of Alaska to trial.

"You're alive," she said with a smile that warmed the very air around me.

"Only just," I replied. "Your mother's a tough cookie."

"Where do you think I get it from?"

She wrapped her arms around my neck and leaned up on her tiptoes to plant a friendly kiss on my unshaven cheek. I wished I had thought to shave that morning.

"Shall we?"

I collected her bags from the pilot, helped her climb into Betty, then stole a glimpse of her backside. She must have seen me, for when our eyes met, she gave me a look that said, *look at my ass again and I'll prosecute yours.*

***

"I'm sorry about your dog," Sophie said. Her olive hues watched as Lake Adamant whizzed by, its frozen surface shimmering under the first sunshine (or what passed as sunshine this far north) that Ukippa had seen since my arrival. Looking back on it now, I'm positive she brought the sun with her.

"Word travels fast," I replied, keeping my eyes fixed on the icy road. I didn't want to talk about Harvey. Every evening, deep in the woods, I searched for him. And every night, I came back with an empty leash.

"Can I tell you something?" she asked.

"As long as you don't tell me that everything is going to be okay."

"I wouldn't be a lawyer if I did," she said. I laughed at that.

"Ok, then. Shoot."

"Don't go into those woods alone, Laz."

"If Old Man Moose can fight off a bear, then so can I," I joked.

"I'm sure you can. Just consider your daughter."

"I do. And that's why I come home every night before the sun sets."

Sophie placed a hand on my arm and squeezed. I turned to look at her. Her eyes were large and hardened, and it was then that I saw her mother in them.

"Those woods are dangerous, Laz. There are things in those trees far more dangerous than a bear."

"Like Moose?"

"More dangerous even than him. All I'm asking is that when you think about going into those woods, think very strongly about how badly Ellie needs her dad. Take somebody with you."

"Because I'm very popular with the Ukippa crowd," I quipped.

"*I'll* go with you," she replied. "Let me help you look for him. At least for the little time I'm here. I know those woods like the back of my hand. I know which paths are safe, and I know which ones aren't."

"I'll make you a deal. You can show me the woods if you introduce me to the fine folks at Galoshes. Drinking alone in the Cabin isn't boding well for my social life."

"Only if you buy my drinks."

"Would Tom like that?" I asked and cocked an eyebrow in her direction.

"Tom isn't here," Sophie said. And when I met her eyes, she smiled.

I parked Betty outside of Galoshes, ran around to open Sophie's door, and caught her as she slipped on a patch of ice.

"Not the best place for heels," I said.

"I've been wearing heels here for ten years," she replied. "Every year, they get higher." Sophie smiled and withdrew from my arms.

She looked around the tiny town square, and her eyes were blank.

From my experience in arson investigation, I'd learned to read people's faces, learned to discern guilt from indifference, fear from shock, sadness from contrition, and longing from nostalgia. From her, I read nothing.

Sophie Dilbrook was a master of her own face.

"Everything okay?" I asked.

"Everything's the same."

"Is that good or bad?"

"Yes," she sighed, suggesting it was both. I was left with the suspicion that she was neither pleased to be home nor keen to fly back to Anchorage. And for just a moment, I saw something in her eyes.

A spark, and then a shadow.

Happy memories. Not so happy memories. And then, cold and hard indifference glazed her eyes once more.

"I'll meet you inside," she said. "I need to visit an old friend. Order me a red zin, would you?"

"They have zin this far north?"

She rolled her eyes. "We're Tundrans. Not Neanderthals."

I watched her beeline across the square, skillfully weaving four-inch heels around patches of invisible black ice. I stood there for a moment, entranced not only by her beauty, but by her intellect, her confidence, and by my own daydream of her fearlessly wandering the dark and mysterious woods behind my new home.

As she disappeared into the Ukippa Village Peace Office, I was left wondering who she might be visiting. What business did she have in the tiny makeshift police station?

I caught myself being nosy, and so, I opened the door to Galoshes and walked inside.

I recoiled as the musk of humidity, melted snow, and old beer flooded my senses. The interior of Galoshes reminded me of a reclaimed old barn, the smell of horses and hay replaced with woodsmoke and whiskey. It was larger than I expected, at least double the size of the Dilbrooks' library, with four long wooden farm tables that stretched to meet an old bar top shaped from a block of chipped mahogany.

I made my way to the end of the farm table closest to the fireplace. Flames whipped and embers popped in an open hearth tall enough for me to comfortably stand within. I looked around at about twenty nameless faces, some laughing with others, some withdrawn into their own sleepy corners, some asleep at the bar. As I tugged off my many layers, more and more eyes began to settle upon me. What I assumed was the usual raucous and laughter of the place dimmed to a gentle whisper, and then an uncomfortable silence.

Every eye was on me.

Inspecting me.

Assessing me.

The news of the Dilbrooks' new groundskeeper had apparently spread. And now here I was, in the flesh. Some watched me with curiosity. Others with trepidation. All with discomfort. I was a new cog introduced into their already well-oiled machine.

I awkwardly raised a hand in introduction.

"Hi," I mumbled.

No one responded.

"Okay."

I walked to the bar, and the eyes followed. Even the bartender, an old Inuit woman with three teeth (and who could have easily passed for Inuksuk's grandmother), scowled at my approach.

"Red zin, please," I said.

At once, the bar erupted in laughter.

"Enough, you clowns," called a familiar voice from the door.

Sophie stood there in her red-bottoms, arms crossed and eyes alight as the locals turned their attention upon her. And then, something amazing happened. They cheered. They whistled. They raised their glasses. She patted large men on the back as if they were long-lost friends, waved at withered widows, and indulged in a bear hug from an old, bearded lumberjack nearly three times her size. From my vantage point, I watched the lumberjack shed a happy tear, one that Sophie quickly wiped away.

"Hush, Bobby. It hasn't been that long," she told him with a smile that could've melted the ice in his glass, then made her way through the crowd aching to greet her and met me at the bar.

"This guy troublin' you, Mags?" Sophie asked the leathery fossil wiping grime from a beer mug. She punched my shoulder, kicked off her heels, and set them on the stool beside her.

It was as though the odorous ambience of Galoshes had stripped away the city girl and revealed the true Sophie Dilbrook underneath. Before my very eyes, the aristocratic attorney turned suddenly into a townie tomboy. The transformation kicked me in the gut, and I found myself falling even harder.

"Red zin for you, cupcake," Mags told me with what I assumed was a smile, sliding a glass across the bar top. Sophie took it from me and swallowed half the burgundy liquid in one gulp. Mags topped her off and then poured me a beer.

"Mags, this is Lazalier. Laz, Mags."

"Nice to meet you, Mags," I said.

"Pleasure's all mine, cupcake."

"That's going to stick, isn't it?" I asked.

Sophie giggled and tugged my shirtsleeve. I grabbed her heels and followed her to a cozy spot by the fire. The locals watched me for a few more moments and (thanks to Sophie's company) decided I wasn't a threat, then went back to their drinks, their laughs, and their naps.

One man, I noticed, continued to watch me from the other end of our long table. At least, I assumed he was watching me. One yellow eye was fixed on mine, the other pointing upward. He was either very interested in me or the ochre water stain on the ceiling. He whispered to himself, digging grimy fingernails into the tabletop.

"Don't stare," Sophie whispered.

"Who is that?" I asked.

"His name is Eldon Gamble."

Eldon continued to stare at me, and I at him. He whispered to himself, grinding his teeth as he did so, digging his nails deeper into the mahogany.

I felt the warmth of Sophie's fingers slide into my palm. It was enough to break my focus, turning my gaze from Eldon Gamble's mismatched yellow eyes to Sophie's illustrious greens.

"He's harmless," she said. "He showed up in Ukippa about six years ago. No one knows where he came from, but it was obvious he needed a little help. My parents took him in, fed him, let him live in the Mansion. My mom gave him some simple work to do around the house and paid him a little bit here and there. My dad taught him how to save his money, taught him how to read – nothing big, mostly children's books – and let him stay until he was well enough on his own. They would have let him stay forever, but he, uh, got himself into some trouble."

"What did he do?"

"He broke into the Cabin one night. The guy that was the groundskeeper at the time woke up and found Eldon at the foot of his bed, just watching him sleep."

"That's creepy."

"The groundskeeper shrugged it off and told my parents it was fine." Sophie swirled the wine in her glass and glanced at Eldon. "But it kept happening. He changed the lock twice, but Eldon kept finding a way in. The guy threatened to quit, so my mom had to find Eldon his own place down here in town. He can't drive, and he'd freeze to death if he even tried walking halfway to Horseshoe Hill." She squeezed my hand and then pulled it away. "Harmless."

"The groundskeeper. Was it that Kelsey guy?"

Sophie's eyes widened. "How do you – "

"Gloria mentioned him. She said he went missing. Do you think – "

"Absolutely not," Sophie insisted. "Eldon can barely spell his own name."

"There was some leftover whiskey in the Cabin," I said. "Malamute. Kelsey had good taste, I'll give him that."

I met Sophie's eyes, and decided to press the subject I had been too timid to press with Gloria.

"What do you know about him?"

"About Adam?" she asked and averted my gaze. A flush rose up in her cheeks. Judging by the inflection in her voice when she spoke his first name, I was finally able to read her face, if only for just a moment.

I saw desire.

I saw anger.

And I saw fear.

"You knew him," I deduced.

She took a moment, sighed, and then nodded. "Better than most."

"It's just me and my daughter in that house, Sophie. If the last guy that lived there went missing, I'd like to know why."

"I don't know why," she said and gulped down the rest of her zin.

I took her glass and left her to her thoughts as I went to the bar and got her a refill. And when I returned, it was with two shots of whiskey.

"Here." I slid one of the shots into her fingertips and took mine down in one swallow, savoring the familiar, satisfying burn. She regarded it for a moment, lost in her own head.

"Just consider my daughter," I whispered, using her own line against her.

She sighed, then swallowed the shot of Malamute.

That afternoon, Sophie answered many of my questions about Adam Kelsey. To this day, I wish I'd never asked.

9

THE MYSTERY OF ADAM KELSEY

To understand Adam Kelsey, one must first understand his parents. Adam's father, Amos Kelsey, was a newly hired police deputy for the Juneau Police Department. Because his father before him had been the police chief for two decades, the first year of Amos' law enforcement career was spent patrolling Douglas Island, an area made up of multimillion-dollar homes where the only crimes committed involved haughty domestic disputes between rich white couples. Arguments over prenuptial agreements. Catfights between wealthy businessmen's wives and mistresses. The occasional transient drifting over the Juneau-Douglas Bridge in search of unlocked doors and pearl necklaces.

The nepotism wasn't overlooked.

Fellow deputies envied the fact that Amos wasn't required to spend his first obligatory year on the job in the jails. Senior officers despised his brazen-faced arrogance. The luxury granted to him by his police chief father led most men and women on the force to find ways to taunt and discredit him. Colleagues stole his badge. Deflated the tires on his assigned unit. Some went as far as replacing the ballistic plate in his bulletproof vest with a fragile porcelain sheet. Luckily for Deputy Amos Kelsey, he never came under gunfire.

Amos knew he was disliked, but he mistook his colleagues' contempt for jealousy. This further prompted the swelling of his already abnormally large head. He focused his inherent bitterness on the homeless; when they had already fallen to their knees, he laughed at their misfortune and kicked them onto their backs. He frequented Douglas Island's local bars and nightclubs while on patrol. He intimidated bartenders for free booze. He touched waitresses, even after they asked him to stop. He worked overtime night shifts without getting the hours first approved, and then utilized his time-and-a-half pay to venture off of Douglas Island and drive to the seedier parts of downtown Juneau. There, Deputy Amos Kelsey arrested local prostitutes on street corners, took them to back alleys, and coerced them into doing their best work for the simple fee of not being tossed into the clink.

***

Laura-Jean Duntz was new to Juneau. A Wyoming woman who had recently escaped a violent marriage, she spent what little pennies she had left after the divorce to purchase a plane ticket to visit her estranged mother in Juneau. Upon arrival, Laura-Jean discovered that her mother had been dead for two years, a victim of the AIDS epidemic that had swept the continent.

The only thing she had left of her mother was a silver necklace with a jade pendant in the shape of a howling wolf.

With no money, no high school diploma, and no way of getting back to Wyoming, Laura-Jean sold off the only thing she had left – her body.

A timid girl of only nineteen, Laura-Jean had a tough time learning the tricks of the trade. Often, she allowed men to take her home simply for the opportunity of sleeping in a bed that wasn't made of soggy cardboard. She cried during the first dozen encounters.

And then, she learned to shut it out.

During these encounters, she disappeared into the tall grasses of her mind. She dreamt of Wyoming skies, wild horses, and snow-capped mountains that burst with burning orange during winter sunsets.

One cold October evening, Laura-Jean emerged from those tall grasses, alone and tangled in filthy motel bedsheets. She was ashamed, but she was warm. Her client was long gone, a rich man in the oil business who had left her a sizable tip on the bedside dresser.

She attempted to drift back to sleep, but was suddenly roused by loud, hurried knocks on the motel room door. She tugged on her clothes and looked through the peephole.

Her heart stopped.

"I know you're in there! Where's my money?!" her pimp screamed. "It's been two months! I protect you and you steal from me?!"

With no escape, Laura-Jean huddled in a damp corner to await her fate.

The pimp kicked open the door, and as he lunged at her, Laura-Jean disappeared into those tall grasses once more.

She awoke in an alley six hours later, eyes swollen shut. Every inch of her body was battered and bruised, money gone, clothes soaked through with blood and rain. She heard footsteps crunching on asphalt, growing louder as a shadow descended upon her. She tried to scream, but her windpipe exuded only a faint rasp.

"It's okay. It's okay," she heard a man say. "Jesus, what the hell happened?"

She felt strong hands grip her bruised shoulders, making her recoil in pain. He let go instantly.

"It's okay," the man repeated. "I'm a cop. Can you stand up?"

Laura-Jean Duntz was helped to her feet by the stranger. Unable to see through her puffy eyelids, she relied on her other senses. He stunk of body odor and whiskey. His speech was slurred and heavy with intoxication. She strongly doubted he was a police officer, but as she reached out to his chest, her fingertips felt the unmistakable grooves of cold metal over his heart. A badge.

"I'm Deputy Kelsey," he said. "Everything is going to be all right. Come with me." He led her to his police unit, and instead of stuffing her into the backseat (a place she was all too familiar with), he let her ride shotgun.

But Deputy Amos Kelsey never took Laura-Jean Duntz to the police station. He never took her to a doctor. Instead, he took her back to his home, a small guesthouse behind his father's sprawling estate. He carefully washed the blood, gravel, and grime off her purple, swollen flesh and out of her matted hair. He fed her hot meals stolen from the kitchen in his father's home. He gave her his bed. He tended to her wounds. He bought her new clothes. Many might argue that

95

because of these selfless acts, Deputy Amos Kelsey was, in fact, a hero.

Many, however, never understood his true intention.

A week passed, and Laura-Jean's swelling went down. She could see again. She could talk. She thanked Amos for all he had done for her, then decided it was time to do better for herself. Time to stop selling herself for money. Time to get off the streets. Time to go back to school. Back to Wyoming.

But those dreams lasted only a few seconds.

Laura-Jean asked Amos for a ride to the police station. He denied her request, claiming she needed more rest. He led her back to bed, gave her a benzo, and as drowsiness clouded her senses, something odd happened.

Amos Kelsey snapped a Polaroid picture of her and then kissed her lips.

"Sleep tight," he whispered.

When Laura-Jean awoke nine hours later, Amos was on top of her. Naked. Snoring. Reeking of beer and cigarettes. She cried silently to herself, knowing he had taken her. This man who had saved her. Fed her. Washed her. Clothed her.

He defiled her.

She waited until he rolled off of her, and then reached for his gun on the dresser. She pointed it at his chest, put her finger on the trigger...

And then slowly lowered the gun.

As much as she hated him, he had saved her life. So instead of killing him, Laura-Jean stole all of the money in Amos's wallet, left him snoring in his bed, and disappeared into the night.

Nine months later, alone in a halfway house, Laura-Jean Duntz gave birth to a baby boy. For the entirety of her pregnancy, she considered aborting the child. But for the first time in her life, she no longer needed protecting. The kind women at the halfway house had seen to that.

She was now the protector of this child. She had purpose. She felt a calling to care for something other than herself. She began to read the Bible, and though she only made it halfway through Genesis before calling it quits, she decided on a name.

Adam.

The first man. God's chosen.

Purity, tainted by shame and deceit.

***

The first six years of Adam Kelsey's life were spent in the women's halfway house, in close proximity to Laura-Jean. She kept him within her sight at all times, fearful that Amos Kelsey would slither out of the shadows and snatch up her son.

His son.

Adam grew among a group of steadfast women who helped raise him and his mother, who was still a child herself. He saw strength in them, and from that strength, he discovered his own independence. For hours and hours, he sat in front of the television watching *Sesame Street*, his spongey young brain soaking up each lesson. By age four, he taught himself to read. His favorites were the *Goosebumps* series, but when he exhausted his resources of R.L. Stein, Adam perused the halfway house's tiny library of cookbooks and nature magazines.

Adam Kelsey became obsessed with animals. He liked wolves most of all. In particular, he loved the jade wolf pendant his mother wore around her neck.

Birthdays came and went. Every Christmas was spent huddled around a fire while the women of the halfway house gave him a new pair of shoes, a bag of apples, and a toothbrush. Every year it was the same, and every year he was elated.

Shoes. Apples. And a toothbrush.

Adam was happy, and because her son was happy, so was Laura-Jean. But as her life had always demonstrated, happiness was quick to evaporate.

The halfway house came under new management. Women were fired. Men filtered in. *Sesame Street* was replaced with *Jerry Springer*. Books were thrown away, and the library was converted into a gym.

Adam witnessed male orderlies taunting the women he'd grown to love as his "other mothers." Watched male workers cut in line in the cafeteria, stuffing themselves while young mothers, addicts, and children were left with scraps. Christmas came, and he received no shoes, no apples, and no toothbrush.

He grew to hate men.

On his sixth birthday, Adam walked in on his mother being groped by her doctor. He didn't know how to react. He just stood in the doorway, watching her cry. Too young to recognize the hate seeping into his veins, Adam imagined he was a wolf. He rushed at the doctor, kicking and scratching and biting.

Laura-Jean Duntz, her son, and their bags were tossed out into the street.

There was no room at the local homeless shelter. Instead, they found shelter in an alley under the lid of an upturned dumpster.

Laura-Jean reverted into the tall grasses of her mind. She began hooking again, more out of a desire to stay numb than to make money. While she worked, Adam remained in their alleyway, begging for food and for pennies.

One autumn evening, dressed in fishnets and lace, Laura-Jean Duntz wiped the tears from her eyes. She kissed her son's forehead, placed the jade wolf necklace around his neck, and went off to work.

It was the last time Adam Kelsey ever saw his mother.

Days passed. The warmth of the sun weakened, and with it, so did his health. Slowly starving, Adam rummaged in dumpsters around downtown Juneau. He wandered through the city. Followed Porsches and Bentleys across the Juneau-Douglas Bridge and onto Douglas Island.

His nose tracked the smell of a Thanksgiving feast. He watched from the street, through the dining room window of a mansion, as a family devoured their feast. Father carved the turkey. Mother kissed her children. Daughter looked out the window, caught Adam's gaze and smiled.

"Hey!"

Filthy and disheveled, Adam turned and found a police officer advancing on him. Wolf instincts kicking in, he ran. The deputy chased him down and tackled him to the concrete. Adam fought, hit, scratched, and bit. The deputy pinned him down and raised his fist. Adam closed his eyes, willing to accept his fate.

But the pain never came. He opened his eyes.

The deputy sat on top of him, eyes wide, mouth agape. Large fingertips touched the jade wolf pendant.

"Where did you get that?" the deputy asked.

"It's mine," he growled.

"Did you steal it?"

"Mommy gave it to me!"

The deputy kept him pinned but loosened his grip. He reached into the breast pocket of his shirt and removed a Polaroid. He showed it to Adam.

"Is this her?" the deputy asked.

Adam was stunned. He stared at the picture of his mother. She looked bruised and sleepy, but there was no denying the jade wolf necklace around her neck was the same one he now wore. Adam looked up at the deputy, and he nodded.

"Where is she?" the deputy asked.

"I don't know," he said.

"What's your name?"

"Adam."

"Adam," the deputy repeated, and smiled. "Well, Adam, my name is Amos. It's a pleasure to meet you."

"How do you know mommy?"

"Because, Adam, I'm your daddy."

***

Deputy Amos Kelsey never took the little boy called Adam to the police station. He never took him to a doctor. Instead, he took him back to his home, a newly purchased townhouse in Auke Bay, twelve miles northwest as the ptarmigan flies.

Shortly after, Amos's father suffered a massive coronary and never got to meet his grandson. Amos put in his bid for the position of police chief, but due to the shift in local politics (as well as the fact that every police officer in Juneau still despised him), he lost by an enormous margin.

His father was dead. He would never be promoted. Fate had returned his son to him, but the boy's mother might still be looking for him. Might try to steal him back.

All the signs pointed to what Amos had been considering for many months now...

It was time to leave Juneau.

Amos Kelsey sold his townhouse for a fraction of what he (or rather, his father) had paid. Calling up an old friend of his late father's, Amos made a lucrative career shift and weaseled his way into becoming an Alaska State Trooper.

The catch was, he was assigned to patrol the tiny towns and villages north of the Arctic Circle.

From the warmth and luxury of Douglas Island to the frozen misery of the Arctic, Amos and Adam settled in the small town of Bettles. Amos provided Adam with everything he needed. Food. Clothes. Books, both educational and entertaining.

And though Amos finally seemed to push aside his immaturity and incompetence and proved to be one hell of a father to Adam, the little boy couldn't shake the feeling that, quite possibly, he had been stolen.

***

During the summer months of Adam Kelsey's teenage years, Amos hired a local Inuit man named Nukilik to teach Adam to hunt. Nukilik forbade the use of guns, and taught Adam how to properly handle a compound bow.

On Adam's fifteenth birthday, Nukilik took him out into the woods beyond the eastern shore of Lake Adamant. Huddled down on the shale, water lapping at his ankles, Adam nocked his arrow, pulled back on the bowstring, and closed one eye. On Nukilik's mark, the boy slowed his breathing.

A velveteen rack of magnificent, flowering antlers emerged from the tree line as a massive bull caribou treaded slowly down the beach for an icy drink.

Nukilik watched as the boy bared his teeth, a soft growl rumbling in his throat.

And then…

Sthwit—

Fump.

The arrow pierced the bull's heart. The bull gave a snort, then went down, face-first into the freezing ripples.

Nukilik's jaw hit the beach. Never had he witnessed a *naluagmiu*, a white boy, so effortlessly take down a bull.

That afternoon, in a small hut in the woods cast in shadow by a large horseshoe-shaped hill, Nukilik taught Adam Kelsey how to skin and butcher the beast. Adam wasn't frightened of death. He did as he was told and carved hunks of meat from the bull's flanks, wiping sweat from his forehead and leaving blood smeared across his face.

"Here," Nukilik said. He cut a small piece of raw meat and

handed it to Adam. "Is your kill. You eat first."

"It isn't cooked," the boy observed.

"Amaruq no cook his kill."

"Amaruq?"

Nukilik smiled and nodded at the wall. Adam looked up.

There, painted on an old sealskin canvas, was the face of a wolf. Nukilik pointed at the painting, then placed his hand on Adam's heart.

"Is in you. Eat, young wolf." The old Inuit man sat back on his haunches and stoked a popping fire. "Eat, Amaruq."

Adam couldn't take his eyes off the sealskin canvas. He stared deep into the wolf's yellow eyes, and then ate the raw flesh.

As they do, the seasons changed.

The world spun.

The young wolf became a young man.

At eighteen, Adam set his heart on returning to Juneau. To opening his own halfway house to care for young women and children who shared the misfortune he'd known as a child. To finding his mother, if she was still alive.

He witnessed the slow decline of his father's health. Amos Kelsey never adapted to the cold of the Arctic. His bones clicked. Fat melted away under chapped skin that ripped like tissue paper. Every winter, influenza became harsher and lasted for weeks on end. Bedridden, Amos Kelsey was forced to retire from the state troopers. And with his resignation, so Adam was forced to resign his own dreams.

Juneau would have to wait.

Amos continued his descent into deterioration. Lesions spread over his chest and down his arms. He coughed up blood. Specialists were flown in from Fairbanks, and all gave the same diagnosis. Unchecked for two decades, HIV had advanced into an aggressive form of AIDS.

Three months after the diagnosis, Amos's squalid and verminous past returned to claim him. Diseased blood flooded his lungs, and he drowned in his sleep.

Adam Kelsey buried his father on the eastern shore of Lake Adamant. Nukilik was the only other person to attend Amos's funeral. He was the only one to help Adam lower the body into a hole. He was the only one to whisper words of condolence, though they fell on deaf ears.

For as they piled dirt, sand, and shale atop Amos's body, Nukilik was also the only one to witness Adam's pleased, wolfish grin.

***

Adam Kelsey met Sophie Dilbrook three years before I did.

She had just completed her second year of law school when her mother called and told her that her father's health was quickly fading. She hopped into a schoolfriend's Cessna and flew direct into Bettles. The snowfall was thick and the roads treacherous, and the fifteen-mile trek to Ukippa was damn near impossible.

Desperate to be by her father's side, Sophie wandered into the town lodge.

In her red-bottomed heels and olive pea coat, every eye fell upon her. She announced then and there that she needed a brave soul to get her to Ukippa, that she would pay whatever was asked, so long as she got there in one piece. Most Bettlans knew the drive to Ukippa was akin to suicide and remained glued to their seats.

A young man sat in a corner booth, his nose buried in the pages of an issue of *Archery Alaska*. He looked up at Sophie, grabbed the keys to his late father's V8, and stood up.

"I can get you there," he said.

Sophie accepted the young man's offer. Always cautious, Sophie's purse (and the 38-caliber revolver inside) was never far from her reach.

Chained tires bit through black ice as they sped out of Bettles. Without warning, the stranger pulled off the icy main road and sped into the trees.

"What the hell are you doing?" she yelled, fingers reaching into her purse for the comfort of the revolver's handle. If he thought he was taking her into the woods, she would be ready.

"Trust me," he said.

"I don't know you!"

"I'm Adam."

And with that, he tore through the underbrush, finding the snowy forest paths he and Nukilik had traversed thousands of times. Adam wove the truck around familiar tree trunks, up and across hillocks, and over frozen creek beds. After only twenty minutes, the truck emerged from the trees on the eastern bank of Lake Adamant.

A mile to the east, the Dilbrook Mansion glittered atop Horseshoe Hill.

"You can let go of the gun," he told her. He rolled the muddy, snowy tires onto the highway that encircled the lake, and drove onward toward the hill with three houses.

One massive, one quaint, and one miniscule.

Sophie kept her eyes on the stranger called Adam. In the dark of the moon, his eyes were gray. Soft, yet hardened. Young, but possessing a wisdom beyond even her father's years. He'd done as he said he would. He'd had all the opportunity in the world to take her into the trees and do whatever he liked. Even with the gun, he could have overpowered her, though she would have put up one hell of a fight.

He caught her staring at him, and then offered her a smile. It was a coy smile, one that ignited his sharp cheekbones and electrified his mischievous stare. It was a smile that made her chew the inside of her bottom lip.

Fascinated by him, Sophie moved in closer.

Adam ignored her advances and drove Sophie home.

***

Sophie ended her story there, but I knew she had only just scratched the surface. I was tempted to press her, to know what happened next. But when I looked at her, I thought better of it.

Her eyes were rimmed in redness, glistening pools of melancholy memories.

Later that night, after Sophie and I read you a collection of old Shel Silverstein favorites from the Dilbrooks' library, I bid her goodnight, carried you back to the Cabin, and put you to bed.

I grabbed a pair of binoculars from the garage, went out onto the front porch, and put the cups to my eyes. I focused the lenses to the west and watched the dark, magnified outline of the Shack. Whether or not Moose was home, I couldn't tell. The windows were black.

But Harvey was in there. I was sure of it.

Then and there, I made my decision: I was going to get my dog back.

As I turned to head back inside, I noticed something odd. A faint glow in the distance, out on Lake Adamant. I put the binoculars back to my eyes, focused the optics upon the icy surface, and saw the ice shanty with its windows ablaze. The door was open, and a lone silhouette stood in the doorway, casting a long velvety shadow across the lake's frozen surface. As I strained my eyes against the optics, I saw her...

The girl in the snow.

10

AT THE END OF THE FORK

The days were getting darker.

A week before Thanksgiving, Gloria had me uproot a particularly rotten black fir, which proved even more difficult than I imagined. Sawing off the branches and the trunk had been simple enough. The burl took a great deal longer, as it weighed ten times as much as I did. I used a thick rope to procure a fireman's cinch, a technique I'd used countless times to lift bariatric geriatrics from the sinkholes of their beds, and then hoisted it from the earth. I spent the morning chopping the burl into firewood, embracing the yearned aches of my back and shoulders.

Unearthing the roots took much of the afternoon. I chopped at the spidery tendrils stiff with the clutching chill of permafrost, cursing the cold and kneading the warmth back into my knuckles.

I looked up at the Dilbrook Mansion, high turrets glinting in the fading light, the edges of the windows glistening with frost. I wondered what Sophie and Gloria were doing, what they were talking about, whether I had become the subject of their conversation.

Hoping that Gloria was singing my praises to her daughter.

He is perfect for you, Soph, I imagined Gloria say. *A good man with strong hands and an even stronger heart.*

I imagined Sophie bouncing you in her lap, imagined you giggling and gazing up at her with trust and adoration. I imagined her holding you close, wanting you as her own, and wanting me because of it.

It was then that my conscience whispered a sobering reminder into my ear…

Tom Clark.

As much as I hated to admit it, Tom Clark and Sophie Dilbrook were perfect for each other. He confident and commanding, she subtle and steadfast. He righteous and respectable, she immaculate and chaste. He successful and longing for the eternal embrace of a woman with principles and piety to the law, she meeting all the requisite requirements.

And me, performing grunt work for pennies in the dead of impending winter. I sighed and went back to work, brooding beneath the shade of my own solitude.

An hour later, Sophie emerged from the house wrapped in her olive pea coat and her mother's parka. She presented me with a smile and a soppressata sandwich. I wolfed it down without restraint.

"Come with me," she said.

"Where are we going?" I asked.

"Where I promised we'd go," she replied. "Into the woods."

Our boots waded through freshly fallen snow as we meandered into the trees behind the Cabin. I kept my eyes on the ground, attempting to navigate the trail buried under nearly a foot of snowfall.

Sophie, however, fixed her gaze upon the trees and the canopy above.

"You recognize these trees, don't you?" I observed.

"Like old friends," she said.

She caressed a few gnarled trunks as we walked, then called out Harvey's name while I whistled through the throng of spruce and cedar. She led me deeper into the woods than I had ever ventured, and as the day began to darken, I began to look over my shoulder. Completely disoriented save for the boot prints we'd left in the snow, I couldn't shake the feeling that we were being watched.

"I know how to get back," Sophie reassured me.

"You sure?"

"Relax," she giggled. "Take your mind off the trees. Tell me about Harvey."

I did as she instructed, taking my mind off the woods and settling my thoughts upon my dog.

"He's a borador," I began.

"A what?"

"A mix of border collie and Labrador."

"Two very smart breeds," she said. "Did you adopt him?"

"Rescued him," I told her. "About three years ago, I was on call during a pretty horrible house fire. An elderly woman who recently lost her husband to a heart attack. Her name was Doris Harvey. To keep her from being lonely, Mrs. Harvey's daughter bought her a puppy."

As Sophie and I scrambled over an icy creek bed, I let out another sharp whistle, but I felt my hope waning.

"One night, she fell asleep with a cobbler in the oven. House caught fire and by the time we got there, she was already dead from smoke inhalation. As I was carrying her body out of the house, I heard these high-pitched little yips upstairs. Nearly killed myself running back inside, but I finally found him huddled under her bed. Managed to get him outside right before the roof collapsed."

"Jesus," she said.

"First time I'd ever given oxygen to an animal," I mused with a scruffy smile. "Brave little guy held on all the way to the vet. Vanessa, my ex, and I weren't doing very well. Ellie was very sick. We drained our savings trying to get her the care she needed. Tensions were very high. I figured a puppy might lighten the mood around the apartment. And he did, for a week or so. Then everything went belly-up and she took everything. The little money we had. The car. And Ellie. She took everything. Everything except the dog."

"I'm sorry, Laz."

"As lonely as I was, Ness and I were only married a couple years. I thought about the old lady a lot, thought about how lonely she must have felt after losing her husband of fifty-eight years. I thought about how much warmth the little pup must have given Mrs. Harvey."

"And that's where he got his name," Sophie deduced. She looked over her shoulder and gave me a smile.

"Harvey was with me during all the shit Ness put me through. I focused what little energy I had left on work. Harvey grew up in the fire station. Became our little mascot. I was promoted to an arson investigator, and thought it only made sense that Harvey be trained as an arson dog. He went through a year of training, but I was done with fire before he was ever certified."

"Why did you quit?" she asked.

I considered stopping the conversation there. It seemed only fair, considering how abruptly she had ended our conversation of Adam Kelsey. But I wanted to know Sophie Dilbrook. Really know her. And I wanted her to know me.

The *real* me.

"I never said I quit."

"You were fired?"

"Let go," I said. "It was a horrible fire, worse than the one that killed Doris Harvey. A little over a year ago, a retirement community near the Anchorage airport went up in flames. It was huge. Biggest one the department's seen in thirty years."

Sophie stopped for a moment, then turned and met my eyes.

"Turnagain Home?" she asked.

I nodded.

"Laz, I had no idea. We had cases flooding in because of Turnagain."

She stepped closer and slowly wrapped me in a hug. It seemed friendly enough, but how I longed to melt into her body. She must have read my mind, for as quickly as she pulled me into her embrace, she pulled away. As she stepped ahead and led us deeper into the trees, I noticed a reddish tinge upon her cheeks. Whether this was from the arctic air or a sudden spark of combustive chemistry, I chose not to guess.

"What happened?" she asked.

I thought of that day, of the panic, how I rushed to the engine without grabbing my helmet. I thought of the blaze, of the elderly who had melted into their mattresses. I thought of Smitty, the way my captain so fearlessly gave up his helmet before running into the burning building.

I thought of the axe.

My axe.

"Negligence," I answered.

I walked straight into Sophie's back, and looked up to find us in the middle of a small clearing. Ahead, the trees were thick and the snow was dark. To the west, the brush had been chopped away high and wide, and though the trail wasn't evident beneath the snow, I had a sense that this was our way out. To the east, a much smaller path existed, but only just, hidden almost entirely by low hanging branches and angry brambles.

We'd reached a fork in the trail.

I watched her for a moment, watched how Sophie stared into the dark abyss of the small, dark, eastern path. I followed her gaze to the ground, and there, etched in the snow, were compacted boot prints.

Sophie snapped back to reality, grabbed my arm, and tugged me down the larger, western path.

"Wait, Sophie – "

"It's getting late. We need to get back."

"What's down that trail?"

"Forget it."

"Harvey could be down there."

"Then he's already dead."

I planted my feet firmly in the snow and wrenched my arm out of her grasp. Like a stubborn toddler, I stood fixed in place.

"You want to freeze? Fine," she admonished, then walked further down the western path. "Stay here and freeze."

I found it odd how quickly her countenance had changed from cool and collected to perplexed and panicked. I watched her disappear beyond a bend in the western path, and though my curiosity threatened to get the better of me, I knew I would become lost in the woods if I didn't follow her.

I glanced back at the gloomy entrance to the eastern path. To the boot prints in the snow. I knew those prints. Had seen them in the woods the night Harvey disappeared.

I knew then that the girl in the snow was waiting at the end of the fork.

***

By the time I made my way up to the Dilbrook Mansion the next morning, Sophie was already in the air, halfway back to Anchorage.

"It was good to see her," I said over a plate of bacon.

Gloria looked up from the pan of eggs she was cooking. She eyed me suspiciously for a moment, her wrinkled lips curving upward into a grin.

"Yes, it was," she agreed. She adjusted your bib, spooned some eggs onto the tray of your highchair, and smiled as you clumsily stabbed at your food with a plastic toddler's fork.

"Does she visit often?" I asked, doing my best (yet failing) to remain nonchalant.

"Not often, no. She used to visit a lot when her dad first got sick. Now that he's sort of leveled out, hardly ever." Gloria scooped a heap of scrambled eggs onto my plate. "This is the first time she's visited in three years."

"You're kidding."

"I wish I was," Gloria said. "It's the same as last time. She doesn't visit unless there's someone worth visiting."

"What do you mean?"

"She didn't come to visit me or Don," she said. "She came to visit *you*."

I snorted into my morning mug, the burn of black coffee searing my nostrils.

"Bullshit," I laughed.

"I know my daughter better than anyone," Gloria replied. "She likes you."

"She's with my best friend."

"So?"

"So, Tom Clark is about as perfect a man as you can get."

"Well, between you and me, Sophie has never been drawn to perfection." Gloria topped off my mug with a smile. "Perfect is boring."

"Did she say something to you?" I asked, a little too eager.

"She didn't have to."

I sat there for a moment, stewing in Gloria's prediction and feeling my head starting to swell. And then, something Gloria said came back to me.

"You said 'it's the same as last time.'"

"Uh huh," she replied, wetting a hand towel and wiping eggs off your chin.

"Did she used to fly up to visit Adam Kelsey?"

I watched her drop the hand towel to the floor. Her eyes became misty. She stared into a distant corner of the room, lost in a memory.

"Gloria?"

"What did she tell you about Adam Kelsey?" she asked.

"Not much. A little about his past, how he ended up in Bettles, how he drove her up here when she got the call that Don was sick. I made my own assumption that's how he got the job I have now."

"Did she tell you about Sam?"

I watched her shoulders weaken, watched her face grow heavy as she slumped into the chair across from me.

"No," I said. "Who's Sam?"

"Sam was her brother," Gloria sighed. "Her twin."

"Was?"

"He died," she said.

"When?"

"Three years ago," she said. The timeline began to fall into place. "That was the last time she visited."

And though I wasn't yet finished, Gloria collected my plate and my mug and dropped them into the sink. I sensed I had struck a nerve.

"Gloria, I – "

"Adam Kelsey is the reason my son is dead."

And with that, she sulked out of the kitchen and left me to my thoughts.

***

I finished trenching the black fir's rotted roots from the frozen earth just after noon. I found Gloria in the library, sitting at Don's old writing desk, the diamond-shaped onyx paperweight set aside as she flipped through the pages of *The Girl in the Snow*. You sat at her heels, sliding multicolored beads across the rungs of an ancient abacus, similar to the ones I used to play with when I was a tot. There was a moment of pride on my part, pride that my toddler was one of the few on this modern earth who actually took joy in playing with a toy rather than gluing herself to the screen of an iPad.

"All done?" Gloria asked without looking up.

"All done," I answered. I wanted to apologize for bringing up Adam Kelsey, but in truth, I wasn't sorry. It seemed as though every time he was mentioned, the mood over the illustrious Dilbrook Mansion fell into shadow.

And I wanted to know why.

"I have nothing else for you today," she said. She closed the book and peered up at me. I could tell she was still in a sour mood. She didn't smile, but at least she was talking. "Take the afternoon off."

"Are you sure?"

"You've been working like a beaver on that tree. I insist. Go into town. This is one of the few sunny days we'll have left until March. Trust me."

"Ellie – "

"She can stay here with me. Go on and enjoy yourself." Finally, a smile broke through, and I knew the reminiscent visions of her dead son had faded.

For now, at least.

"I'll be back by six," I said. I walked over and lowered to my haunches, picked you up, and planted a series of kisses on your chubby cheeks. You looked a little pale, so I readjusted the cannula in your nose and increased the flow of your oxygen.

"I'll take good care of her. As if she were my own," Gloria said. "Go on."

I did as she said, but I had no intention of spending my afternoon in Ukippa.

***

Grateful as I was for the warmth of the summer sun, I was more grateful still that no snow had fallen overnight. Yesterday's boot prints were clear as ever, etched in the snow and leading deep into the woods.

I took heed of Sophie's warning by bringing along the shotgun I found in the gun safe in the garage. It lay strapped to my back, the weight of its cold steel not doing much to alleviate the cloud of worry over my head. If a bear came along, two rounds of birdshot weren't going to save my life.

I followed mine and Sophie's tracks around the trees and through thorny brambles until, after what seemed like an hour, I found it.

The clearing.

The fork.

My feet told me to turn left. To follow the western path back to the safety of Horseshoe Hill. To take Gloria's advice and spend my afternoon at Galoshes, drinking away my curiosity. To come home to the warm safety of my bed and forget I ever heard the name Adam

Kelsey.

Then, I turned my attention to the small, dark eastern path.

I peered into its dusky depths. Knew that somewhere beyond that crepuscular corridor, Harvey might be waiting for me to rescue him for the second time in his life.

Without thinking, I ducked under the overhanging branches and trudged down the eastern path. The canopy overhead was so thick that hardly any snow made it to the forest floor. Instead, I crunched over the frosty crust of mud and stones, ankle-deep in rotting foliage while sharpened woody fingers reached out of the darkness and scratched my face and neck.

Deeper still I pressed on.

More than once, I lost the trail amid vast spiderwebs and twisted roots, and had to double-back to relocate my path.

Then, I stopped. The hair on the back of my neck stood on end.

I heard the distant, unmistakable snap of a twig and the low growl of some great beast deep within the trees. Eager not to meet whatever made those noises, I quickened my pace, glanced over my shoulder to peer into the rustling trees –

And felt my feet leave the path entirely.

My stomach performed a sickening backflip as I tumbled over a precipice. My vision spun in all directions, blurs of brown and green and gray unfolding in a kaleidoscope of terror. My fingers grasped at vertical earth, flesh and bones assaulted by unyielding boulders, sharpened stones, and battering branches.

I landed with an earsplitting thud.

The breath left my body, and with it, my consciousness.

11

COLD BONES

The first image I saw when I awoke was that of my face, perfectly impacted in the snow. The concave impression my nose left behind was flooded with bloody slush. I tried to breathe through my nostrils, but all that passed were wet and bubbling wheezes. I wiped fresh blood from my mouth and chin as a sharp and excruciating pain pulsed across the bridge of my nose, and as I reached up to inspect it, my guess unfortunately proved correct.

Broken.

With a groan, I rolled onto my back and allowed my watery gaze to drift skyward. Twilight was no longer the placid petal pink of days past. It was now ghostly gray and growing darker by the second.

In just a few days, Horseshoe Hill, Ukippa, and the whole of the Arctic Circle would be engulfed in the soft, wintry darkness of perpetual night.

I lie there a minute longer, staring up at the sheer, jagged rockface I had tumbled over. Nearly vertical, with sharp, unforgiveable overhangs, a seventy-foot cliff of mud and shrubs towered high above me, leaving me in bone-numbing shadow. The recent snowfall had cushioned my fall, leaving me with a broken nose, but thankfully nothing else. Had it been summer (or the snowmelt had been even two inches less), I most certainly would have fallen to my death.

As I looked up, I noticed a narrow ribbon of hard-packed snow forming a switchback trail up the cliff face. Halfway up, however, a recent mudslide had obliterated any hope of reaching the top. I would have to find another way home.

Sophie warned me. I shouldn't have come out here on my own.

My body ached from the fall and from the bitter cold. Exhaustion beckoned like a missed lover. I knew that if I fell asleep, I wouldn't wake up again. But the promise of sleepy warmth lulled me into a cool and quiet calm. Fresh snowflakes fell on my eyelashes as I closed my eyes to the darkness.

And then, your face flashed behind my eyelids, Ellie-bear.

Get up, my conscience grunted. Oddly enough, my conscience sounded very much like Gloria Dilbrook.

A sharp kick to my side brought new life to my cold bones. My eyes bolted open to find her hovering over me, dirt streaked across her wrinkled forehead and mud clumped in her hair.

"What in the holiest of hells were you thinkin'?" she shrieked. "Broke your damn nose, you dummy."

"Gloria, how – "

"I followed you, you dingbat! Here I am, a sweet woman givin' you the day off. I take a peek out the window, expecting to see that godawful orange Bronco headin' into town, but what do I see instead?"

She scoffed and walked a circle around me. For a moment, I wondered if she would ever give me a hand, or just chastise me until I froze to death.

"What do I see?" she repeated, as if expecting an answer. "I see you, walking off into the trees by yourself. Tell me, Laz, is it that damn dog again? Because if it is, I can assure you that it's dead by now, either from the cold or the wolves."

She reached down to grip my wrist and helped me to my feet. My vision swirled about like oil in milk.

"How did you get down the cliff?" I asked, gazing up at the murderous precipice.

"Very carefully. Took a tumble near the bottom. The mud gave out under me," she said, blowing a mud-caked clump of hair from her cheek. "We won't be able to go up. We'll have to find another way back."

And then, something occurred to me.

"Where's Ellie?" I asked, gripping her shoulders.

"At the Mansion, where she ought to be," she snapped and pushed me away. "Her father, on the other hand – "

"Who's with her?!"

I imagined you sitting alone at Don Dilbrook's bedside, the pair of you sipping from your respective cannulas. And then I imagined your face turning purple, your lips an icy blue as you choked on the final breath of your oxygen tank. I imagined Don Dilbrook worlds away in his comatose slumber, unable to help as you slipped into unconsciousness on the cold floor. And me, miles away in the woods, searching for a lost dog that was probably already dead.

I must have been panicking, because Gloria slapped me.

"Calm down," she said. "She's with Lizanne."

As if that made anything better.

"You left her with the nurse? Lord knows what that woman is teaching my daughter right now."

"At least she's teaching your daughter something," she rebuked. Gloria grabbed me by the combined collar of my three sweaters and pulled my face in close.

"Listen here," she growled. "That girl needs her father. Not me. Not the nurse. She needs *you*. For the rest of her life. And judging by your actions lately, leaving her alone in the Cabin for me to find, leaving her with me while you go running off a cliff, I'm starting to suspect that you need *me* more than she needs you."

She stared at me with hard, disapproving eyes. And then, as they always did, I watched them soften. Her knuckles followed suit as she released my collar.

"You could have died, Lazalier. You're lucky the snowdrift was so high."

"You're right," I conceded. I looked off into the trees, hoping against hope that Harvey's face would appear through the brush.

"He's gone. You have to let him go," Gloria said. "She needs you now."

***

I'm not afraid of the dark. I prefer it, actually. I was beginning to crave it. There above the Arctic Circle, I patiently waited for twilight to be swallowed by the moon, the stars, and an inky black sky.

The infinite twilight had me on edge.

"Do you know where we are?" I asked.

"Nope," Gloria grunted.

In this cold, I knew better than to check if my phone would work. Desperate to open Google Maps, I pulled it out anyway. As always, mother nature's icy breath had sucked the battery dry.

"There's no signal out here anyway," Gloria grumbled. For what seemed like an hour, we walked aimlessly through the snow. And then, she grabbed my wrist.

"What is it?"

She tugged me through the trees until we stood under a large black fir.

"There!" she whooped. I followed her pointed finger up the trunk and saw, embedded just under the ragged branches, an unusually straight branch. And where leaves should have been, there were feathers.

"*Katjuk*," Gloria said.

"Gesundheit."

"Hush, dummy," she chuckled, a little more lighthearted than she had been upon finding me. This, then, was a good sign. "*Katjuk*. It means *arrow*. The eskimos in this region used to use them to mark their way through the woods. This one will point to the next, and so on."

"A marker," I said, astounded.

"And there are bound to be others."

We followed the direction of the arrow's compass. Just as Gloria predicted, we found another *katjuk*, its sharp stone head buried deep in the trunk of a gnarled old cypress. We changed our course and followed suit until we found a third arrow, almost invisible under the needly skirt of a great lodgepole pine. Again, we followed.

We were led to a small clearing, and in the center of the clearing was a small hut. At least, what remained of it.

The hut had very recently burned down, its wooden frame black and charred. Embers glowed like rubies where the roof had caved in. Wispy tendrils of smoke swirled upward like upside-down ink blots dripped in water. This was a fresh burn.

And on instinct alone, I reacted.

I bolted through the doorway, my eyes scanning scorched floorboards and blistering paint, searching for anything suspicious, or an ignition point.

And oddly enough, I found three.

"This wasn't an accident," I said.

"How do you know?" Gloria asked. She climbed into the burnt wreckage behind me, holding her shirt over her nose and mouth.

"Three ignition paths. Look."

I pointed out three separate walls where blackened wood in the shape of a V spread upward.

"Three ignition paths on three separate walls, none of which has an electrical socket. It's sloppy, actually. This wasn't a veteran arson."

I continued my search around the husk of the hut, my feet leaving snowy boot prints in the soot and ash. But as I looked closer, I noticed a separate set of boot prints scuffed along the wood. The scuffed prints of the arsonist, no doubt.

And then I saw them.

Beside the scuffed boot prints, etched in fresh soot, were paw prints. Four toes and a pad. Canine prints. Too small for a wolf, but exactly the size of a set of paws I instantly recognized.

"Harvey."

Behind me, Gloria let out a yelp.

I turned to find her eyes wide and glassy, skin as white as the snow around her. She pointed a sooty finger at a charred, overturned wardrobe. A sudden breeze kicked up, and on the wind, I smelled a foul odor I knew all too well.

It was the rancid perfume of burnt hair and charred flesh.

I covered my nose and mouth, my stomach twisting into knots as I approached the blackened wardrobe. I knew better than to disturb a crime scene.

Wedged underneath the enormous wardrobe were the blackened remains of a naked body. The fire must have been intensely hot because the entire face was burned away, leaving nothing but waxy cords of tendon and eyeless sockets that stared back at me. While most of the corpse was hidden beneath the heavy wardrobe, the trunk and arms of the body were completely seared, cold bones poking through the little muscle and flesh that hadn't fully burned away. I noticed a pair of blackened handcuffs imprisoning the bony wrists. Had Harvey been with me, I had no doubt he would have sniffed the body and barked to indicate the scent of an accelerant.

This was murder in the most brutal degree.

But whether this person had been burned alive or was killed before being doused in oil and set on fire, that remained a mystery.

I heard a horrible retching sound and turned to find Gloria

vomiting into the snow. As I turned back to the remains of the body, I noticed something that made the breath catch in my throat.

A silver chain was slung loosely about the neck. A necklace. And hanging from the end of the necklace was a green stone.

A jade pendant in the shape of a howling wolf.

The same pendant Laura-Jean Duntz gave to her son all those years ago.

***

Convinced we would freeze to death if we lingered at the crime scene deep in those woods, I decided it was time to go. I discovered another *katjuk* pointing us away from the hut, and then led a shaken Gloria through the trees.

After an hour, we found our way through the scrub and onto the shore of Lake Adamant. A star-studded night sky impregnated the milieu with a silvery moon casting milky ribbons across Adamant's icy surface. Out on the frozen lake, the windows of the ice shanty were black.

Apparently, the girl in the snow had abandoned her post.

We followed a snowy path that led the mile back to Horseshoe Hill. Gloria Dilbrook was a tough woman, but discovering the corpse had done something to her. I couldn't decipher whether she was shocked, saddened, scared, or otherwise.

"That was Adam Kelsey, wasn't it?" I asked.

I expected her to remain silent, but as she always did, she surprised me.

"Hard to say," she said. "Face all melted to shit. That necklace, though… that was his necklace."

"You're sure?"

"No doubt about it."

"Who do you think did it?"

She stopped then. I watched her gaze drift upward to the crescent-moon hilltop we called home. But she wasn't staring at the Mansion or the Cabin to the east. Instead, her hardened stare remained fixed to the west.

At the Shack.

"Moose?" I asked.

To this, she said nothing. But she didn't have to. As she walked onward, I watched the Shack, wondering what the great bear of a man was doing within the confines of his wooded, shadowy cottage.

By the time we made it back to the Mansion, it was well after midnight, and you were fast asleep. As much as I didn't trust her, I couldn't deny that Lizanne was, in fact, one hell of a babysitter. I grunted as the nurse forced my nasal bone back into place and fashioned a nose cast out of water, flour, glue, and newspaper.

Before Gloria and I had a chance to discuss what we had seen that night and how we were going to proceed, she retired to her bedroom. I found solace on an old Chesterfield sofa in the front parlor, my brain a fuzzy haze of pain, exhaustion, cold, and confusion.

And as I dozed off, I meditated on a single thought. Large, scuffed boot prints in the soot, and Harvey's paw prints beside them.

The devil had my dog.

***

The next morning, I awoke to the slam of a car door.

Nose throbbing but held in place by the papier-mâché plaster, I opened my eyes to a pale sun drifting into the dusty parlor. The morning light was weaker than yesterday's, and it would be gone in three or four hours. Polar night would arrive in less than a week.

I rolled off the Chesterfield and moved to the window.

The Silverado grumbled in the driveway, steam heat rising from the tailpipe. I watched Gloria trudge up the Mansion's snowy front steps, then heard her open and close the oak front door out of my view. I stretched, left the ancient front parlor, and met her in the grand foyer.

"Here," she said, shoving a thermos of hot coffee into my palms. "No need to grab Betty. I'll drive."

"Where's Ellie?" I asked, rubbing the sleep from my eyes. My knuckles grazed the bridge of my broken nose, and the jolt of pain made my eyes water.

"Asleep in Sophie's old room," she said. "Lizanne will look after her. Come on. They're waiting for us."

"Who's waiting for us?"

***

Police tape whipped and popped on a sharp, frosty breeze.

It stretched from one tree to the next, forming a wide misshapen square around the husk of the old, burned hut. The embers had completely gone out. Black ash mixed with freshly fallen snow, giving the appearance of salt and pepper upon the frozen forest floor.

Three Alaska State Troopers crunched around in the snow, taking pictures of the hut from every angle, dusting for prints, collecting samples. Gloria led one of the men around the clearing, re-enacting the trajectory of our forest wandering from the day before.

I wondered if the arsonist assumed that a fire, even one doused in accelerant, would be enough to remove the evidence. It surely hadn't gotten rid of the body, at least not all of it.

I decided to offer my expertise to help in the investigation.

"Who you?" a crusty voice petitioned behind me. I turned and found myself eye-to-eye with a sixty-something Inuit man, his weather-beaten face hardened into a sullen scowl.

Gloria wrenched herself away from the trooper and took up a post between me and the old man.

"Mornin', Nuk," she said. "I didn't know you'd be here."

"Likewise," he growled.

"Laz," she addressed me. "This is Nukilik, Ukippa's Village Peace Officer." The name rang a bell, but I couldn't quite put a finger on it.

"This a crime scene," he barked at her in a thick accent and broken English. "Leave. You two, out. No right be here."

"We have every right," Gloria barked back.

"Leave!"

"Had it not been for us," I piped in, "that body never would have been found."

Nukilik set his hawk-like eyes on me, jowls hung so low that I feared they might fall off his face entirely. The old man took a step toward me, shoved me, and then Gloria shoved him back.

"Nukilik, look at the necklace," she snapped. "It's him. It's Kelsey."

And then, like a sack of potatoes, it hit me. Sophie mentioned

Nukilik's name during her story at Galoshes. The old Inuit man was hired by Amos Kelsey to teach Adam how to shoot a bow and arrow. Taught him how to hunt. Had been by Adam's side when he put his father in the ground on the eastern shore of Lake Adamant.

Nukilik had named Adam Kelsey *Amaruq*, the Wolf.

"I seen it," Nukilik grumbled. "Don't need see it again."

"Nuk – "

"It not him."

"It has to be."

"Not him," he repeated.

And with that, Nukilik glared at the burnt shell of the hut he'd shared with Adam Kelsey on so many hunts. Glared at the cold, charred corpse lying frozen stiff beneath the wardrobe. Glared at Gloria, glared at me, and then stalked off into the trees.

I harbored no ill will toward Nukilik. From what Gloria told me that afternoon, Adam Kelsey had been the closest thing to a son the old man ever had. I pitied him.

We stayed as long as the dwindling sun would allow. We finally left when the troopers wrapped up the body for transport on a floatplane. Final destination, a forensics lab in Fairbanks.

The sleepy town of Ukippa, Alaska was about to get one hell of a wake-up call.

12

WATCHING

I didn't sleep for three nights.

Instead, I watched.

The binoculars became a piece of me, tucked away in my jacket during the ever-fading daylight while I performed odd jobs around the Dilbrook Mansion. At night, while you snored in your crib across the hall, the binoculars were glued to my face. From the silent warmth of the Cabin's master bedroom, I watched the Shack for hours on end.

What does he want with Harvey?

At first, I gave Moose the benefit of the doubt. Perhaps he'd found Harvey alone and shivering in the woods, thought him a stray, and taken him home.

But no, he must have seen Harvey's collar.

Was it a threat, then? Did he steal my dog as a way of telling me I wasn't welcome on Horseshoe Hill?

I wondered if the boot prints I found in the hut belonged to Moose. The prints hadn't been overly massive, and he was a very large man... but maybe he had average-sized feet. And what about the corpse, now suspected to be the remains of Adam Kelsey? Was Moose responsible for Adam Kelsey's disappearance? For his murder?

I considered the possibilities.

Moose had been accused of murdering a female employee of Don Dilbrook's but was never convicted. During his time as groundskeeper for the Dilbrooks, Adam Kelsey uncovered the truth about the murder. Had found the evidence needed to put Moose away... but Moose got to him first. Knocked him out, cuffed him, dragged him out to the hut in the woods, locked him away for three years.

But why wait until now to set the place on fire?

It didn't completely add up.

I needed to know the truth. I needed Harvey back. I needed to keep watch. And so, for three nights, I did just that.

I watched.

Watched the scarred, bearded giant thump around his property, a black and elephantine shadow in the darkness. Watched him chop firewood, the sharpened head of his massive axe glinting in the moonlight. Watched him drag a bloody caribou carcass out of the woods and into the Shack. Watched him through the singular window as he sliced and stripped meat from bone.

In the early hours of the morning, before the faintest of dawn's periwinkle pink threatened to taint the night's inky black, Moose had a habit of disappearing into the woods, never to emerge until the stars came out again.

Time was running out. Tomorrow, the wintry sun would abandon the Arctic Circle in favor of the southern hemisphere, and six weeks of darkness would take over.

If I planned on stealing Harvey back, it had to be today.

***

Moose left before sunrise with a rifle strung across his back.

I watched him disappear into the trees behind the Shack, and then I lowered the binoculars. I made sure you were still fast asleep in your crib, checked your oxygen tank, and prayed that Gloria would never find out I'd left you alone again.

I made my way down the short flight of steps that led into the garage, retrieved the Post-It behind the gun safe, and used the code scrawled upon it to open the hatch. I saw the glint of a handgun tucked away in the back corner of the safe, withdrew the snub-nose revolver, checked to make sure it was loaded, then hopped into the orange Ford Bronco.

And then, I noticed something strange.

Betty's interior stank of decay and the faintest hints of iron. I deduced it was merely her age. How many others had rented her, used her, and abused her before me? But God, she smelled bad. I woke her up with a chortle of her engine, opened the garage door, and I was off. My intention was to drive in complete darkness, but the fresh falling snow made it hard to see. To compensate, I turned on the fog lights. I took the long way around the Dilbrook Mansion, determined to keep my business entirely that – *my* business. I liked Gloria Dilbrook (admittedly, I often daydreamed about her as my future mother-in-law, if ever Sophie could see past her attraction to Tom Clark), but I was beginning to wonder if the old woman was starting to enjoy butting in on my life.

I followed the natural, descending crescent of Horseshoe Hill. Betty's wipers whipped back and forth across the windshield, worsening instead of aiding my vision. The road hugged a steep grade as I drove westward along a series of switchbacks, and even with chains, Betty's tires slipped on the slush and ice, causing my guts to contort into knots with each ghostly twist of the steering wheel.

At the western base of the hill, the road ascended once more. I came around a final turn and had to slam on the brakes as the road suddenly disappeared. In its place stood a rusted, steel tube gate.

A battered, frosty sign warned:

T RN AR UND

I shut off the fog lights and kept the engine running. If the devil (as Gloria referred to him) decided to end his hunt early, I needed a quick escape to make sure I didn't end up in his crosshairs. I savored the final warmth of Betty's heater, then opened the door and stepped out into knee-deep snow.

I surveyed the old gate. Barbed wire fencing stretched in all directions, wrapped around splintered wooden posts that disappeared over the snowy rise. I knew that just beyond the rise, fringed by a thicket of trees and scrub, stood the old Shack.

And inside, Harvey.

I hoped.

I hoisted myself over the gate. To my right towered the dark, dense woods Moose disappeared into an hour earlier. I stuffed one hand into the pocket of my snow jacket and found the handle of the revolver nestled firmly in my grip. I waded up the snowy rise with my eyes fixed on the trees. The temperature was well below freezing, and while my limbs were used to the chill, my lungs ached for the moist warmth of Betty's cab.

Ribbons of purple and green danced in the sky above me. Two weeks ago, the aurora had hypnotized me, had coaxed me to sleep. Here and now, it illuminated my every movement. I felt exposed, vulnerable. I imagined Moose just beyond the tree line, his scarred, yellow eyes watching me.

A twig snapped.

The hairs on the back of my neck stood on end. I drew the pistol, my hands shaking as I pointed the gun into the aspens. Their white trunks and black knots casted ghostly visions as they swayed in the darkness.

Easy, old boy.

I tucked the gun away and continued my ascent. And once over the rise, I saw it. Nestled within a sparse patch of trees on the edge of the woods stood the old Shack.

Even from a distance, I noticed signs of decay. The wooden beams and oaken logs forming its miniscule structure creaked as a sharp gust of wind battered the shutters. The single window I had watched Moose through every night looked as though a rock had been thrown at it, cracks in the glass stretching like an intricate spiderweb. A gate crafted from thin pine branches and chicken wire wrapped around the perimeter of the Shack.

I glanced around at the trees to ensure that I was alone, and then swung my leg over the gate. I looked around for any signs of Harvey, hoping to find a shed where he might be locked up. But there was nothing except me and the tiny cottage.

I shifted my gaze to the Shack, and it seemed to stare right back.

I thought about my mission, and then weighed my options. If I were Moose, I wouldn't want some strange person snooping around my property. I considered knocking on the door. Introducing myself. Talking to him. Earning his trust. Becoming his friend in order to steal Harvey back. From what Gloria told me, Adam Kelsey proved it was possible to befriend the devil.

Then again, look where it led him.

But I knew Moose wasn't inside. I knew his movements. I'd been watching him for days and memorizing his agenda. I knew he wouldn't be back until late, well after the dwindling winter sunlight had disappeared.

Knocking on the door made no sense.

With my mind made up, I approached the steps leading to the Shack's front door. The wood creaked loudly beneath my feet as I stepped up onto the porch. I tried the doorknob and, as expected, it was locked. I hopped down from the porch and moved to the cracked, dusty window, cupping my hands to the edges of my eyes and pressing my face to the glass.

The interior was dark, a mess of black and blotchy shapes sitting eerily and idly beside cardboard boxes and trinkets wrapped in old potato sacks. I watched for any sign of movement, but there was none.

I tapped my fingertips on the glass, waiting to see Harvey's head pop up from among the shadows.

And then, a pair of powerful, muscular hands seized my shoulders.

My bones went rigid. My mind went cold. I'd forgotten about the gun in my pocket. I was dead. Your future flashed before my eyes, and there you were, fatherless and abandoned.

"What the fuck do you think you are doing?"

I knew that voice. I spun around, and there she was.

"Gloria."

I exhaled, but not before she slapped me hard across the cheek. The icy sting brought me out of my trance.

"We need to go," she whispered in a fearful hush, her hardened eagle eyes swiveling to the trees. "Now."

Without waiting for a response, she grabbed my wrist and yanked me away from the Shack, over the gate, and into the trees. A grumbling snowmobile waited for us in a small clearing, and it was there that she shoved me against the trunk of a black pine, and the wind was knocked from my chest.

I was always astounded how strong this tiny woman truly was.

"What did I tell you about coming here?" Gloria whispered. Her eyes were dark, her hair wind-whipped and wild, her usual cocky grimace replaced with a venomous snarl. For the first time since I'd met Gloria Dilbrook, she looked rabid. Threatening.

Unstable.

"I was just – "

"What did I tell you?!" she repeated, her face an inch from mine. I smelled whiskey on her breath.

"You told me not to."

"And you did anyway."

"I'm a grown man," I growled back and shoved her away.

"Like hell you are," she spat. "You left her alone again, didn't you?"

I didn't answer. I didn't have to.

"What are you doing here?" she asked.

"He's got my dog."

"Fuck the dog!" she yelled and swung at me again. This time, I caught her wrist in midair and squeezed hard enough to make her eyes widen. She tugged herself out of my grip, walked over to the snowmobile, and swung her leg over the seat.

"Are you trying to get yourself killed?" she barked. "We find a body in the woods, and you walk right up to the killer's front door?"

"We don't know that he killed – "

"Who the hell else would it be?"

My mind flashed to the ice shanty on Lake Adamant. To the dark-skinned mystery woman whose shadow I'd watched stretch across the ice a few nights earlier. I thought of Ukippa, of the dozens of unfriendly faces inside Galoshes who scowled in my direction. I thought of Lizanne, how she secretly gave something to someone in the trees in the dead of night. I thought of Nukilik, of his history with Adam Kelsey and the burned hut.

But without a motive –

"It could be anyone," I said. "Anyone down in that damned town."

She scoffed.

"Get on," she said. "I'll take you back to Betty."

I didn't want to be in her company at the moment, but I didn't want to walk across Moose's property again. Didn't want to leave anymore tracks. Didn't want to risk my life.

Or yours.

"A bit of advice, Laz. Put the binoculars away."

"Are you watching me?" I asked.

"Someone has to."

***

We sped off through the woods, following the tree line to the barbed wire fence on the edge of Moose's property, abandoning my rescue mission and the hope of finding Harvey along with it.

At least, that's what I let Gloria think.

I would return.

I was hell-bent on it.

I told Gloria where I parked the Bronco. We followed the fence line all the way to the steel tube gate and the warning sign, but there was something wrong.

My heart sank.

Betty was gone.

13

PARANOIA

First Harvey, and now Betty.

My first instinct was to blame Gloria. She was punishing me for leaving you alone again. She followed me that morning and noticed that I'd left Betty's engine on. Once I disappeared over the rise to Moose's property, she stole the Bronco, hid it, then doubled back to park the snowmobile in the woods higher up on Moose's property. She trudged a quarter mile through knee-deep snow and found me with my nose pressed to the Shack's broken window like a Peeping Tom.

But it didn't entirely make sense.

"How could I accomplish all that in ten minutes?" she laughed over the roar of the wind. "Bit paranoid, are ya?"

I clung tightly to her waist as she whipped the snowmobile through the trees, headlights following the direction of Betty's tire prints in the snow. We followed the prints down the switchbacks of Horseshoe Hill. A flurry of snowflakes collected on my eyelashes as

Gloria did her best to keep her goggles clear. We reached the base of the hill and followed the disappearing prints to the eastern bank of Lake Adamant. By then, however, the blizzard made it impossible to see anything else.

We lost the tracks, and Betty with them.

"We'll have to come back," Gloria yelled over the wind. She turned the snowmobile around, and we began the ascent back to the Mansion.

"Nukilik called this morning," she said. "We're needed in town."

"For what?"

"State troopers. They want us to answer a few questions."

I didn't like the way she said it. It sounded inquisitorial. Insinuating. Accusatory.

Maybe I *was* being paranoid.

***

"Mr. Brady, my name is Detective Marjorie Weekes. I'm an investigator for the Regional Major Crimes Unit of the Alaska Bureau of Investigation."

The room was bare, save for a single file cabinet. The walls were off-white and streaked with dark smudges where picture frames and furniture had left their marks over the years. A single phosphorescent beam flickered overhead. We sat across from each other at a hard steel desk, butts crammed into equally hard steel chairs. It was comical how perfectly the atmosphere resembled a typical questioning room you might find in a low-budget crime drama. It was, much to my enjoyment, overly cliché and exactly what I was expecting.

I wanted to laugh, but this was no laughing matter.

Detective Weekes yawned and then sucked down the rest of whatever was in her thermos. Judging by the redness of her eyes, I wondered whether it was coffee or something a bit stronger.

"You and Mrs. Dilbrook discovered the hut during a walk in the woods?"

"I guess you could call it a walk."

"Some pretty dense foliage back there," she said. "Why were you two on a walk that deep in the woods?"

"It wasn't a casual stroll," I answered. "I was out alone, looking for my dog. Like I said earlier, I took a tumble over the cliff and when I woke up, there she was. We couldn't go back the way we came – mudslide – so we wandered until we found a path we *could* follow."

"Pretty lucky you walked in the right direction," Weekes mused.

"I assumed Gloria knew her way around," I answered.

"And you'd never been to the hut before."

"Is that a question?"

Detective Weekes offered a tired smile. "Had you ever been to the hut before?"

"No."

She shuffled through a file, read a line, and set her reddened eyes back on mine.

"You told Peace Officer Nukilik that it was arson. Is that true?"

"Yes."

"How did you know it was arson?"

"Because I know what arson looks like."

Weekes rifled through the pages and read some more. "You were

143

a deputy with the Anchorage Fire Department."

"And an arson investigator," I added.

"Only for a few months, though," she said. "What happened?"

I closed and rubbed my eyes. And when I opened them, we were no longer alone. Smitty stood in the corner of the room, my fireman's axe jutting from the crown of his skull. His melted face remained obscure in the shadows, but I knew he was smiling.

"A fire," I said.

"Pretty typical in your line of work," she quipped.

"Not like this. This was – this one was different."

"Geriatric living facility. Five people dead. Including one of your own," Weekes said, then closed the file and fixed me with her hardened eyes. "You were let go two weeks later?"

"I was."

"Charges were filed against you by a Mrs. Jessica Smitson for the death of her husband, your Captain, but the charges were later dropped. Why?"

"Because I was let go."

"Let me rephrase," she sighed. "Why did Mrs. Smitson file charges against you in the first place?"

"What does any of this have to do with the body we found in the woods?" I asked.

"Just a simple character assessment."

"Am I a suspect?"

"We're not ruling anyone out at this point. Until we have an identity of the victim – "

"Adam Kelsey."

Weekes watched me closely, her eyes narrowing. "What did you say?" she asked.

"The body we found. It's a man named Adam Kelsey."

"And how do you know that?"

"I just know."

Detective Weekes stood up, left the room, and for a minute or so, I wondered if our interrogation was over. She'd made no conclusive remark. Just left. But as quickly as she'd left, she returned and handed me a cup of steaming hot coffee.

And for a moment, I wondered if she'd spiked it with something. Scopolamine, maybe? Sodium Pentothal? Hell, even a good triple shot of whiskey to help loosen my tongue?

Bit paranoid, are ya?

"What is your relationship to Adam Kelsey?" Weekes asked.

"I've never met him. He was the Dilbrooks' groundskeeper before me. He went missing a few years back."

"And you think it was his body you found?" she asked.

"Gloria recognized the necklace."

***

Gloria never met my gaze.

Instead, she brushed past me on her way into the interrogation room to meet with Detective Weekes. I knew the investigator was far from through with me, and I wondered if Gloria's account of that day in the woods would help or hinder my alibi.

The Ukippa Peace Office seemed even smaller inside than out. The plain white walls pressed in on me, and I needed air. I walked down the maze of small, sharp hallways, and suddenly set eyes on winter's final, feeble rays of sunlight pressing in through the small windows of the waiting room. I passed an open door on my right, noticed something out of the corner of my eye, and stopped. I doubled back, peeked my head into the small office, and flipped on the light.

Like the rest of the station, this office was small and overly cramped. A desk and a bookshelf were cluttered with file folders and stray papers, but it was the walls that caught my attention. Unlike the rest of the bland and boring station, these walls were adorned in photographs. Some candid, some professional. I perused each picture, my eyes drawn to the same familiar landscape present in each one...

Lake Adamant.

In one massive print, the rippling water glowed during a summer sunset. In another, winter ice glowed beneath amethyst ribbons of the aurora borealis. One canvas covered an entire wall, a bird's eye view of the lake and, hugging its southern shore, the crescent of Horseshoe Hill. Squinting my eyes, I noticed the turrets and towers of the Dilbrook Mansion on its eastern peak and the Cabin beside it. And to the west, a single dot among the aspens, stood the Shack.

Moose will be back in a few hours.

I had to get back.

I turned to leave, considered leaving Gloria in the interrogation room and stealing the Silverado like I'd assumed she'd stolen Betty, and then noticed a final photograph...

Framed in silver and propped against the computer, it was the only photograph on the desk. I picked it up, and there they were, standing on the shore of the lake.

It was the Dilbrooks. All four of them.

Don, awake and well, with broad shoulders, a proud, upturned nose, and not even the faintest shadow of a smile. Gloria at his side, a decade younger, her complexion free of wrinkles, her hair a sleek and lustrous black. Sophie between them, maybe seventeen or eighteen, as beautiful as ever, determined eyes displaying a glimpse of her future success.

And standing a few feet from the rest of the family stood a young man. His olive skin, chestnut hair, and green eyes perfectly matched Sophie's.

So, here was the brother that nobody wanted to talk about.

"She made us pose like that."

I looked up to find Gloria leaning against the doorframe.

"Told us not to smile, just to stand there with our arms at our sides. Said she wanted us to look regal," she mused.

Gloria took the picture off the desk and stared at it for a few moments, a smile on her face and sadness in her eyes.

"Handsome, ain't he? My boy."

"I'm sorry," I said. "What happened?"

"Story for another time," she said. She set the photograph back on the desk and looked around the walls, at the seasonal panorama of Lake Adamant. "She's one hell of a photographer. Always was."

"Who took all these?"

"Same person that sits behind this desk," she said. "Her name is Evie Brooks."

Evie Brooks.

The name rang a bell. Gloria had mentioned her before.

"The live-in nurse before Lizanne," I recalled.

"Much more than our live-in nurse," Gloria replied. "We took Evie in when her mother moved south to Texas. Ol' Jackie Brooks said she was afraid of Evie's dad, though she never said who he was, just up and moved to some place called Lubbock. Evie spent a few years with us, then went off to Anchorage to get her nursing degree. When Don got sick, she quit the program and moved up here to be with us. Did all she could for him."

Gloria set down the photograph and sighed.

"By that time, though, we'd taken in a troubled young man who had wandered into town with nothing but the shirt on his back."

"Eldon Gamble," I said.

I remembered the disturbed man from Galoshes, the man who had watched me while I sat and drank with Sophie. The man with distant anger in his mismatched, yellow eyes. The man who spoke to himself in whispers.

"Evie did her best to help him too, but it became too much. After a while, he frightened her. Snuck into her room at night, watched her while she slept. She moved out, lost interest in nursing, and decided she wanted to work in law enforcement instead."

"Why is that?"

"I always assumed it was because she was afraid of people like Eldon. People like Moose. People who should be watched or incarcerated, but who wandered freely. Nukilik took her on, and she's been here ever since."

Gloria shrugged. She ran her fingertips along the print, along the ridges of Horseshoe Hill.

"Never lost her interest in photography, though. Evie used to walk around the Mansion, just snappin' pictures," she said. "She and Sophie were joined at the hip."

I now understood who Sophie had visited at the Peace Office two weeks earlier. I couldn't help wondering if getting in good with Sophie's friends would give me a better chance with her in the future (if Tom Clark ever left the picture).

"Can I meet Evie Brooks?" I asked.

"Depends how long you stay," Gloria replied. "She flies south during the winter months – hates the darkness this far north. She stays with her mother in Texas, but she'll return in the spring, all fattened up and tanned. She always does."

I examined Evie Brooks' impressive photography a moment longer, then followed Gloria out of the station. She hopped in the truck and revved the engine, and just as I was about to follow suit, I saw him.

He sat crouched among the pines just beyond Ukippa's tiny town square.

Staring. Whispering.

Eldon Gamble kept his good eye fixed on me, and I stared right back. I watched his lips move, unable to hear his murmured secrets. He scratched at his arms, let out a hodgepodge of coarse, raving laughter...

And then, almost as quickly, he began to sob.

I took a few steps in his direction, and then he disappeared into the trees.

I stood rooted to the spot, watching the patch of trees where he'd stood. The hairs on the back of my neck stood on end, and it wasn't due to the chilly breeze that suddenly kicked up.

I was left with the sudden paranoia that Sophie hadn't told me everything about Eldon Gamble.

14

WOLVES AND WRINKLES

As much as I was dying to break into the Shack, to unearth the secrets that impregnated the old wooden house, I decided to shift my focus from Moose to Eldon Gamble.

If he was going to spy on me, I would spy right back.

The dying sun peeked the crown of its head over the horizon line. The final dregs of wintry light spilled like a thin film of honey over the imposing shoulder of Mount Poe, casting peony tinges on wispy clouds dancing across a frigid sky. I knew the day's sunlight would only last an hour before darkness settled once more, but I planned on relishing the sunlight while I could. Betty was still gone, taken from under my nose, the warmth of her radiant orange paint job stolen into the shadows, and with her, my mind's only link to the comfort I once enjoyed in Anchorage.

Ukippa had finally and fully engulfed me, and it made me uneasy.

Gloria allowed me to borrow the old Silverado for the day. As I drove along the eastern rim of Lake Adamant, I absorbed the weak sunlight into every corner of my body, knowing it would completely vanish in a day or so. Now fully frozen over, Adamant's icy surface glowed as though lit from beneath, a brilliant gold and blue mirror cradled within the bowl created by Mount Poe to the north, Horseshoe Hill to the south, and dense tundran woods to the east and west.

I glanced into the rearview mirror and smiled.

You sat in your car seat, wrapped tightly in three different coats. The outermost layer was a deep blue, giving you the appearance of Violet Beauregarde just after she's consumed Willy Wonka's infamous three-course-dinner chewing gum and swells into a gigantic blueberry. (A favorite childhood film of mine. If you get the chance, Ellie-bear, watch it and think of me.)

You watched the snowy spruces whiz past before you caught me staring, our eyes linked in the reflection of the rearview mirror. I saw your mother in your eyes, tenderness and curiosity manifested in a single glance.

At least, that's how she used to look at me.

My last memory of your mother's eyes harbored hesitation, hurt, and even the earliest signs of hatred. Not to mention the shifty deceit of cocaine abuse.

Your gaze shifted to the front windshield, and suddenly, your eyes became wide as tennis balls. I glanced forward and my heart stopped.

A wolf sat in the road, big yellow eyes ablaze.

I punched the brake. Ice and snow whipped up behind the Silverado as the truck's back tires fishtailed viciously against black ice. I heard you scream from the backseat as I swerved and struggled to re-right the steering wheel.

We stopped a foot from the wolf's billowing breath. Fearless and unmoving, it watched us calmly, its feathery white and gray fur flitting in the breeze, its massive shoulders blocking our path. The snowbanks on either side of the road were too high to drive over and around the animal.

So, I honked the horn.

The wolf stared through the windshield, big yellow eyes patient and testing. Maybe it was my imagination, but I surmised that it wasn't staring at me at all.

It was staring at *you*. Small, sick, and fragile.

A predator staring down its prey.

And all that stood between the two of you was the hood of a truck, two millimeters of glass… and me.

I honked again, eased my foot off the brake, and inched the Silverado slowly forward.

The wolf finally stood up. It shook the snowflakes from its coat, yawned its great sharp maw, and then moved off the road. It didn't run off into the trees as I would have expected. Instead, the beast climbed up over the snowbank, walked down the snowy shoreline, and padded onto the glowing surface of Lake Adamant, its sharp nails raking over the ice.

I watched as the beast turned its head to glance at us once more. It held my stare, and then it walked further out onto the surface of the lake. Before too long, it disappeared behind a bend in the shoreline.

"Dawgy," you giggled from the backseat. "Where go dawgy?"

"Good question, El," I said. But I knew exactly where the animal was headed. And it was another mystery I was determined to solve.

What awaited the wolf inside the old ice shanty?

One thing at a time, old boy, I thought. *For now, let's focus on Eldon Gamble.*

***

The snow began to fall as we parked outside of Galoshes.

"Hungry, El?"

I killed the engine, climbed out into the snow, and helped you out of your car seat. I made sure the cannula was fixed into your little button nose, then strapped the tiny backpack to your shoulders, the small oxygen tank gently hissing as you sipped from your lifeline. Hand in hand, we crunched our boots up the snowy steps.

The familiar warmth and musty interior of Galoshes ensnared us as we settled down at the bar top. The restaurant was completely empty, and for a moment, I wondered if our trip here was for naught.

Yes, lunch with my daughter was top of the queue for the afternoon, but a singularly important task sat just below on my list of to-dos...

To my dismay, Eldon Gamble was nowhere to be found.

Galoshes was the one place in Ukippa I'd seen him most often, a refuge from the biting cold and, from what Sophie had told me, his lack of an actual home. I suppose you could say I pitied him, but the stories I'd heard about him so far had been nothing short of suspicious.

He snuck into people's homes and watched them sleep.

He whispered sinister secrets to himself.

He spied on me from the shade of the pines.

My efforts to learn more about Eldon Gamble weren't for my own entertainment or my longing to oust him from Ukippa. I was afraid for you, Ellie, afraid that he might sneak into the Cabin in the middle of the night. After all, he'd done it once before when Adam Kelsey was the Dilbrooks' groundskeeper. What was stopping him from doing it again? What was stopping him from stealing you right out of your crib?

Or worse.

The familiar musk of burning whale oil entranced my senses. I thought of Anchorage, of my countless visits to Anchors. I thought of my old friend, Inuksuk the bartender, of his generous pour hand. I thought of an olive-green pea coat, a pair of matching green eyes glancing up from pages of discovery to land upon mine.

And then, I thought of Tom Clark, the way my best friend's lips landed effortlessly upon Sophie's.

My daydream dissipated into the musky haze.

I was seconds from relinquishing all thoughts of Eldon Gamble, seconds from grabbing your chubby little fist, leading you back to the truck, and heading back to the Cabin. But just as I bent down to button your three layers of coats, a familiar face with weather-worn, raisin skin appeared from under the bar top.

"Zin for you, princess?"

The toothless old bar matron of Galoshes smacked her tongue against her gums and let out a crusty chuckle. Gnarled and arthritic hands slapped a couple steaming rags on the wooden bar top, polishing the lacquered mahogany until it gleamed and glittered with the reflection of the large *qulliq* set upon the bar, its sheet of flame swaying and popping.

"Not today, Mags," I said. "Are you open for lunch?"

"Not for another hour," she answered. Her silvery blue eyes scanned me before looking at you. And then, she smiled.

"Who is this little caribou?"

"This is my daughter, Ellie."

"S'wrong with her?" Mags asked.

"Nothing's wrong with her," I growled.

The old woman reached slender, bony arms across the bar and lifted you with a strength I wasn't expecting. She held you at arm's length, examining you as though deciding whether or not you were contagious.

"'Course there ain't," she finally decided. And with a smile, she held you against her like a great-great-great-grandmother, and stared deep into your face. Whether she was envious of your youth or simply reminiscing of a time when she held her own grandchild that close, I couldn't tell, but I allowed her to hold you as long as she wished.

"Pulmonary lymphoma," I said. "At least, it used to be."

"Ah," Mags sighed, then brushed back your hair. "Well, you seem to be doin' good by her."

I smiled at that. Really smiled. I'd needed that, more than anything.

"I'll open 'er up a little early for the two o' ya," Mags said.

"Thank you." I met her eyes fully for the first time. The blue, vulpine glow of her cataracts glistened with decades of deep, cold memories. "A burger for me, no pickles, and a grilled cheese for the lady."

"Comin' up."

She set you down and let you wander the restaurant. I took a seat near the cold, damp hearth where Sophie had shared with me her story of Adam Kelsey. I peered into the velvety black soot carpeting the brick walls of the hearth and allowed the whale oil's scent to bewitch me once again.

I thought of Adam Kelsey and of his mysterious disappearance. I thought of him waking to find the mismatched yellow eyes and oily demeanor of Eldon Gamble at his bedside.

Whispering vicious, wicked secrets.

Were the two events related? And if they were, who in Ukippa would know?

Mags trundled out from the kitchen, back hunched, her arms effortlessly carrying our food to the table beside the hearth. And then, it hit me. Who better to know the town's secrets than the only barkeep?

"When does it start to pick up?" I asked.

"'Round six o'clock, the boys start bumblin' in. Dilbrook's got 'em workin' like dogs in them fields," she grumbled and smacked her gums as she helped you into your highchair.

"The oil fields?" I asked.

"Ayuh," she said. "Y'ain't never seen the Mainstay fields?"

"Not yet."

"It don't surprise me," she went on. "Not after what happened."

"What happened?"

"Ah, hell," she said. "Now you got me gossipin'."

"Curiosity isn't gossip. I'm curious, Mags. I know next to nothing about the Dilbrooks and I've been living there over a month."

"Ain't my place to – "

"Gloria and I discovered a body behind Horseshoe Hill," I said bluntly.

"So, it *was* you that found it," she said. "That's why them troopers been here."

"And they'll be back," I replied. "They'll be looking for whoever burned that hut and the person inside, and they'll start the questioning with the guy who just happened to stumble upon it. I need to know these things, Mags. I need to know that my daughter and I are safe here. There's something odd going on up on that hill."

"The trees behind that hill, they change folks," Mags said with a shrug of her bony shoulders. "Stay out there long 'nuff, you might not come back at all."

"They're saying the remains belong to Adam Kelsey." And by *they*, I meant *me*.

"Not everyone is sayin' that."

"What do you mean?"

Mags sighed. She took a seat across from you, picked up a French fry, and helped herself.

"Nukilik," she said. "Man's been tellin' folks around here that body ain't Adam Kelsey. He knew Kelsey better than anyone. *Too small to be Amaruq*, he say."

"Kelsey's necklace was hanging around its neck."

"Hangin' from?" she asked. "Or wrapped around?"

I hadn't thought of that.

"So, you're saying whoever was burned in that hut was first

strangled with Adam Kelsey's necklace."

"Ain't sayin' nothin'," she said, and stole another fry. "Just repeatin'."

"What can you tell me about Eldon Gamble?" I asked.

Mags cocked a hairless eyebrow in my direction, smoky blue cataracts watching me carefully. "Why?" she asked.

"There's something about him. Something… not quite right."

"You think he had somethin' to do with it?"

"All I know is, I found a body, and he's been watching me ever since."

Mags sat back in her chair and stared deep into the blackened hearth. The silence that settled between us lasted long enough to leave me wondering if Mags had nodded off to sleep with her eyes open. At last, she looked down at you, and made the decision to tell me what she knew.

"Deep down, he's a good boy," she said. "A good man."

"And on the surface?"

"Misunderstood. People steer clear of 'im, but what they don' know is that he's the one who's terrified. He don' do well in crowds or with new people."

"What's wrong with him?"

"A lot o' things," she sighed. "He wandered into town a few years back and no one really knows where he come from. Rumor is, he drifted into Ukippa with no lodgin' or nothin', just kept repeatin' the same word over and over."

"What word?" I asked.

"*Wolf*," Mags said. "Whether he been chased by a wolf on his way into town, or just talkin' nonsense, he kept sayin' it. *Wolf, wolf, wolf.*"

I thought of the wolf we saw on the road not an hour earlier. My mind began to spin, and I suddenly remembered a small detail from Sophie's story.

Adam Kelsey liked wolves.

"Mags, do you think Eldon had anything to do with Adam Kelsey's disappearance?" I watched her face become shriveled as an old plum, and then I noticed her shoulders slump.

"I've wondered that m'self," she said. "Don't really know."

I sighed, rubbed my face into my palms, and was about to abandon my would-be interrogation of Mags when she said the words that piqued my interest.

"But I know of some'ne that might."

***

Our bellies full to bursting, we left Galoshes with a new destination in mind. Following a map Mags had scribbled onto the back of a greasy old napkin, I wove the Silverado around the town square, past the Ukippa Peace Office, beyond the large pine tree where Eldon had watched me, and onto the main highway that led back to the lake.

But instead of following the road south as I always did, I found the small turnoff Mags had outlined on the makeshift map. I'd never noticed the turnoff before – a small, snowy path led into the trees and disappeared into the woods at the base of Mount Poe. The snow was too deep, the trees too thick, the climb too steep for the Silverado.

We would have to hike.

I found a pair of Don Dilbrook's old snowshoes in the back of the truck and strapped them to my feet. Intent never to leave you behind again, I hoisted you out of your car seat and considered how to keep you out of the snow. It was then that I set my eyes upon the car seat itself.

I've only ever had a few strokes of genius in my life, El, and this was one of them.

Careful not to damage the car seat too terribly, I ripped the foam and fabric of the seat pad from the plastic harness and canopy. I found a bundle of rope under the passenger seat and threaded the ends through the harness slots, looping them twice over. Having perfected dozens of slipknots in my time with the Anchorage Fire Department, I tied off the ropes to create a makeshift baby carrier. I strapped you and your oxygen tank firmly to my chest, tied off the rope around my shoulders and waist, and we were off.

My legs burned as we hiked up the trail, but it was a burn I now eagerly invited. Weeks of hard labor had brought the firmness back to my muscles. The Lazalier Brady who had found himself nearly homeless on the streets of Anchorage was gone, and in his place stood the man I had been before Smitty's death. Before I had lost my job, my wife, and my child. The man I had once been proud to be.

The fighter. The father. The fearless.

I was back, baby.

15

THE HERMIT OF MOUNT POE

S *huhf. Shuhf. Shuhf.*
I'll admit my first time in snowshoes wasn't a stroll in the woods, especially with a thirty-pound toddler strapped to my chest. I waddled like a punch-drunk penguin through the dense, fresh snow, sinking a few inches with each stride, though I knew I might have been groin-deep in powder had it not been for my lucky find. The sun was long gone, and I knew it wouldn't find its way back over the horizon by morning.

Black spruce and white birch surrounded us as we penetrated the western woods, their high, dense canopies looming over us like dark wraiths and pale ghosts in the night. The world stood still in a wintry grayscale, all whites and blacks and grays saturated in sepulchral silence.

I climbed onward, the steep and steady misery of Mount Poe's incline freezing its way into my lungs. I sacrificed my scarf to keep you warm, the crocheted wool wrapped delicately around your nose and forehead, your big cornflower blue eyes peering up the mountain. I stopped to rest once or twice, hands on my knees, brain going numb as my vision swam. And each time I stopped to breathe, I thought of the charred and twisted corpse in the hut. I thought of Horseshoe Hill, of Ukippa, and of each crooked character that had twisted its way into my psyche.

Eldon Gamble...

Adam Kelsey...

Moose...

Sam Dilbrook...

The girl in the snow...

I had taken up a cause to figure out exactly what was going on. I wouldn't rest until I did. And so, I lumbered on.

Shuhf. Shuhf. Shuhf.

An hour after we'd abandoned the Silverado by the wayside, we broke through the trees. I looked up, and my breath caught in my chest.

Mount Poe stood like a snowy sentinel against an obsidian canvas. Jagged ridges stretched skyward, slicing through the stars and leaving a white, lifeless void across the cosmos. The sheer mass of the mountain was daunting, ancestral in its towering silence. And though it exuded immense size and strength, I noticed its delicate southern face shift under the slightest breeze, a curtain of snow spilling down the ridge toward the northern shore of Lake Adamant.

If I'm not careful, I thought, *Poe will bury me.*

The snowy mug of the mountain began to glow and glitter a stark and vivid green. I looked up, and there to light our way were the shimmering ribbons of the aurora borealis. It's true what they say about the northern lights, El. With each viewing, they grow more spellbinding. My mother used to beckon me to sleep with the story of an old Inuit fisherman who watched the aurora once a year during his ninety-eight year lifetime, and each time, he cried a river of tears that brought the seasonal salmon north from the ocean. I thought of my mother then, and of my father, and the strenuous and violent relationship that led to her demise.

Together, you and I watched the ribbons dance, pirouetting gracefully between the moon and stars, igniting the lifeless whites and blacks and grays of the night into a chartreuse ballet.

Encouraging us to continue on.

I lifted one snowshoe out of the snow, then the other, then forced my thighs to press on up the mountain.

Shuhf. Shuhf. Shuhf.

I looked down for a moment, and from between the crocheted wrapping of my scarf, your big glassy eyes remained fixed on the glowing sky. Enraptured by the light. As I lie here writing our story, awaiting death's cold kiss, I wonder if you remember that night. If you remember being strapped to my chest in the seat of a throwaway car seat. If you remember your first glance at the aurora. Have you watched them since? Do you watch them still? Do you think of me?

Excuse me, Ellie-bear, while I digress.

Let's continue.

Mags' greasy map led us up and around a crumbling ridge and, finally, I saw it.

A small, dark rectangle sat perched on a snowy ledge, tucked beneath a rocky overhang dripping with icicles. Had I not been looking for it, I would have missed the structure entirely, mistaken it for an oddly angular boulder wedged between the fangs and the maw of the mountain. I took a deep breath. Tucked the napkin back into my pocket. And then, I heard a swift crunch in the snow behind me.

A cold, hard something touched the nape of my skull.

Chk-chnk!

"Move and I'll paint your brains on the snow."

So, I didn't.

I remained stock still. Blood pounded in my ears, pulsed behind my retinas. My fatherly instincts screamed at me to fight, to duck, to lunge, to swing my leg and level my opponent. Steal his gun. Blast his face apart. Paint the snow with *his* brains. I wanted it so bad. It would be risky… what if he shot before I gained the upper hand? Chances are, you and I would both die.

I was about to risk it all, a moment from fighting to kill, when I noticed the soft glow of eyes in the trees beyond.

Ol' Smitty stood between two conifers, his milky, lifeless eyes glittering green with the shimmering skylights.

I've killed enough men in my life, I decided.

"Please," I whispered.

"Who are yeh?" spoke a deep and thorny voice.

"My name is Lazalier Brady."

"Rich ol' Dilbrook's lawn-bitch, huh?" the Gunman snorted. "This here ain't Horsehoe Hill, boy. You lost. Begs the question, 'chu doin' all the way up here?"

"Mags sent me."

"Mags? The hell she sent you for?"

"I need to speak with Denali Shaw."

"Denali don't like visitors," he spat.

"It's important," I said.

"What's it about?"

"Please, I just—"

"Nobody talks't Denali without gettin' through me first. I'll ask yeh again. The fuck you need to talk to Denali Shaw 'bout?"

"Eldon Gamble."

He was silent for a full minute. All I heard was the sound of pine needles whispering in the breeze, the pounding of my heart, and the raggedness of his breath.

"Turn around," the Gunman said.

"You told me not to move."

"Turn. Around."

I did as I was told, slowly turned, and stared into the circular darkness of a sawed-off shotgun's twin barrels. I glanced up to meet the eyes of the Gunman. Judging by his harsh tone, I expected him to be an old, bearded, frightening Moose-type. Instead, the eyes peering down the scope belonged to a man younger than I was. No more than a boy, early twenties, perhaps. And though his tone was confident, the shotgun trembled in his grip. Whether from fear or from cold, I couldn't tell. I was taller than he was, broader in shoulder, wider in stance. He stared into my face, and then I watched his gaze move to my chest.

His hardened eyes met your big blues, and all at once, they softened.

"Ah, shit," he grumbled.

"My daughter and I are cold," I said. "We hiked all the way from the turnoff. All I need is ten minutes of her time."

"She don't like people," he stated. "Don't like strangers."

"Then consider me a neighbor," I replied, and held my hands higher.

"What's in the bag?"

"A gift. Mags made it special for Denali."

I kept eye contact with him, slowly pulled the backpack from my shoulders, unzipped it, and let the scent of a cold cheeseburger and fries waft in the winter chill. "I would have asked her to pack two if I knew Denali had a companion."

"Ain't a companion," the Gunman grunted. "Just a nephew." He slung the shotgun over his shoulder, wiped the frozen snot from the end of his nose, and scuffed past me.

"Zip it up," he grunted. "S'go before I change my mind."

I glanced down at you and smiled, then followed the Gunman in silence. Don's snowshoes were two sizes too small and clumsily *shuhf*-ed along behind the Gunman's smooth, practiced steps. He led us higher up the balding ridge until the edge of my snowshoe scraped against what I thought was Mount Poe's granite face.

"You'll want to leave them floaters," he grunted over his shoulder.

I had no idea what he meant until he unstrapped and kicked off his own snowshoes, and then I followed suit. What I initially thought was granite were actually large, flattened rectangles of concrete that had recently been shoveled clean of fresh powder. The smooth, flat, and wide manmade steps led further up the mountain.

I looked to my right, and there was nothing but cold air and a steep drop. I clutched my arms tighter around you and pressed my back against the side of the mountain. The Gunman must have noticed, because he laughed and continued on.

"See 'em there?" he called over the whistling wind. I looked ahead and watched as he pointed across the darkened canvas of the night sky. Had it not been for his instruction, I would have missed them altogether. But there they were, far below and miles away.

Three specks of light in the darkness. They could have been stars, but I knew their identities in an instant.

One tiny speck, off on its own at the western edge of a large, horseshoe-shaped shadow. A second, immensely larger speck that, like a miniature galaxy, was actually a collection of smaller specks. Windows upon windows upon windows. And just to the left and down a little way, a third speck flickered every few seconds. I knew that particular light very well, a light I'd seen almost every night for the past month.

As I stood there on the freezing ridge, I was left to wonder who (or what) was causing the Cabin's automatic porchlight to ignite over and over.

"Don' fall behind now," I heard the Gunman call.

I pulled my gaze from the lights of Horseshoe Hill's three houses, then pushed onward. I rounded a crumbling corner and gently bumped you against the Gunman's back.

"Air's a little thin up here," he said, and nodded ahead.

There, pressed against the vertical face of Mount Poe, was a large black shipping container. How anyone had ever managed to get it this far up, I couldn't fathom. As though sensing my thoughts, the Gunman spoke up.

"Helicopter was carryin' it over Poe on the way to the Gates of the Arctic. Somehow lost hold of it."

"What is it?" I asked.

"Home," he answered.

As we approached the jet-black, horizontal monolith, I noticed the edges of the shipping container shimmering, as though the mountain itself glowed from within. The Gunman wrenched open the door, and light flooded out onto the snow.

"C'mon then. Denali'll be wantin' that grub. Close the door behind you."

With that, he descended and simply vanished into the floor of the shipping container. Half of me wanted to turn around, to head back down the mountain, and to forget all about Eldon Gamble, the Gunman, and the hermit of Mount Poe.

The other half was far too intrigued.

Following the Gunman's lead, I carried you up and over a final snowbank and set foot inside the shipping container. Inside, there was nothing but four black steel walls strung with gaslit lanterns and a small square hole in the floor. I stepped carefully into the hole and followed a set of concrete steps down into a narrow, winding tunnel that had been carved out of the rock. For more than a few moments, I wondered if I was being led into a trap by the Gunman, every paternal nerve and fatherly fiber of my being screaming at me to get you out of there.

But then, as the tunnel widened into an opening, all the breath left my chest.

We stood at the precipice of a granite cliff, at the edge of a monstrous, illuminated cavern within the bowels of Mount Poe. String lights hung from the ceiling of the cave, interwoven among dozens of dripping stalactites stretching ten feet or more, casting tentacular shadows among the alcoves of the cave. On the floor of the cavern, storage racks housing hundreds of paper-wrapped packages and cardboard boxes lined the vast walls. Towers upon towers of stacked tin cans rose like spires from the floor.

In the middle of the floor were two tents erected upon a stony outcrop, polyester walls flapping softly in the cavern's moist, humid breeze. Down below, I heard the soft hum of an electrical generator. High above, the unmistakable chittering of bats.

"Most of 'em fly south for winter," the Gunman said. He sat at the edge of the precipice, legs dangling over the edge. "Some of 'em stay behind, chew through the boxes for food. Spam and raisins, more often'n not."

I had to rub my eyes to make sure I wasn't dreaming. When I opened them again, it was to find a hermit's cathedral, just as it was.

"How long – "

"Denali's been here more'n ten years," he said, chewing off a fingernail. "I been here a year or so. Once you get used to shittin' in a hole, it ain't too bad."

The Gunman stood up and walked over to a ladder that led down to the cave floor.

"Careful with the little miss," he said and smiled at you. "It's a helluva drop."

***

Denali Shaw watched me closely, firelight crackling within her hard and calculating gaze. We sat across from each other on the cave floor, warm flames dancing in a stone firepit between us.

The Gunman had graciously lit the fire for us and offered to play with you while I spoke to the old hermit woman alone. I was hesitant at first, but there was a kindness in the Gunman's eyes that I hadn't seen much of since arriving in Ukippa. I agreed under the stipulation that he leave his shotgun by the fire, which he did. I watched as he took your hand in his own, lifted you gently over a few jagged rocks, sat Indian-style and presented you with a crate of empty bean cans.

"He's harmless," the old woman croaked.

I turned to look at Denali Shaw through the fire, watching as she ripped open the paper bag, fished out the cold cheeseburger, unwrapped it, and began to feed.

"What is it yeh want?" she grumbled, her mouth full of meat and bread. Her voice was hoarse, as though she hadn't used it in years. She had a thick Scottish drawl... or perhaps it was Irish. (To tell you the truth, I've never been able to tell the difference.)

"I'm being watched by someone," I replied.

"Airn't we all?"

She stuffed her gullet once more, her gnarled, greasy hand pushing strands of cobweb hair out of her eyes.

"Who's a-watchin' ya?" she asked.

"Eldon Gamble."

"Aye? The window licker."

"The what?"

"The ree-tard."

My lips thinned. I was many things, but a bigot wasn't one of them. She must have noticed, because she showed me her teeth in what I assumed was a smile, food and slime stuck between her blackened gums.

"City boy, eh? Sowtheh?" *Southie.* "Don't like me speech."

"I didn't – "

"Fact is, I don' give a feck."

She slurped a glob of mayonnaise from the butt of the burger, savored it on her tongue, then gulped it down. I wondered how long it had been since she'd eaten anything other than non-perishables from a tin can.

"So. Eldon Gamble. What is it yeh know of 'im so far?"

"Not much," I confessed. "From what I've been told, he showed up in Ukippa a few years back. Was taken in by the Dilbrooks until he could land on his feet. Creeped out everyone else who worked for them."

"Oh, aye? How so?"

"He whispers to himself. Watches people while they sleep. And he's, uh – well, I've caught him staring at me on more than one occasion."

"Aye, he can't be the only one," she replied. "Is it a crime to stare at someone in Anchorage or Juneau or wherever it is you come from, Sowtheh?"

"Nobody else in town hides in the trees and spies on me and my daughter."

I glanced over to find you and the Gunman building an impressively tall pyramid out of old soup cans.

"Hmm," Denali grunted softly. She almost sounded amused. She took the second half of the burger down in a single bite, chewing it open-mouthed like a moose chewing cud. Getting it all down with a gluttonous gulp, she sat back in her chair and rubbed her bloated, malnourished belly.

"To really know Eldon Gamble," Denali said, "Yeh need to know his mammy."

"His mother?"

"Prudence Gamble and I were dear friends. Worked together for twelve years. Side b' side all deh, every deh. Answerin' phones. Draftin' checks. Doin' all the shite the man in charge didn't want to do."

"Where did you work?"

"Where we all used to work. Where most folk still work," she said, and I had a hunch.

"Mainstay," I said. "The oil field."

"'Cept back then, it wasn't Mainstay. It was Dilbrook Enterprises."

She snorted deep and low, hacking an impressive green wad into the fire.

"*Enterprises*, ha! The rich, stupid feck thought a lot of 'imself. We only had two wells back then. Two!" She held up an arthritic forefinger and half a pinkie. "Nothin' but a tiny plot o' land given to Dilbrook by his bastard father, may 'e rot in hell."

"We're getting off topic," I noticed, attempting to reel her focus

173

back to Eldon.

"Aye, we're just gettin' started," she retorted. "As I's sayin', Pru and I worked admin for old Don Dilbrook. I say old, but he was young then. Young and 'andsome, feck me for sayin' it."

Her greasy grin collapsed, chapped lips sinking into a sad, old scowl.

"Pru thought so, anyway. Stupid betch."

"Did she like him?" I asked.

"Oh, it was much more'n a crush, for both of 'em. Pru'd spend hours in his office, *filin' papers.*" She made quotes in midair with grubby fingertips. "They'd been feckin' around under Gloria Dilbrook's nose for years, even before I arrived on the job."

A loud, metallic crash suddenly echoed from all corners of the cave. I looked around and found you giggling like a madwoman among the toppled pyramid of tin cans. I even noticed a grin on the Gunman's unshaven mug.

Denali closed her eyes and rocked in her chair. Her wrinkled eyelids shifted back and forth as she became enveloped in her memories.

"One day, Dilbrook hired a new man," she said, a slight tremble in her tone. "Big, burly, murderous-lookin' metherfecker." She opened her eyes and offered me a leering smile, one I didn't return. "You've probably seen 'im stalkin' 'round that old hill."

"Moose," I said.

"The big beast took a fancy to Pru from day one. Watched 'er constantly. Licked his lips in 'er direction. Made 'er nervous. Never said a word, but always watched 'er with those big, yellow eyes."

I had indeed seen those eyes.

"Pru told me time 'n again she was afraid of 'im, but I could tell she liked bein' looked at. After a while, she began to quietly flirt with 'im. Bend over to pick up a pencil as he was thumpin' past. She'd do it right in front of Don jus' to irritate him. Moose's eyes got hungry, like a wolf stalkin' a fox."

I watched Denali Shaw's eyes become entranced by the flames, lids growing dark as demons in shadow.

"Pru took it too far."

"How do you mean?"

"She came in late one mornin', and the Prudence Gamble that I knew for twelve years was dead. She was a husk. Nothin' but silence."

The old woman looked up at me, and I saw wetness in her eyes.

"Some men shouldn't have a dick," Denali whispered.

"Prudence was raped?" I asked.

"More than once. Got pregnant by it."

"Was it Moose?"

"She never said 'is name, curse it forever, but I knew it was 'im," she said. "Pru thought maybe she should abort the baby. But, stupid me, I convinced her to keep it. No life should be taken early."

"And did she keep it?"

Denali looked into my eyes, and then I realized.

"Eldon Gamble," I said.

"He came out of the womb an odd boy. Pru couldn't afford childcare, so she'd bring him into work. His whole childhood was spent at the oil field. Don Dilbrook hated havin' him around the office. Would kick the boy. Lock 'im in a storage closet for hours. I'd

175

hear 'im screamin' and I'd have to rescue 'im."

"What about his mother?" I asked.

"Like I said, Pru was a shell. Was never the same after the assault. She didn't want to upset Don. He would take Pru into his office, but it wasn't to do what they used to do. He would scream at 'er. Try to break 'er down. Threaten to fire 'er."

"And Moose?"

"Moose went 'bout his business. Acted like nothin' ever happened with Pru. Even *he* stopped lookin' at 'er. Feckin' ogre."

Denali Shaw took a moment to collect her thoughts. The old woman stood up and rested her back against the cave wall, stretching her neck side to side.

"Then it happened," she said.

"What happened?" I asked, though I had an idea where Denali's memories were leading. I recalled the conversation I had with Gloria a month earlier while rebuilding the shed. The terrible situation she'd mentioned.

"Pru came in to work one day and told me she'd had enough of it all. That she was goin' to leave. Take Eldon and fly down to Oregon to be with her mam. Moose heard everything. Tried to talk to her, but she shoved him off. The next mornin', I came in, and – "

She shuddered.

"A few broken teeth and bits of brain on her desk were all the troopers ever found of Prudence Gamble."

The silence that followed was intensely uncomfortable.

"Moose?" I asked again.

"Not enough evidence to convict him. *Could have been anyone,* they said. Pru just vanished. Filin' papers one day, and *poof.*"

I glanced across the cave and found you dozing soundly atop the Gunman's chest. And while I watched you both snooze among the toppled heap of tin cans, I let the weight of Denali's memory sink into the present.

I wondered if Eldon knew of his mother's murder. If that's why he came back to Ukippa after so many years away. If he planned on confronting his mother's killer, or exacting revenge on Moose.

I wondered if Sophie knew of her father's infidelity. Of his cruelty. I assumed Gloria Dilbrook knew everything about her husband. Perhaps that was why she didn't mind his constant vegetative state.

And that – *that* got me thinking…

Gloria always said Moose was a devil. And like it or not, I had always been good at playing the part of devil's advocate.

And so, I asked the question that needed asking.

"Could Moose be innocent?"

"What d'yeh mean?" Denali asked.

"You mentioned Pru used to flirt with Moose in front of Don just to irritate him. You also mentioned that after she was assaulted, Moose went about his business as though nothing had happened. You said he had eyes for her from the start, and once she became pregnant, he stopped looking at her."

"Aye."

"What if nothing happened between them?" I asked. "Why would Moose ignore Pru after he'd raped her? After he'd gotten her pregnant? It's obvious she didn't want anyone to know. Most predators would continue to pursue a silent victim. If Moose had assaulted and impregnated her, why ignore her? I would expect Don Dilbrook to be the one ignoring her, to recognize that he'd gotten involved in a lust triangle. To steer well clear of it, considering he had the most to lose. A successful business. A big home. A good wife."

I stood up and began to pace.

"But according to you, Don didn't act like that. He became hostile. He became mean. He became verbally abusive. Domineering, almost."

I sat back down, this time a little closer to Denali.

"She never verbally told you who raped her, right? Never told anyone?"

"Aye, tha's right."

"Moose was just some guy she worked with. Why not immediately tell Don, the rich and powerful man she's sleeping with, that one of his employees had assaulted her? Don could have easily fired Moose, gotten him arrested, and Pru could have gone on living her life as normal. Other than being physically terrifying, Moose had no actual power over her."

Denali watched me carefully, and I watched her. Watched the puzzle pieces behind those cataracts being dusted off and rearranged after decades of disuse.

"Victims often keep quiet because their attacker has some sort of control over them. Don had physical, emotional, and financial control over Prudence Gamble. They were physically intimate on the job, away from his wife. He became possessive over her. And then, a new man took notice of her. And even though she had no interest in Moose, she loved the attention and flaunted it in front of Don."

I let that sink in for a moment.

"You never mentioned if Don became upset at Pru for flirting with Moose."

"I never saw him get angry," Denali said. "I just assumed he didn't care."

"Or he was bottling it up," I replied. "Successful people don't become successful without a sense of dominance. Maybe Don felt as though he was losing his grip on the woman he'd taken possession of. Decided to show Pru that, yes, in fact, he *did* own her."

"Yeh think Don Dilbrook did it?"

"He's the person in all this that had the most to lose. Maybe he said something to Prudence to try and keep her quiet. Maybe he threatened to fire her if she said anything… or worse. And then she found out she was pregnant. Don loved his wife and was planning a family with *her*, not with Pru. It was all fun and games until there was a baby involved."

"You don't think Moose killed Pru?" Denali asked.

"I think the signs point elsewhere."

"To Don?"

"There's no way to know for sure," I said. "At least, not yet. And unless Prudence Gamble was involved with more men than just Don Dilbrook – "

"She never mentioned anyone else," the old woman said. "Always *Don this*, and *Don that*."

"Then there's one thing we *can* say with certainty."

I watched the final puzzle piece click into place behind Denali Shaw's firelit eyes.

"Eldon Gamble is Eldon Dilbrook."

16

PHOTOGRAPHS

I awoke to hot, stale air blowing in my face.

My head was foggy and dense, my eyes swimming as they adjusted to the small strip of peachy light skimming the blackened horizon line. The perpetual wintry darkness was beginning to make a mess of my ability to keep time, and I wondered how long I'd been asleep.

I sat in the driver seat of the Silverado with the heater on full blast. I heard a gentle hiss of oxygen and looked over my shoulder to find you asleep in the backseat, long sleepy lashes reminiscent of your mother's, drool glistening on your crimson pouts. Our midnight meeting with Denali Shaw seemed like a far-off dream, but sleep suddenly gave way to a waking yawn and, all at once, I recalled my final conversation with the Gunman as he led us away from the hermit's cave and back to the trailhead.

As I strapped the snowshoes to my feet and you to my chest, he spoke over the chill.

"Be careful."

"Should be simpler going down than up," I chuckled.

"Not that," he said. And when I looked up, his eyes were focused on the lunular shadow of Horseshoe Hill. "Be careful."

"What do you know?"

"Not much, but there's somethin' about that hill. Denali says it's cursed."

"Cursed?"

"Last groundskeeper gone missin'. Dilbrook boy threw himself over a cliff. Now that body, all burned to shit."

And then, something clicked.

"Do you think they're all connected?" I asked.

"I don't know nothin', man. I just keep to this mountain. I just live my own life."

"Smart," I said. And as we turned to leave, he spoke up one last time.

"If you want to know more about Eldon Gamble, you should talk to the Dilbrooks' live-in nurse."

"Lizanne?"

"Nah. The first one," he said. "Evie Brooks."

"I'll do that. Thanks."

I vaguely recalled hiking back down the slopes of Mount Poe, vaguely recalled the icy breath of winter attempting to lull me to sleep in those trees. And I probably would have succumbed, would have stopped to take a rest, would have fallen asleep against the trunk of a ghostly aspen and froze to death.

But I had you, Ellie, and you kept me awake with your endless jabbering.

So, thanks.

***

I fully intended to pay Evie Brooks a visit, but the carpet in the Mansion's eastern sitting room needed replacing.

Imagine that. A room just for sitting. And there was also a *western* sitting room.

It was simple enough work, though I'll admit prying up the tack strips was a bit backbreaking. The carpet had originally been a hideous yolk yellow, though as I ripped up the musty shag, I noticed beautiful oak planks beneath. I planned on cleaning, staining, and polishing the old floorboards as a Christmas present for Gloria, a small token of gratitude for all she had done for me.

And all she had done for *you.*

Once I rolled up the final strip of carpet, I tossed it out into the hall and surveyed the old wooden floor. I wasn't entirely certain how old the Mansion was, or even if the Dilbrooks were the original owners. Judging by the weathered scratches and the matured chips in the oak, I assumed the house was very old, older than the Dilbrooks themselves. As disheveled as the wooden planks were, they were beautiful and gave plenty of character to the small sitting room.

Well, all except one plank.

It warped at an unholy angle, one I imagined had stubbed plenty of toes in its time. It would need to be replaced, I decided.

I wedged my fingers under the warped, rotting edge of the awkward plank and gave a swift yank. The plank cracked and split as I

183

ripped it up, and as I tossed it out into the hallway with the old carpet, I noticed something tucked away in the hole it left behind.

A shoebox.

Treasure, the boy in me guffawed with glee.

I lifted the old box out of the hole and opened the lid. Inside were dozens, hundreds even, of small photographs. It wasn't the sheer amount of photos in the box that seemed strange, nor the fact that the box had been hidden at all. Everyone needed their memories, and sometimes, memories were better left tucked away.

I knew that all too well.

No, what I found strange was that every single picture was taken of the exact same person. A young man in his late twenties, perhaps, with lank, shaggy brown hair and dark circles under eyes that were black as caviar. What I also found strange was the fact that he never looked into the camera, that each photograph showed him at different angles, from different vantage points, performing different activities.

As though he didn't know he was being photographed.

At first, I wondered if the man in the photographs was Sam Dilbrook. I'd only ever seen him in the family photo in Evie's office, and I tried recalling his features. And if it was Sam, I wondered if Gloria or Sophie or even Don had hidden all of the photographs they'd ever taken of Sam in an effort to subdue their grief after his suicide. The man in the photographs looked somewhat similar to Sophie, but enough to be her twin? I wasn't so sure.

Perhaps my eyes were playing tricks on me.

I was halfway to tucking the photographs back into the shoebox, and the shoebox back into the hole, when one photograph in particular made my stomach leap. I pulled it out, held it up to the light, and squinted my eyes.

In it, the same man was asleep on top of tree-print bedsheets that seemed eerily familiar. I recognized them suddenly as the bedsheets I had been sleeping on since my first night in the Cabin. The photograph was taken from above, and while the man slept, a small jade wolf's head rested on his chest.

So, *this* was Adam Kelsey.

But who had taken all the pictures?

I recalled my time at the Ukippa Peace Office after answering Detective Weekes' questions about the body in the hut. I recalled Evie Brooks' office, how it had been littered with photographs. And while the photographs in her office had been taken of beautifully extravagant landscapes and looked entirely professional, the photographs hidden in the shoebox were sloppy, candid, and voyeuristic.

Sophie said that Adam Kelsey had woken up in the middle of the night to Eldon Gamble standing over him, watching him sleep. I thought of Eldon watching me from the trees. Whispering to himself.

A chill ran down my spine.

I knew then it was imperative that I speak with Evie Brooks.

***

"Was it always a sitting room?" I asked Gloria as we sat down for a lunchtime bowl of caribou stew.

"Not always," she said, blowing the steam from her spoon. "Used to be a bedroom."

"Sophie's?"

"No," she said. "Soph isn't a fan of heights."

"It must have been Evie's then, when she lived here?" I tossed in casually.

"Why do you ask?"

"You said she loved photography," I said. "In my opinion, it's got the best view in the house. I can only imagine the sunrise over Lake Adamant in the summertime."

She watched me a moment, considered my words, and shrugged.

"No, no, it was never Evie's room. Evie liked to sleep in the room next to the library," she said. "That room was Sam's room."

Sam?

That threw me for a loop.

"But now that I think of it," she added. "Eldon slept in there too, when he was living here."

Bingo.

"They were friends?"

"Well, neither of 'em were necessarily all together in the head. Eldon's slower than molasses. And Sam, well… we never got him checked out, but I'm certain he was pretty severely autistic. Neither of 'em liked to be left alone, so Sam and Eldon shared that room."

Her eyes remained fixed on me while I slurped my stew, and I decided to change the subject.

"I've been thinking about Betty," I lied.

"The Bronco?"

"Yeah. I was supposed to return her to a mechanic's garage in Bettles. Sitka Slim's?"

"I know of it. Ol' Slim is a friend."

"I figured if you didn't need it this afternoon, I'd take the Silverado and drive on over to let Slim know Betty'd been stolen. I'd rather tell him in person."

"Well, he won't be happy. Fixed her up himself. Want me to go with you to dampen his hot head?"

I smiled.

"I'll manage. But, would you mind watching Ellie while I'm gone?"

"I never mind watching Ellie."

"I'll tell Slim you say hi," I said, then I stood up and took my bowl to the sink. But Sitka Slim's was the last place I had in mind for the afternoon.

***

It was easy enough to figure out where Evie Brooks lived. All it took was a quick stop in Galoshes, a small chat over coffee with Mags, and a swift and simple lie as I walked out the door.

"By the way, Gloria asked me to deliver some old clothes to Evie Brooks. Which house is hers?"

"Evie? Well, she's in the ol' shiplap place up on Ricketts Knob," Mags replied as she rubbed the morning kinks out of her lower back. "Although, I 'magine she's already down in Texas."

My heart deflated.

"Flies down every winter to visit Jackie. Tha's her ma," she added. "Might make more sense just to leave 'em in her office." She nodded toward the frosted window, and through the glass stood the Ukippa Peace Office.

187

I thanked Mags and left, then made my way across the tiny town square and noticed the station appeared to be abandoned, save for a single lightbulb flickering from within. I found the front door unlocked, decided that at least one person was present, and let myself in.

"Hello?"

I was met with silence.

I pressed on through the door that led from the waiting area to the back offices, followed the familiarly tight hallway around one corner, then another, and pushed open the door to Evie's office. When I flipped on the light, I found it exactly how Gloria and I had left it.

Marvelous landscape photographs lined the walls and desk, and once again, I was drawn to the enormous canvas of Lake Adamant and Horseshoe Hill. I found the Cabin, the dense copse of trees surrounding the Dilbrook Mansion, and then looked at the rundown Shack on the western ridge. And as I surveyed the landscape, I noticed various soft, frozen glints of sunlight on glass...

The front windows of the Mansion and the Cabin.

I suddenly realized the uncomfortable truth of it all. Up on the hill, we were a spectacle to be photographed. We were exposed.

Exposed and alone.

"Mr. Brady," a voice spoke behind me, and I froze. "Turn around slowly, please."

On instinct, I raised my arms and turned my back on the canvas print, instead setting my gaze on Detective Weekes. She stood with her arms crossed, one shoulder resting against the doorframe.

"There's no need for that," she said, nodding at my arms. "Unless, of course, you're concealing."

"No guns on me, no," I replied, then lowered my arms.

"What are you doing in here?" she asked. Even though there was a smile on her face, her voice was firm, her eyes hard and sharp. Her stare made me uncomfortable, and I suddenly longed to be anywhere else.

"I'm looking for Evie Brooks."

"Why?" she asked calmly. She continued to stare, as though anxiously awaiting my response.

"She, uh, used to work for the Dilbrooks, like I do now, and I had some questions for her."

"Is that right?"

I glanced at the hallway beyond the door, and she adjusted her body to block the doorframe.

"I'm sorry, have I done something wrong?" I asked.

She didn't respond, just continued to smile and stare, and I felt my patience wearing thin.

"Did you need something from me, Detective?" I asked finally.

"Not yet."

I didn't like the way she said that.

"Ms. Brooks," she continued, "is apparently in Lubbock, Texas at the moment. Have you tried calling?"

"I don't have her number."

She moved to the desk, opened the top left drawer, removed a black business card, and set it face up on the desk.

"Have a good day, Mr. Brady."

And with that, Detective Weekes disappeared down the hallway.

It had been a strange interaction, one that left me feeling confused and uneasy. Whatever Detective Weekes knew, she wasn't telling me.

At least, not yet.

***

I put you to bed earlier than usual that night, singing you a lullaby that your mother and I had composed entirely on our own. But halfway through, I found that I couldn't remember the rest of the lyrics. As you closed your eyes and drifted off to sleep, I had to wipe the wetness away from my own. In forgetting those lyrics, I began to understand that the long-ago memory of our happy little family was simply that...

A memory.

Your mother was gone. Harvey was gone. Anchorage was gone. And I had the distinct feeling that none of them were coming back.

I made my way downstairs, poured four fingers of Malamute, sucked it down, and then poured four more. I gave the whiskey a few moments to do its work, feeling the warmth spread from my gut to my arms and finally to my head, dulling my emotions and setting my mind back on what was important.

I took Evie Brooks' business card out of my pocket and dialed the listed number. When she didn't answer, I called two more times and decided on leaving a simple voicemail.

Instead, I was met by a digital voice.

"The inbox for the person you have dialed is full and cannot accept any voice messages at this time. Goodbye."

Evie Brooks was proving harder to find than I'd anticipated.

I took down the second glass of Malamute, choked back the urge to gag it up, then poured one more. I was moments from abandoning all thoughts of Evie Brooks to the wind when one final idea popped into my head.

I turned on the computer the Dilbrooks had left in the Cabin, created a fake Facebook account, typed "Evie Brooks" into the search bar, and watched as hundreds of Evies, Eves, and Evelyn Brookses smiled back at me. Most were listed in the lower forty-eight, some across the pond in the UK and Ireland, two in Australia, and finally, I saw it.

Evelyn Brooks
Lives in Bettles, Alaska

The circular profile photo wasn't of a woman's face. Instead, it was a black void, save for a single, horizontal blue line scored through its middle.

The thin blue line. A symbol of the police force.

It was her.

I clicked on her name and cursed when I discovered that her profile was private. I had found Evie Brooks, sure, but I still couldn't make contact. Out of desperation, I sent her a Friend Request but had the distinct feeling that she wouldn't accept. Why would she? She didn't know me, after all.

I leaned back in my chair, took a sip of whiskey, and rubbed my eyes. And then, I remembered something Mags had said over coffee.

Flies down every winter to visit Jackie.

And then, I remembered Detective Weekes' words.

Ms. Brooks is apparently in Lubbock, Texas at the moment.

I set down the Malamute and typed "Jackie Brooks" into the search bar. Thousands of profiles popped up from all over the world, and as I scrolled, I prayed that luck would be on my side. I narrowed the search criteria to focus on profiles in the United States, and again to just Texas. Dozens of Jackie Brookses were scattered across El Paso, Austin, Dallas, Houston, San Antonio, until finally, I found the only Jackie Brooks listed in Lubbock. The profile photo revealed a smiling woman in her fifties or sixties, with piercing almond eyes that seemed oddly familiar. I clicked the profile and, to my astonishment, found that it was public.

Luck had indeed been on my side.

I chose to bypass sending Jackie Brooks a Friend Request, and instead clicked on the Message button.

Hi, Ms. Brooks. My name is Lazalier Brady. I live in Ukippa, AK, and currently work for Don and Gloria Dilbrook. I am trying to get in touch with your daughter, Evie, regarding a photograph I would like to purchase.

Liar.

I was told she spends winters in Texas. I tried calling, but I am having trouble reaching her. Would you be kind enough to pass along my message? She can call me anytime, at her own convenience. Thank you.

I added my phone number underneath and hit Send. Content that I had done everything in my power to make contact with Evie

Brooks, I swallowed the rest of the Malamute, shut off the monitor, and stumbled to bed.

And as I lie there waiting for the whiskey to lull me to sleep, I couldn't help picturing Jackie Brooks' eyes, and wondered where I had seen them before.

***

Lazalier, thanks for ur message. Unfortunately, Evie isn't here. She decided not to fly to Lubbock this winter. She told me she was stayin behind to finish work on a case. I tried callin her this morning, but it seems as though her voicemail inbox is full. U might try visitin her office in Ukippa. I will message u when I get a hold of her. Hope y'all are stayin warm up there. Hugs, Jaxx.

I read Jackie's response over and over, a cup of joe steaming in my hand and a hangover aching in my skull.

It made no sense.

Everyone in Ukippa was under the impression that Evie had flown south like she did every winter, but apparently, she'd made plans to stay in Alaska. I'd never met the woman, but my desire to speak with her about Eldon Gamble had now become a sort of concern for her well-being.

There was only one more course of action.

***

Ricketts Knob is a small hillock nestled over the highway connecting Ukippa and Bettles. On a clear summer day, you can see

193

all the way to the Gates of the Arctic, the spine of sharp, sawtooth peaks slicing a gash in the sky. During winter's perpetual darkness, however, you can see nothing but small pinpricks of light glittering from Bettles to the east and Ukippa to the west.

Evie's was the only house atop the Knob. A modest structure of cedarwood, the façade of the house showcased one enormous glass window, no doubt designed to exploit the spectacular view. A single white truck sat in the driveway with snow caked over the windshield. Not wanting to frighten Evie by my sudden appearance (I'm a semi-large man, imposing to some, and she had no idea who I was), I brought you along to soften the shock of finding a stranger on her doorstep.

I hiked you up on my shoulders, knocked on the door, and waited.

And waited.

And waited.

"Ms. Brooks?" I called out. "You home?"

I knocked again.

"I work for Gloria Dilbrook. I'm a friend of Sophie's. Are you there?"

The firefighter in me told me that something wasn't right, told me to kick down the door to make sure she was okay. We walked around the side porch and arrived at a sliding glass door, and I immediately knew something was wrong.

The door was wide open, leading into a den that was flooded with snow.

17

THE DARKROOM

My boots crunched along the frosted carpet and my breath billowed in thick white clouds as I surveyed the spacious den and connecting kitchen.

Much like her office in Ukippa, the walls of Evie Brooks' home were covered in canvases and photographs of mountainous landscapes, dense foliage, and silhouettes of wildlife ranging from willow ptarmigans and tufted puffins to black bears and muskoxen.

"Ms. Brooks," I called out again, though I was almost entirely sure I would get no answer. Considering the temperature inside Evie's home matched the blistering cold outside, I knew I wouldn't find her inside the house.

Then again, maybe I would.

I pictured a body, frozen solid and stuffed carelessly inside a hall closet, then shuddered and shook the image from my mind.

Not wanting you to catch a cold, I closed the sliding door behind us and sat you down on a squashy armchair by the façade window, it being the only piece of furniture that wasn't dusted with snow. I tightened the straps of your oxygen cannister backpack and wrapped a spare throw blanket around you. Your eyes were focused on the glass, watching the far-off lights of Ukippa glittering in the darkness.

"Stay here, El," I said.

I used the flashlight of my cell phone to illuminate a long hallway stretching out of the den. I followed the fuzzy beam of light and began my search of the rest of the darkened home.

The first door I came to stood ajar, and as I stepped inside, I cast my light upon a small bedroom that had been transformed into a home office. A futon in the corner had been pulled out into a bed. Either Evie had been working long nights and sleeping on the futon, or she'd recently had a guest.

I moved along into a second room, twice as large as the first, sporting a king-size bed and its own modest bathroom. Evie's master bedroom, I assumed. The bedsheets were crumpled and messy, a pile of women's clothes and undergarments piled high within a teetering hamper beside the open closet door. I shined my light inside the large walk-in, looked down, and felt the hairs on the back of my neck stand on end.

Jutting out from beneath the wall of clothes were the muddy soles of women's snow boots.

I held my breath, ripped aside the wall of clothes...

And saw nothing but a muddy pair of women's snow boots.

Relax.

Evie Brooks' home appeared to be both unoriginal and uninhabited, and I was moments from abandoning our visit altogether when I walked out into the hall and noticed a third door at the far end of the hall. This door was closed, and as I approached it, I noticed a faint rectangle of dim scarlet light glowing around the edges of the blackened door jamb.

I tried the door handle, but it was locked.

"Evie Brooks," I called through the red-rimmed door. "Evie, are you in there?"

When I heard no answer, I decided enough was enough. My brain screamed, *Get in there, you idiot! She needs help!*

I shouldered the door as hard as I could, but it wouldn't budge. Stepping back, I pressed my hands to the walls on either side of me, launched my foot at the door stile, and kicked it open with a resounding *crack!*

Blood red light flooded the hallway.

The source of the sanguine glow came from the bottom of a stairwell that led into what I assumed was a basement, or quite possibly, the entrance to hell. I glanced over my shoulder, at the other end of the hallway and the safety of the den and kitchen, knowing you were waiting patiently for my return. I looked back down at the bottom of the stairwell, and to whatever (or whomever) awaited me in the crimson room below.

I descended into the bowels of Evie's home, one creaky step at a time. When I reached the bottom, I discovered the source of the red glow. The light emanated from a single scarlet lightbulb dangling from the ceiling. A safelight, if I recall the term correctly. Blackened squares and rectangles hung from bands of wire strung across the room, and as I approached them slowly, I noticed that they were photographs developing in the darkness.

I had stumbled into Evie Brooks' darkroom.

It wasn't odd that Evie had a full-blown darkroom in her home. She was a photographer, after all, and a damn good one. What I did find odd, however, was the fact that the safelight had been left on. That the sliding glass door upstairs had been left wide open. That Evie's truck was still parked in the driveway.

The way I saw it, there were three possibilities…

The first possibility was that Evie had fled her home on foot, and in a hurry.

The second, she'd been kidnapped.

The third, she had taken a small break from developing her photographs, gone outside for some reason (possibly for a smoke), and never made it back inside.

Up close, my eyes adjusted to the photographs strung up on the line like dirty laundry. These photographs were very different from any others I had seen from Evie. They weren't taken of mountains, trees, or frozen lakes, nor of birds, bears, or ravenous wolves.

These were taken of people. Very familiar people.

I saw Lizanne, the Dilbrooks' live-in nurse, alone in the woods, her hair disheveled and dirt caking her forehead. I could almost smell the filth and sweat glistening on her leathery skin. Her nervous eyes were fixed over her shoulder, as though making sure she wasn't being followed. A hurried encounter through the woods, it seemed.

I saw Gloria Dilbrook from far below. She stood behind the glass of the Mansion's third-floor bay window at the end of the east wing, the window I knew as Don Dilbrook's bedroom. The man of the house was on his bed beneath her. Gloria simply stood there, eyes glazed over and fixated on the bare stretch of wall over her husband's bed. There was no tenderness in her demeanor. No familiar thin-lipped scowl I'd grown accustomed to seeing her wear. There was nothing. I squinted my eyes, and as I looked closer, I noticed something very peculiar. Gloria held Don's oxygen mask at her side. Don's eyes, normally closed, were open and completely white, fixed upward within his skull. His chest was raised, his bony back arched high off the bed. His jaw hung open, and I could almost hear his wheezing gasps.

I moved on.

There was Sophie, adorned in her telltale olive pea coat, a crisp black pencil skirt, and a pair of Louboutin red bottoms. Her cheeks were pink, her chestnut hair floating on the breeze as she stood in time, mid-stride, in the middle of Ukippa's tiny square. Behind her, I noticed the exterior of Galoshes and a blurry smudge of neon orange. Beside the orange smudge stood the outline of a man, his features out of focus and his jaw darker than the rest of his face. I recognized the man's build and stance, because I saw him every morning in the mirror. It was me, standing there beside Betty, unshaven and wondering who Sophie might be visiting in the Ukippa Peace Office the day I ordered her a red zin.

It made sense now. Sophie had visited Evie Brooks that day.

And Evie felt the need to photograph the impending encounter. To document it.

But why?

Next up on the string of photographs was an image that piqued both my interest and my anger. I instantly recognized a small two-story log structure. It was the backside of the Cabin, as seen from the trees. My gaze was drawn to the arched window of the second floor. There, behind glass reflecting the glowing aurora, I stood with my forearms pressed to the railing of your crib. My eyes were closed and I was smiling. Your small hands tugged hard on my ears, your curly brown tufts thrown back as you laughed like a madwoman.

As I surveyed the image, I glanced down at the back deck, and I was suddenly smacked with a wave of melancholy. Behind the glass door leading onto the deck, I noticed a glistening bubblegum tongue, floppy ears, and big honey-brown eyes peering out from inside the Cabin, staring directly at the camera.

Harvey had been the only witness to Evie's voyeuristic photography.

I thought of that night, after I put you to bed, my ears raw from your hedonistic game of tug-of-war. Harvey and I sat on the back deck as I admired the aurora, effortlessly polishing off a bottle of Malamute. I fell asleep, and when I awoke, it was to the sound of Harvey's growls. I heard a twig snap in the woods beyond, and Harvey bolted into the trees.

And then, like a punch to the gut, I realized something.

I knew what Evie Brooks looked like.

I had seen her before, and I had seen her up close. I'd seen her in the woods that night. I'd seen her again, many nights later behind my binoculars, casting a long shadow across the frozen surface of Lake Adamant. I recognized her in her mother's eyes from a single Facebook profile photo.

Evie Brooks was the girl in the snow.

On and on I went down the neat row of hanging photographs. Here was Horseshoe Hill with its three very different houses, shot most likely from a boat or from the ice shanty in the middle of Lake Adamant. In another, my arms were arced in mid-swing an instant before I split a burl of black cedar with an axe, shot from the woods behind the Mansion. Another showed me and Sophie at the fork in the woods, taken from behind a tree trunk, on the afternoon Sophie first warned me about the eastern path that led to the cliff.

Nearly every single photograph was taken on the hill, of the hill, or in the trees behind the hill. Nearly every photograph was taken in the last few weeks. And nearly every photograph had *me* in it…

One of me and Gloria in the window of the library.

One of the Mansion at dusk, me mid-stride in the background.

One of me shirtless in my bathroom window.

I felt very exposed. I suddenly found the red-black hue of the darkroom terrifying. I'd seen far too many slasher flicks in the late nineties to know that rooms exactly like this one were perfect hiding places for psychotic, knife-wielding murderers. I was ready to leave. And then, I heard it.

A loud *creeeak* in the floorboards above my head.

Gooseflesh spread down my arms. Blood pulsed behind my eardrums. There was someone else in Evie's home, and I'd left you alone upstairs.

I wheeled around and bolted across the darkroom. In my haste, my shoulder caught the dangling safelight and sent it swinging in all directions. Red and black shadows reeled and flashed across the walls in a deranged and demonic dance. My boot caught the steel foot of a deep and ancient porcelain scrub sink. I lost my footing, and I went down.

For a moment, all was silent. All was dark. I heard the softest whoosh of wind in my ears.

And then, all I knew was pain.

My head cracked against the corner edge of the bottommost concrete step. White light exploded behind my eyelids while a phantom steam-whistle screamed against my ear drums. When I opened my eyes, the darkroom was spinning and, combined with the swinging of the safelight, became a chaotic kaleidoscope that sent a wave of nausea into the pit of my stomach, up my esophagus, and into a mess on the floor.

I knew I was concussed, but it didn't matter, for as dizzy as I was, I knew I had to get to you. I stood up, slipped in my sick, and fell back against the stairs. Groaning in pain, I flipped over, clawed my fingertips into the concrete steps, and crawled up the stairwell, my eyes fixed on the dim light from the hallway above. My world continued to spin as I climbed, and when I finally reached the top, my head pulsed so hard and hurt so bad that my stomach lurched and sent me into another bout of loud, gut-twisting dry heaves.

Any chance I had at surprising the intruder (or perhaps Evie Brooks herself) had vanished. I looked up and saw nothing but a dim and blurry tunnel. I squeezed my eyes shut and willed them into focus, and when I opened them again, I saw a dark shape silhouetted against the dim light at the opposite end of the hallway.

The silhouette had broad shoulders. Stocky legs. A small round head. The build of a man.

Not Evie, I thought.

I stared at the unmoving shape, and for the slightest moment, I considered that, quite possibly, it wasn't a man after all. A misshapen coat rack, perhaps.

And then, the silhouette's head slowly tilted to one side.

My blood ran cold. The shape took two steps forward, or perhaps two steps back. With my head spinning like it was, I wasn't quite sure which. I heard hushed, hurried whispers, and that's when I knew.

"Eldon – " I croaked.

The shape stopped. It whispered louder, then turned and disappeared into the room beyond.

Fatherly instincts kicked into overdrive. I leapt in great strides down the length of the darkened hallway and stumbled into the living room. To my great relief, there you were on the same squashy armchair I left you in, cornflower eyes wide and confused, but altogether untouched or, more likely, completely unnoticed by Eldon Gamble.

A cold wind stung my cheek as fresh snowflakes floated in through the open sliding door. Fresh boot prints led outside and disappeared into the trees behind Evie's home. I rewrapped the blanket around you, kissed your forehead, and then slid the door shut behind me before sprinting out into the cold.

The gentle flurry quickly swirled into a blinding, teeth-chattering blizzard, and before I knew it, I shuffled into a waist-deep snowbank piled high between the compacted trees. My skull throbbed and my vision faded in and out of focus. Up ahead, I saw the blurred shoulders of Eldon, desperately clawing his way through the snow. Eldon knew he had been caught, and he knew he had been caught by someone a foot taller than he was, someone in much better shape, someone who could easily wade through the powder he was struggling to penetrate.

"Stop!" I yelled, but he pushed through the snowbank and scrambled up the steep base of a lofty hillock. He'd already climbed to the top when I stopped at the base to regain control of my swirling equilibrium. The snow was much thinner here, and as I began to climb, mud caked under my fingernails while rocks and sticks gouged at my hands. A couple steps from the top of the hillock, I planted my foot on a small pine sapling that had managed to grow out the side of the hill like a snowman's arm. The fragile limb groaned as it bent under my weight, and then...

Snap!

My face hit the permafrost with a sickening crunch. Ice and rock pushed up my jacket and my undershirt, scratching deep gashes into my chest and stomach as I slid down the hill face. I grappled at frozen shrubs and protruding stones buried beneath the snow, scrabbled at anything I could catch in my fingers.

Finally, I managed to grasp one hand around the root of a particularly thorny shrub. Electric pain shot through my palm and my fingers, up my elbow and into my shoulder as the microscopic barbs of a stinging nettle did their work. My cry of agony echoed through the wilderness, and I knew that if I let go, I would slide all the way to the bottom, and Eldon Gamble would once again disappear into the trees.

I sunk my teeth into my tongue to stifle my urge to scream. My right hand gripped the stinging nettle until my left finally unearthed a rocky handhold. I dug the toes of my boots into the side of the hill and, recalling an instance when Smitty had beckoned me to climb a similarly vertical cliff face to escape a wild brushfire, I hoisted myself up.

And up.

And up.

I reached the top of the hillock and, once again, I took a moment to steady my vision. The mound upon which I stood was barren of trees, giving me a clear, 360-degree view of the surrounding forest.

To the south, I could just make out the small sugar cube that was Evie's home, where I had abandoned you, yet again. Had I been thinking clearly, had my concussion not left me drunk and devoid of my better judgment, I never would have chased after Eldon. I would have left him alone. At least, for now.

My head pounded, my clothes were torn, my entire right arm stung, and I was caked in mud, blood, sticks, and scratches. I had to get back to you.

It was time to call off the chase.

And then, I saw him.

Like an ant sifting through spilled sugar, the shadow of Eldon Gamble pressed on toward the base of the hillock. He was knee-deep in snow, moving at a snail's pace toward the tree line. To my left, I noticed a small, rocky gorge at the edge of the hilltop I stood upon, a jagged and unforgiving gash in the hillock that Eldon had carefully carved his way around. Looking down, I watched him make a beeline for the trees, directly below the gorge. If I jumped (and if I survived), I could cut him off.

I had one chance. If he got to the trees, I would never find him.

I took a deep breath, held the image of your face in my mind, set my eyes on the gorge's toothy rim.

And then, I shot forward like a bullet.

My feet carried me across the mound, boots pummeling the earth, blood pounding in my ears. I pressed my boot into the rocky rim of the gorge, held my breath, and leapt.

The earth dropped out from under me and, for a moment, the breath was sucked from my lungs. My legs kicked in midair, searching desperately for solid ground. I never even realized my eyes had closed.

I forgot where I was. I forgot who I was. What I was. Why I was.

When my mind finally caught up, I remembered the jump. I remembered that my feet were in the air when they should have been on the ground. I remembered that I needed to catch Eldon Gamble. I remembered that I needed to get back to my daughter.

I opened my eyes, and the earth came rushing back.

I hit the snow at such speed that I had no time to register what was up and what was down. My feet hit first, and then my shoulder, and then my feet again, and then my back. I cleared the gorge, but I was tumbling out of control, all the way down the hill until finally, I performed a final somersault and landed so hard that the wind was knocked clean from my chest.

No time to breathe, I thought.

When I staggered to my feet, it was to find myself between Eldon Gamble and the tree line. He stood rooted in the snow, jaw hanging slack, mismatched eyes wide in disbelief. He whispered something to himself, turned back the way he came, and tried to run.

I tackled him from behind, flipped him onto his back, and

pinned him down.

"Where is she?!" I screamed.

"Shhhh!"

"Where is Evie?!"

"Shhh! Shhh!"

His mouth was agape and drool slid down one cheek, his eyes shifting in all directions. He shoved his thumbs into his ears and dug the remaining fingers into his eyes.

"SHHH!!!"

"Eldon, where is Evie?"

His long, jagged fingernails carved red streaks into his eyelids, and it was then I realized the severity of his mental handicap. I was overloading his senses, and all he could think to do in order to drown me out was cork his ears and claw his eyes.

"That's enough," I spoke calmly. "Eldon, relax."

"Shhh… shhh…" he answered, and it was only after I rolled off him that he withdrew his hands from his face. I sat back on my haunches, and he rolled onto his knees.

Without warning, Eldon Gamble burst into tears. He sobbed and screamed and drooled in the snow like a troubled toddler who'd just been whipped raw with a belt. (I knew the feeling well. It had been my father's favorite form of discipline – for me *and* my mother.)

"Where is she, Eldon?"

He continued to sob, rocking back and forth on his knees. And then suddenly, he gripped his chest.

But he didn't look up in surprise. He didn't gasp in pain. And he didn't collapse. He simply held his hand to his chest, and I watched his fingers slide into his jacket. When they withdrew, it was to reveal a photograph clutched in his grubby fingers.

"Shhh..." he whispered through his tears, then handed me the photograph.

Judging by the quality of the print, I knew immediately it had been stolen from Evie Brooks' collection, possibly from the darkroom I had recently escaped. It was an older photograph, bent and frayed at the edges. It showed the cliff at the end of the fork in the woods behind the Cabin.

Two men stood upon the precipice, locked in a struggle.

I recognized the first man as Adam Kelsey, whose hands were clenched around the other man's neck. Kelsey's victim had only one foot on the precipice, the other dangling over the edge. This man's eyes were wide in horror, his chestnut hair floating on the wind.

I instantly knew his identity.

18

THE FALL OF SAM DILBROOK

"Yes," she said, holding a shaky hand over her mouth. "That's him."

I adjusted the cold compress, flipped it over, and pressed the still frozen side against my head. I winced as the cold worked its way into the scabbed-over knot above my temple where my head had connected with the concrete step in Evie Brooks' darkroom.

I looked up into Gloria's hardened, watery eyes.

"It's Sam," she said.

"I'm sorry, Gloria."

"All this time, I thought..."

Her voice cracked, and she went silent.

I didn't know what to say. I couldn't comprehend the hurt she must have felt. The confusion. The swirling questions. For so long, Gloria Dilbrook had been told her son committed suicide, that he'd jumped off that cliff of his own accord.

At least, that's what the police and the coroner had agreed upon.

But here was the undeniable proof that Sam Dilbrook had in fact been murdered by Adam Kelsey. Undeniable proof that had been plucked from Evie Brooks' darkroom by someone so unlikely.

"Why this one?" I asked.

"What?"

"Of all the pictures in that house, why did Eldon take this one?"

Gloria pushed the photograph away. She closed her eyes and wiped her cheeks, then stood up and moved to the edge of the Mansion's third-floor balcony. She ran her leathery palm along the crumbling stone, breath billowing in great clouds among the falling snow.

"As a token, I'd venture to guess."

She reached into her parka and withdrew a cigarette, the first I'd ever seen in her possession. She lit in, took a long, slow drag, and let the smoke drift from her flared nostrils like a waking dragon.

"A token of what?"

"Grief," she said. "When he lived with us, he and Sam were like brothers. When Sam died, it wasn't easy for any of us. Don wasn't around to witness it; not mentally, at least. Sophie flew home, cried for a week straight, helped me coordinate the funeral, then slapped on her lawyer face and high-tailed it back to Anchorage."

Gloria sighed and took another drag.

"My own grief was matched only by Eldon's," she said. "He didn't eat. He had manic episodes. I found him hiding in the Cabin. By then, Kelsey, well – "

"Kelsey disappeared," I said, remembering one of the first things Gloria ever told me about the previous groundskeeper. "You said you thought Moose might have done something to him."

"That's what I thought. Now, it makes sense. Adam Kelsey killed my boy. Whether he pushed him on purpose, or on accident, he pushed Sam over the edge and then he fled."

It was then that I remembered something else. Something I'd seen when Gloria and I discovered the charred corpse inside the hut in the woods.

"What if he never left?" I said.

I smelled burnt hair and skin, and when I looked up, Gloria was staring at me with an expression I couldn't quite discern. The cigarette had burned all the way to the quick, singeing the skin and peach hairs of her top lip.

"It doesn't matter."

I did a double-take, certain I had heard her wrong.

"I'm sorry?" I asked.

"It doesn't matter," she said. "None of it matters anymore."

"What do you mean?"

"My son is dead, Laz," Gloria barked. "Nothing is going to change that. Now that I know the truth, it's time to leave it alone."

"Bullshit. You know what I think?" I said, pointing to the trees. "I think Kelsey is out there right now. This photograph right here – this is evidence that he killed your son. Your *son*," I emphasized. "We saw Kelsey's necklace, remember… his mother's necklace, the jade wolf pendant, wrapped around that person's throat before they were burned alive."

"Leave it alone, Laz."

"Why?"

"Because it doesn't involve you. There's no reason for you to get yourself wrapped up in our shit."

"Maybe not, but he used to live in the Cabin, Gloria. He slept in the same bed I sleep in now. You're crazy if you think I'm going to keep my sick daughter in the same house where a murderer lived, what, only three years ago? If he wanted to, he would know exactly how to get inside. He might even still have a *key*!"

"Nobody is asking you to stay."

"I can't afford to go back to Anchorage! There's nothing for me there anymore."

"Then by all means, Lazalier, sleep in the Mansion. Although, if Kelsey is alive, and if he still has a key to the Cabin, it's more than likely he still has a key to the Mansion."

Gloria spat the cigarette filter over the side of the balcony. She took the photograph off the table and handed it to me with a sigh, then brushed past me and moved to the door that led into the interior parlor.

She stopped in the doorway.

"I want to show you something."

***

Sam Dilbrook's headstone was a chest-high, black marble sentinel standing alone on a ridge overlooking a wide, snow-dusted valley that appeared to have no end. Behind us, the sharpened tips of the Mansion's east turrets peeked over the treetops.

Ahead of us, the white valley lay peppered with the strangest animals I'd ever seen. They were black with shiny coats and long necks, their equine heads bobbing up and down, up and down. I squinted my eyes through the near darkness, the softest slivers of the aurora providing a better view as I finally understood the true identity of these strange beasts.

"Nodding donkeys," Gloria said.

Pumpjacks. So, this was the Mainstay oil field. I finally laid eyes on the infamous black jewel of the north. Provider of jobs. Robber of lives.

"This was supposed to belong to him. All of this," she said, sweeping her arm across the valley. "Now, he watches over it."

She picked up a large, prickly pinecone and placed it at the foot of the grave in lieu of fresh flowers.

"Who will it all go to, when – "

I stopped myself.

"Don't be a coward," she grunted. "Just say it."

"Who will get it now, when Don dies?"

"The obvious answer is Sophie," she said. "But seeing as she doesn't want it, I guess the stakeholders will divvy it up, or give it all to the state."

"You realize that Adam Kelsey stole all of this from Sam too," I said. "Stole it right out from under him the moment he pushed Sam over that cliff."

Gloria brushed the frost off the face of Sam's headstone and took a seat on the snow. She pulled her eyes from the black monolith, let out a thick vapory cloud, and gazed out at the vast and unending valley of the oil field.

"No, he didn't."

213

"But you just said – "

"I said it was *supposed* to belong to Sam," she said. "Long before we knew what Sam actually was."

I took a seat next to Gloria, and there on the ridge, she told me everything about her son.

***

Samuel Ezekiel Dilbrook was born in the east wing library, fourteen hours after his sister.

Sophie had been a simple enough birth, a labor that lasted only thirty-four minutes before she slipped out at a healthy six and a half pounds. She cried and slept and shat and suckled, exactly as a newborn should. And though Gloria was happy to be halfway through the process, something inside her whispered that the next child was going to make her life a living hell.

Gloria's screams of agony echoed throughout the Mansion as she fought her son tooth and nail. Sam was backwards, purple legs protruding from between Gloria's thighs as he sat wedged and unmoving inside her.

This is it, she thought to herself. *I need finish to this, or I'm going to die.*

She cried and cursed and bled, the pain so intense that tunnel vision became a constant. She slipped out of consciousness on four separate occasions, each time coming to with a team of hired midwives slapping her cheeks and dousing her in ice water. When the four Inuit women finally succeeded in heaving the son out of the mother by his ankles, it was to find him purple and near death, the umbilical cord wrapped in a devilish knot around his neck. A doctor had been rush-helicoptered to Horseshoe Hill to tend to the fading infant.

Gloria slept for three days after Sam emerged, and when she finally awoke, it was to find her husband at her bedside, having just arrived back from a conference in Ketchikan. He looked well-rested and overtly happy, and Gloria knew all too well what that meant. Don wasn't a happy man by nature. Only the combination of time away from his wife, three glasses of Malamute whiskey, young lips, and red stilettos could beckon the smile out of his hardened scowl.

The eldest midwife interrupted by entering the room with one newborn in each arm and an oxygen tank clunking at her feet. She presented Don's children to him, and Gloria watched as he stared in wonder at his daughter, and then in horror at his son.

Sam was blue-faced and cockeyed, a tiny oxygen mask affixed to his face. A paper cone sat atop Sam's head, and though it resembled a lopsided birthday hat, Gloria knew its true purpose. Sam had been born with entirely collapsed veins, and the medicine he required couldn't be administered into his arms, hands, feet, or legs. The cone concealed an IV port, a long needle that stuck into the only vein large enough to save his life, throbbing just above his temple.

Don Dilbrook's distaste for his son began on that day, and as the years ticked by, it festered.

Typical Ukippans had always considered the Dilbrooks as outsiders, rich and spoiled money-mongers that hid in the shadows of their lavish Mansion, watching over Lake Adamant to ensure the peasants and the bumpkins remained at bay. That is, until Sophie Dilbrook was old enough to brave the cold and accompany her mother to town during daytime outings.

Brash and bold, six-year-old Sophie had the unique ability to help the unhappy citizens of Ukippa shake the dust off their funny bones. She found immense interest in the lives of people who were nothing like her or her family. She asked them questions about their hardships. Offered advice on how to build the best snowmen. Helped the other little girls calmly talk through their disputes over who had the prettier Barbie doll. Drew up contracts with crayon and Post-Its, instructing the other children of the official rules and regulations of hide-and-seek.

She was, and remains to this day, the unofficial and undisputed magistrate of Ukippa, Alaska.

Sam Dilbrook, meanwhile, spent his younger years shut up in the Mansion. Gloria often found him alone in the dark, sitting upright under a sheet in the middle of the floor, whispering to himself, divulging secrets of a dark fantasy world in which he alone belonged. Each time she removed the cover, she found him underneath, crouched over dozens of scraps of paper, watching in both wonder and terror as Sam scribbled in black ink.

He drew incredibly precise depictions of his mother and father, fast asleep in their bed. He drew Sophie, alone with a boy in the woods, their lips locked. He drew the Shack and old Moose staring blankly from his porch, exposing a ghoulish grin.

In one, Sam drew the Mansion, and he drew it in flames.

Gloria did her best to let him be, to give her son the space he needed to grow into the man her husband hoped he would one day become.

Don, however, wasn't so patient.

He reprimanded Sam at every turn. Screamed at him to go outside, to be a *normal* boy, to stop sketching voyeuristic nonsense. To drive his point home, after discovering a box of disturbing drawings under a loose floorboard in Sam's room, he burned them all. Sam screamed for two days straight, then finally fell silent from exhausted vocal cords. From then on, Sam hardly ever spoke to Don. Instead, he simply stared at his father with dark, blank eyes.

Don began to refer to his hermit son as "Sam the Clam," a nickname that stuck to the boy like tree sap. During the rare occasion when Sophie was successful in dragging Sam along to play in the woods, the other kids chanted the nickname, laughing all the while, until Sophie pushed each of them down and threatened to throw them all over the cliff unless they knocked it off.

Sophie was imposing when she needed to be, a trait she took with her all the way to the Anchorage Prosecutors Office.

On Sophie and Sam's thirteenth birthday, Don and Gloria attempted to re-establish their haughty, mysterious image by inviting the entire township to the western shore of Lake Adamant for a barbeque honoring the twins. Eager to get in good with the richest family north of the Gates of the Arctic, nearly everyone in town attended (save for the old hermit woman on Mount Poe), and nearly everyone presented Sophie with a gift. Don gave his daughter a kiss on the forehead and when everyone was watching, told her to close her eyes. And when he instructed her to open them, it was to find a spotted, brown and ginger kitten at her feet.

Through sobs of joy, Sophie named the kitten Juniper.

Sam, however, received only one gift that day. It was a Nikon camera, given to him in secret by his mother behind an old oak tree. Though Don had squashed Sam's love of drawing, Gloria decided to nourish his artistic side by encouraging Sam to pursue photography instead.

The party went off without a hitch, at least until it was time to blow out the candles. Even though everyone in town (and indeed, Don himself) preferred Sophie, they recognized it was just as much Sam's party. Sam, however, was nowhere to be found. And while Sophie tried desperately to remember where she'd last seen Juniper the kitten, Gloria had the sudden realization that something had gone terribly, terribly wrong.

As the adults searched the trees along the bank, a young girl screamed and pointed at the water.

A hundred feet from shore, a string of bubbles broke the surface. "Sam!"

Gloria sprinted into the lake in full dress, the waterlogged fabric of her dress weighing her down, gulping and spluttering water that tasted of weeds and iron. She swam to the spot where the bubbles had been, but there was nothing left except silent ripples. Gloria looked back at the shore, her desperate eyes searching for her husband in the water, but there was only Sophie, knee-deep in the lake and her face a mess of tears. The other Ukippans watched from the shore, holding fast to their wide-eyed children. And way in the back stood Don, leaning against the trunk of a black spruce, lazily chewing a fingernail.

"Mom! There!" Sophie screamed and pointed further out. Gloria turned and saw two objects floating on the surface.

The first was a small mound that looked like a floating log, at least until she recognized the perfectly linear black and green stripes of Sam's shirt. The second was much smaller, a tangled mess of matted brown and ginger hair.

Sam, what have you done?

Still fighting the weight of her sodden sundress, Gloria swam out to her son and pulled him close to her chest. He was unresponsive and not breathing, but under the water, she could feel his slow and uneven heartbeat as she swam. Fifty feet from shore, his added weight finally pulled her under, and Gloria was certain she would drown. As she dipped below the surface, her feet touched the rocky bottom, and when her shoes got a grip of the lakebed, she held her breath and walked the rest of the way, pressing on through the wall of water until finally, her head broke the surface.

Gloria gasped and choked for breath as the rest of the Ukippans pulled her and Sam out of the water. A group of older men began attempting to revive her son.

Don Dilbrook made his way over to his wife, hunched down, and kissed her forehead. "You should have let him be," he whispered in her ear. And before she had time to respond, Don stood up and disappeared into the trees, following the path that led back to Horseshoe Hill.

"Juniper! Where's Juniper?!" Sophie cried, searching the whitecaps.

And when Sophie met her mother's eyes, she knew the truth. Sam tried to drown himself, took the kitten with him, and only one made it back to shore.

After that day, Gloria saw fit to have Sam looked at.

"Schizoid Personality Disorder," the doctor said. "The patient displays a distinct pattern of detachment and withdrawal, and an indifference to social and familial relationships."

"From anxiety?" Gloria asked, heartbroken. "Paranoia? What?"

"Quite the opposite, in fact. Sam possesses an intense lack of emotionality and has little ability to empathize with others, including yourself, your daughter, and your husband." The doctor sighed. "He's empty inside, Mrs. Dilbrook."

Sam was prescribed with a slew of mood stabilizers and antidepressants, none of which could pull him completely out of the dark void within.

At least, not until he met Eldon Gamble.

Gloria took in Eldon after he stumbled into town with nothing but the shirt on his back. She had no idea where he came from or why he ended up in Ukippa, and no one else in town wanted anything to do with him. With a mentally challenged son of her own, Gloria felt compelled to offer sanctuary to the cold and confused young man.

At first, Sam steered clear of Eldon. But after a few weeks shut up inside after a massive snowstorm, Gloria discovered them alone in the upstairs parlor, sitting upright under a sheet, whispering secrets of Sam's dark fantasy world, into which he had apparently invited Eldon. At the time, Sam was in his early twenties, and while Gloria knew she shouldn't condone such childish fantasies, she was elated that her son had found a kindred soul in Eldon Gamble.

Out of earshot of her husband, Gloria encouraged Sam and Eldon to share the upstairs bedroom and eventually, the two young men became joined at the hip.

That is, until Sophie introduced the family to Adam Kelsey.

Kelsey was everything Eldon was not. He was handy, rugged, confident, and capable. He worked hard on the Mansion and around the grounds. More and more often, Gloria discovered Sam at Kelsey's side, holding his tools, supporting his ladder, or making his lunch. Sam began to idolize Adam, and Eldon fell to the wayside.

One night, Adam Kelsey awoke to find Eldon standing over his bed, staring at him while he slept. Kelsey raised a stink about it, and Eldon left the Mansion shortly after. He meandered down into Ukippa, found his way into the heart of Mags the bar matron, and graciously accepted a cot and a pillow in the backroom of Galoshes.

With Eldon gone, Sam spent every waking second around Adam Kelsey.

Given her son's mental and emotional instability, Gloria grew steadily more uncomfortable. She hoped Sophie might notice and intervene, but Sophie was too focused on her law studies to notice anything outside of her textbooks.

And then, on a hot summer afternoon, the whole of Ukippa was shaken to its core by the sudden fall of Sam Dilbrook.

***

"Sometime around noon, I heard Sam and Don fighting in the library. They were screaming at each other. Something about Adam. And then, everything went quiet. When I got there, Don was bleeding, and Sam was gone."

"Where did he go?"

"Into the woods."

"Why?"

"Well, until today, I assumed he did exactly what he'd done on his thirteenth birthday. But instead of walking out into the lake, he threw himself over a cliff. Quick. Simple. Done."

"And now?" I asked. "Now that you've seen the photograph?"

"I'm not sure," she said. "Maybe he panicked and ran off into the woods, ran into Kelsey. Maybe he said something that pissed Kelsey off."

"Enough to *kill* Sam?"

"I don't know."

"But why? Why the woods?"

"Kelsey knew those woods better than he knew his own two feet. Spent a lot of time huntin' and trackin' with Nukilik when he was younger."

Something about the way she said it was odd, but I couldn't put my finger on it.

"Yeah. Sophie told me."

"Sam liked Kelsey a lot. Trusted him more than he ever trusted anyone. Adam Kelsey had no reason to dislike Sam, other than maybe thinking of Sam as clingy or annoying."

"Again, enough to kill him?"

Gloria sighed, pressed her gloved palms against the firm black stone streaked in white-blue veins, and was silent. While I watched her, I noticed her feet shift uncomfortably.

She's hiding something.

"What is it that Kelsey wants?" I asked.

"Why do you think I know?"

"Why else would he come back? Why kill again? You know something and you're not telling me."

"I don't know anything, Laz. Not anymore," she stated firmly. She began walking up the trail that led back to the Mansion. And then, she turned around.

"And that's what scares me."

19

BREADCRUMBS

When we returned from our hike to Sam's Overlook (as Gloria liked to call it), we found you right where we left you, asleep in the spare third-floor bedroom Lizanne had abandoned a week prior.

"What happened to her?" I asked Gloria, more than a little paranoid. It seemed more and more as though people who associated with the Dilbrooks had a habit of disappearing or dying.

Prudence Gamble.

Sam Dilbrook.

Adam Kelsey.

Evie Brooks.

And now Lizanne, apparently.

"I promise, she's alive and well," Gloria huffed as I followed her down the main spiral staircase. "Flies south for winter to be with her family."

"Like Evie?"

"Like Evie," Gloria repeated.

"Except Evie never made it," I said.

Gloria stopped halfway down the second-floor landing and turned to face me. The sudden stop made me slightly nauseous, standing forty feet in the air on a rickety steel corkscrew, a swift drop to the oakwood floors kept at bay by nothing more than a coiled steel railing. I imagined the railing suddenly twist around my wrist and forearm, a metallic serpent tugging me over the side. I shook my head, casting away the daydream.

"What are you talking about?" she asked.

"She never made it to Texas."

"How do you know?"

"I went to talk to her about Eldon."

"About Eldon? Why?"

"He spied on me," I said. "I don't trust him. I thought he might have something to do with the body we found."

Gloria stared at me for a moment. A hard, calculating stare. And then, she burst out in laughter.

"Eldon? You think Eldon, of all people, killed that person?"

"He just seems – "

"Why? Because he whispers to himself?"

"I just – "

"And why the hell would Evie know?"

"They lived here at the same time. I thought maybe – "

"Well, you thought wrong. Evie wanted nothin' to do with Eldon while she was here. She went about her business with Don, spent some of her off-days hikin' with Sophie, and spent all of her nights down at the Cabin. That was the extent of her time here."

"Nights down at the Cabin?" I asked,

"*Adam and Evie*, we called 'em, just like the Holy fuckin' Bible."
She laughed harder at that.

"They were a couple?" I asked.

"Humped like rabbits, but I don't know if I'd call 'em a couple. I think she was infatuated with him, sure, but Kelsey had a dark heart. He didn't – couldn't love anything or anyone, least as far as I know."

We continued our descent, the constant twist making my eyes spin.

"I went to her office," I confessed. "They said she'd gone to Texas to be with her mother. So, I reached out to Jackie Brooks on social media, and she told me Evie decided to stay behind in Ukippa this winter to work on a case."

"Stayed behind?" Gloria grumbled. "That's not like her."

"So I've heard. I went to Evie's house, Gloria. The side door was wide open, had been open for days. The furniture was all frozen. That's where I found Eldon. And that's where Eldon found the photograph."

I heard the soft, distant shuffling of boots on marble twenty feet below. Gloria and I looked down.

Eldon stood in the middle of the vast and elaborate rotunda that graced the Mansion's foyer. He held a half-eaten PB&J in both hands, the sticky contents smeared across his lips and chin.

Gloria smiled and shook her head, then spiraled down to the bottom before sweeping her hands across Eldon's cheeks, brushing away the breadcrumbs.

"That's a good boy," I heard her say. "Help yourself, just like always. You know you're always welcome here."

She pulled him into a bearhug, clutching his head to her chest and rocking him side to side. It was strange, but after our conversation at Sam's grave, I now knew that the Dilbrooks' relationship with Eldon Gamble (with the exception of cold-hearted Don) was nothing short of familial. They took him in when he arrived in Ukippa with nothing and no one. He became something of a second sibling to Sophie and Sam. And now, it appeared as though Gloria loved him like one of her own, albeit from a bit of a distance.

For so many weeks now, I'd painted a mental portrait of Eldon Gamble as some sort of sinister psychopath, a whispering goblin that lurked in the shadows.

Looking at him now, he was nothing more than a lost child.

***

Later that afternoon, I was busy shoveling mounds of snow from the Mansion's wide, circular stone driveway, when the sound of rubber on gravel made my ears prick up. I buried the business end of my shovel into the snow and glanced up to see Detective Weekes emerge from a sleek, black SUV.

"Hi there, Mr. Brady," she said with a wave of her arm.

"Detective," I nodded, suddenly wary of her visit.

"Wolverines, huh?" Weekes asked with a smile, glancing at my snow boots.

"My favorites," I said.

"My husband owns a pair."

"There ain't a better brand."

"Christ, your feet are huge," she laughed. "What are you, like a size eleven?"

"Twelve and a half," I answered with a smile of my own. It appeared that Detective Weekes had begun warming up to me.

Gloria emerged from the Mansion in a bit of a huff.

"Laz, you missed a little snow on the back p – "

She noticed the large SUV billowing clouds from its tailpipe, her eyes swinging right to fix upon Weekes. Gloria stopped halfway down the freshly shoveled front steps, holding the higher ground and keeping her gaze fixed upon the detective.

"How can we help you?" she asked sharply.

"Some bad business, unfortunately," Weekes said. She sighed a vaporous cloud of her own, then withdrew an envelope from her coat and handed it to Gloria. Eyes still fixed on the detective, Gloria pulled out the contents, unfolded two sheets paper, and began to read.

"What is that?" I asked.

"Coroner's report," Weekes said. "As well as a DNA analysis of the body from the woods."

Gloria clapped a hand to her mouth, her eyes wide as dinner plates.

"Oh, my god," she whimpered into her palm. "No, it can't be."

"Who is it?" I asked.

Weekes sighed. "The body belongs – well, belonged – to Evie Brooks."

I felt a sudden chill course through my veins that had nothing to do with the weather. All this time, I'd been searching for someone I'd already stumbled upon weeks earlier. I recalled the last time I saw Evie Brooks, throwing a long black shadow across the surface of

Lake Adamant from the light of the ice shanty. It was only two days later that Gloria and I discovered her charred skeleton. Someone had murdered Evie only hours after I saw her, and that realization alone was enough to make me dizzy.

"There was enough of her lungs left to deduce that she didn't die from smoke inhalation," said Weekes. "In fact, her inner lungs were still perfectly intact and without residue, which suggests she didn't die in the fire.

"So then – "

"Evie Brooks was killed prior to being placed in that hut."

"Then what killed her?" Gloria asked.

"We found – "

"A necklace," I interjected. Weekes' hardened eyes landed on mine like a hawk to prey. "A jade pendant in the shape of a wolf's head."

"That's right," said Weekes.

"She was strangled," I said. "It was Adam Kelsey. He's out there, and – "

"No, actually," Weekes interrupted.

"I'm sorry?"

"Evie Brooks was not strangled to death. In addition to her lungs, her trachea was undamaged."

"I don't understand."

"Blunt force trauma to the skull, right above the left temple," Weekes said. "That's how she was killed." Her eyes made a beeline to my own damaged temple, and I saw the beginnings of a smirk tug at the corner of her thin, wormy mouth.

"A really interesting wound, actually," she continued. "Wide, shallow, and sharp. Something pointy punctured her brain, but it left a large, concave impression."

I was stumped.

"You mentioned Adam Kelsey," Weekes stated, her eyes on me. "He was the previous groundskeeper before Mr. Brady. Is that right, Mrs. Dilbrook?"

"That's correct," Gloria said.

"Nukilik told me all about Adam Kelsey. He is under the impression that Kelsey is dead."

"He's wrong," I said.

"Why do you say that?" Weekes asked, calm and collected, but entirely accusatory. "Have you seen him?"

"No."

"Then why are you so convinced he's alive?"

"How do you explain the necklace?"

Weekes stared at me for a moment, her gaze piercing my own in a way I'd never experienced before. "Mrs. Dilbrook, when was the Cabin built?" she asked.

"It would've been, let's see, 1984."

"And why was it built?"

"I beg your pardon?"

"*Why?* Why build the Cabin when you have this big house all to yourselves?"

"We decided to hire a groundskeeper," Gloria answered.

"In 1984?"

"Yes."

"And who was that groundskeeper?"

Gloria was silent for a moment. She looked at me, then back at Weekes.

"Moose," she said. "Moose was our first groundskeeper."

I couldn't believe it. All this time, I'd believed a murderer to have slept in the same bed I slept in now, but now I realized that there'd been not just one, but two. All this time, and she never mentioned a thing about Moose.

"When did Moose stop being your groundskeeper?" Weekes asked.

"In 2010."

"So, Moose was your groundskeeper for twenty-six years. And now he lives on the other side of the hill?"

Gloria nodded, glancing over her shoulder at the front door. Evidently, she wanted this conversation to end.

"What happened?" asked Weekes.

"A dispute with my husband."

"Nukilik informed me it was a bit more than a dispute," she said. "A woman, Prudence Gamble, went missing from the Mainstay oil field in 1984, is that correct?"

"That's right, but – "

"Moose was arrested in accordance with her disappearance, but he was never convicted?"

"What you don't underst – "

"And immediately upon his release, your husband fired him from the oil field, but then quietly hired him on as groundskeeper at your home. I've talked to a few people in town, and they all agree on the same thing, Mrs. Dilbrook."

"And what's that?"

"You continue to maintain that Moose killed Prudence Gamble all those years ago. And yet, you stood by while he was hired to work and live on your property with your children running around... and for twenty-six years, no less."

"It's complicated," Gloria sneered.

"Is it safe to assume that, in the twenty-six years Moose lived in the Cabin, he may have possibly left some belongings behind?"

"It's possible."

"By the same token, is it possible that in the seven months Adam Kelsey lived in the Cabin, he too left some belongings behind? Say, perhaps, a necklace?"

"Again, it's possible."

"So then, it's also safe to assume that anyone with access into the Cabin might also have access to items left behind by previous occupants."

"What are you saying?"

"I'm saying it's entirely possible that Adam Kelsey, for whatever reason, left behind the jade necklace when he disappeared. And the only people with access into the Cabin are you, Mrs. Dilbrook; Moose, assuming he still possesses a key; and you, Mr. Brady."

"You're saying one of us killed Evie," Gloria scoffed. "Jesus Christ."

"I've never even met Evie Brooks," I said.

Weekes looked at me, and she smiled.

"Then why were you in her office last week?"

Shit.

232

"I was looking for her," I said.

"You were looking for her?" Weekes replied, wearing a sweet smile laced with strychnine. Apparently, her warmth toward me had been for lowering my walls.

"To ask her some questions."

"We searched Evie's home, Mr. Brady, and we found boot prints," Weekes said. "Men's Wolverines, size twelve and a half."

Double shit.

"What were you doing in her house, Mr. Brady?"

"Again, I was looking for her."

"To ask her some questions?" she mocked quietly.

"Yes."

"But you've never met her, remember?" she reminded me. "What incredibly important questions could you possibly have for someone you've never met?"

I was on the verge of telling Weekes all about my suspicions of Eldon Gamble, suspicions that had led me to Evie's office and then to her home. Suspicions that, after watching the way Gloria interacted with Eldon on the marble rotunda in the Mansion's foyer, I knew held no water.

I didn't believe Eldon Gamble killed anyone.

"It sounds to me like you've already made up your mind," I said. "You've already decided who's responsible."

"I'm unbiased, actually," Weekes said. "Just following the breadcrumbs. And so far, they all lead back to this hill. And as for Adam Kelsey murdering Ms. Brooks, I see no motive."

"Motive?!"

This outburst came from Gloria. Without warning, she reached into my pocket and with a flash of her hand, shoved the photograph a little too hard into Weekes' nose, causing the detective to slip and fall on a patch of ice.

"Adam Kelsey killed my fucking son," she spat, her fuse far from extinguished. "Pushed him over a cliff, and Evie Brooks caught it on camera. There's your fucking motive."

Gloria spun on her heel and walked off in the direction of the Mansion. I looked down at Detective Weekes and watched as she wiped a bead of blood from her left nostril. I shrugged my shoulders, then turned and left her to her own devices. I followed behind Gloria from a distance, and I smiled. Never before, not in my entire life, had I possessed such respect for a human being.

I knew then that I was on Gloria Dilbrook's side, whatever the outcome.

20

THE DOG AND THE WOLF

The first week of December came and went with nothing but a single snowfall, and a light one at that.

Gloria suggested I take full advantage of what she called the "recent beach weather," pack up yours and my belongings, and hitch a waterplane back to Anchorage. And though much of me agreed that we should indeed restart fresh in the city I'd missed for months, another part of me now felt a pull towards this place. As though Horseshoe Hill was not a hill at all, but a magnificent magnet set within the earth, a magnet that refused to release the soles of my shoes.

It wasn't just the hill, though.

After the way she asserted herself against Detective Weekes, I felt a newfound respect for and connection with Gloria Dilbrook, a connection that could only be compared to one I'd shared with my mother's older sister in my teen years.

Aunt Franny had gone to pasture after a sudden heart attack

during my first semester at UAA. The woman had always been a saint, as far as I was concerned, a woman who never let anyone pass judgment upon her or any member of her family. A woman who never passed up the chance to slip me a nugget of fresh sativa or the Bob Marley record she favored above all others. Aunt Franny never married or had any children, and that was A-okay with me. She spent every Christmas with us. Chortling at my father's stupid jokes. Secretly sharing a cigarette (or three) with my mother who, admittedly, was a closet smoker. Watching with glee as I unwrapped the very peculiar (yet very unique) beadwork socks she knitted for me every year, always with some mythological depiction woven into the wool.

Aunt Franny had been obsessed with Inuit folklore, particularly the story of the Great Wolf, a deity as beautiful as it was deadly, one she claimed devoured any person foolish enough to wander too close and attempt to touch its enchanted white fur.

The Great Wolf, whom Aunt Franny had called Amarok.

Amaruq.

Adam Kelsey.

I couldn't help noticing the similarities between the myth and the ex-groundskeeper. Kelsey had preyed upon Sam Dilbrook, a young man foolish enough to wander too close. Now it appeared that Kelsey had also preyed upon Evie Brooks, a woman with whom he'd shared an intimate relationship, a woman who (for lack of a better analogy) had actually succeeded in touching his enchanted white fur.

Who will he stalk next?

I asked myself this question over and over as I perused the old wooden shelves of Bannock General, Ukippa's one and only food pantry, automobile depot, drugstore, and jewelry boutique all rolled into one. And as I pulled a brand spankin' new bundle of Christmas lights from aisle four's top rack, the answer washed over me like icy lake water…

The first Ukippan to grow fond of Adam Kelsey. The person who led him directly to Horseshoe Hill.

Sophie.

But Sophie was alive and well in Anchorage. A long way from Ukippa, and a long way from Kelsey. As I considered this, I felt a little better. I carried Gloria's Christmas lights to the register and smiled at the old man behind the counter.

"How much do I owe you, Harry?" I asked, sifting through the dollar bills Gloria had given me. When he didn't reply, I looked up and found him staring at me with hardened, silver eyes and a thin, quivering line where his chapped, toothless smile normally sat.

"How much?" I repeated.

His thin grimace descended further down his jowls.

"Everything all right, Harry?"

I watched the bulge of the old man's tongue push a large wad of chaw from one side of his inner bottom lip to the other, and still he stared. Finally, he took eight dollars out of my hand, stuffed it in the register, and shoved the bundle of lights against my chest. His gaze shifted from my face to somewhere over my left shoulder, and as I turned, I noticed twelve other shoppers, all with their eyes fixed on me.

Staring.

Scowling.

Seething.

"Get out," I heard Harry grumble behind me. "And don't come back."

"What do you – "

"She was a good girl," he said. "A nice girl, all burnt to shit."

"Harry, I had nothing to do with – "

"Didn't you fuckin' hear 'im?" this came from a big, burly guy wearing a parka with the Mainstay logo etched on the breast pocket. "Get the fuck out."

"Go back to your hill," spat a Ukippan woman with balding, stringy hair.

"Murderin' fuck!" someone else barked.

"Look, whatever you heard from Weekes or from Nukilik – "

Chk-chink.

For the second time since arriving in Ukippa, I turned to peer deep into the sooty blackness of twin shotgun barrels. Harry had the butt held to his shoulder, nostrils flared as he stared me down, a thousand times more confident behind his trusty slugthower.

"I said get out," he said. "I ain't gonna tell you again. Take yer lights and go."

I really do hate the cliché of small towns, the washed-up notion that a simple smear by the town's only authority (in this case, Nukilik or Detective Weekes) became the pure and simple truth, no matter how you looked at it. But sadly, Ukippa fit the bill. Here, the stereotype rang true. Ukippans either feared, loathed, or pitied everyone who had ever lived on Horseshoe Hill.

Everyone except Sophie.

And while Gloria made me feel like you and I were members of the family up on the hill, the townsfolk of Ukippa made sure I knew where I stood with all of them.

When one of their own wound up a smoking husk in a fiery shack, all of a sudden, the main culprit was the outsider.

The main culprit was me.

***

For the next few days, I noticed Nukilik's truck parked on the icy gravel of Lake Adamant's southern shore, at the base of Horseshoe Hill. Whenever I raised the binoculars to my eyes, it was to find binoculars of his own, pressed between his face and the windshield.

Watching Moose's Shack.

Watching the Dilbrook Mansion.

Watching my Cabin.

More than once, I stepped out onto the front porch, waved, and watched as his headlights switched on. The tires rolled back onto the highway before zipping off around the lake and back toward Ukippa.

Back to Detective Weekes.

A dog to his master.

Gloria made sure Eldon remained inside the Mansion at all times, feeding him and loving him like only a mother knew how. I knew, however, that her affection and her intention for keeping him locked away inside were for our own good as much as his. At the first opportunity, Weekes and Nukilik would surely bring him in for questioning and, knowing his fragile state of mind, might be

239

successful in coaxing out a false confession.

"Or inject him with some lie about us bashing in Evie's skull," Gloria grumbled as she held the ladder steady.

I sat high upon the ladder, my legs straddled over the top rung as I punched another staple into the new string of Christmas lights dangling from the eaves like swirling icicles. We'd spent the better part of a week hanging what had to be tens of thousands of red and white twinklers from the Mansion's turrets, gables, and hand-carved fascia (and by *we*, I mean Gloria held the ladder and complained about Detective Weekes while I scaled the Mansion's dizziest drops).

It was work that seemed pointless to me, considering no one but myself, Gloria, and the peeping Nukilik and Weekes would see the Mansion glowing like a candy-coated beacon in the night. But when I grunted my contention, she shushed and waved me away like a mosquito.

"Oh, hush. Ellie will love it," she said. "And so will Sophie."

"Sophie?" I muttered, trying not to sound too excited. "Sophie's coming home for Christmas?"

"Didn't I mention that?"

I shrugged, placed the staple gun to the eave, completely missed the string of lights, and nearly stapled clean through my hand as my mind swiftly drifted.

Drifted to a vision of Sophie holding you in her lap beside a thirty-foot-high Christmas tree dotted in reds and silvers and golds. And there I stood beside her, my hand on her shoulder. And the Mansion was ours. The Cabin too. And there, on the rug, sat Harvey, nibbling a crumb out of the bear rug.

One big happy family.

"Yes, and Tom too."

My vision faded as quickly as it had come.

"Tom Clark?"

"Are there any other Toms?" Gloria chuckled. "That's all right, isn't it?"

As I looked down, I noticed the hint of a cheeky grin on her face, her crow's feet a tad more crinkled than usual as she struggled to hide her smile.

"Why wouldn't it be all right? Tom's my best friend."

"I know he is," she said, and I knew precisely what she meant. "I wouldn't be too worried about it."

"Why should I be worried?"

"You shouldn't be."

"Well, I'm not."

"Good."

She closed her eyes and bit her tongue, desperately attempting to keep her smile at bay.

"Oh, shut up," I grunted, then went back to my stapling.

Sophie was coming for Christmas, and as excited as I was, I couldn't shake what I had convinced myself of earlier in the week.

Adam Kelsey wants Sophie next.

***

There was a certain warmth in the air as Christmas drew closer. And though the constant twilight and inky skies always put a damper on my mood, somehow the sight of you scribbling a letter to Santa

Claus in a language only you could understand was enough to make me hopeful.

Hopeful enough to pick up my career where I'd left it burned to the ground. Hopeful that once winter had come and gone, we could leave Ukippa forever. Hopeful we could go back to Anchorage and live semi-normal lives in a semi-normal city.

My recent confrontation in Bannock General had loosened Horseshoe Hill's magnetic pull. In the course of three days, I found myself aching to get back to that which was semi-normal.

After all, nothing about life in Alaska will ever be completely normal.

As I prepared to leave for the airport in Allakaket, Gloria decided to stay behind at the Mansion to tidy up the guest rooms where Tom and Sophie would be sleeping (she made sure I knew the term was plural, that Sophie preferred to sleep alone). She insisted that you also stay behind and pick through a chipped wooden box of Sophie and Sam's old toys. As Gloria liked to remind me, "Yuletide pickin's will be slim under the tree this year." I gave you a kiss on the forehead as you pulled out a truly raggedy Raggedy Ann doll. I laced up my Wolverines, grabbed the keys to the Silverado, and was out the door.

The "recent beach weather" was short-lived. As I drove down Horseshoe Hill's winding, slippery switchbacks, the back tires squealed and sung. Chains or no chains, the white flurry and black ice didn't give a rip. My toes made sweet, sweet love with the brake pedal as I weaseled my way down the unforgiving path, certain beyond certainty I was going to slip up and send the truck tumbling over the edge and down the snowy scree slope.

Nope, I told myself. *Everything is going to be fine.*

I'd slept in a little later than I intended, and I knew Sophie and Tom would be waiting for me in the warmth of the waterplane docked at the jetty. The drive to Allakaket should have taken only two hours or so.

That is, if I hadn't seen a black shadow out in the middle of Lake Adamant.

It skittered along the ice just beyond the old fishing shanty. The shadow immediately reminded me of the girl in the snow, but I knew it was impossible. Evie Brooks was now nothing but a charred corpse awaiting cremation and a one-way trip to Lubbock, Texas in a cardboard shoebox.

Was the shadow on Lake Adamant her ghost, perhaps?

I thought of Smitty, of Nurse Joy, of Mr. Guthrie, and of the fused twins. My eternal guilt over their fiery deaths had resulted in their ghostly manifestations. Had I also added Evie Brooks' name to my black book of spectral pals?

I doubted it.

She had been long dead by the time Gloria and I found her. I was neither her killer nor her rescuer.

The shadow slid and stumbled on the ice, and the closer the road took me to the edge of the lake, the more I realized how inhuman the shadow appeared. It didn't possess two legs, but four. The constant twilight made everything appear darker, but this particular shadow was pitch, pitch black.

The shadow on the lake was a black dog.

My heart stopped.

243

I punched the brake and fishtailed onto the snowy shoulder.

Wide-eyed, bone-thin, and shivering, Harvey's skinny black paws scratched and slipped along the ice. He fell hard onto his face, legs splaying out in all directions. He tried to get up, but slipped again, accepted defeat, and was still. Plumes of fog poured from his maw as he panted in exhaustion and, I assumed, dehydration.

I jumped out of the truck and nearly slipped on the black ice myself. I waded through knee-high snow that had been pushed to the shoulder by Ukippa's single snowplow, leapt over the barrier between the road and the white shoreline, and ventured out onto the ice.

He was over a hundred yards away, and as I shuffled slowly along, I was hit by a sudden howling gale, lost my balance and my footing, and then slipped. My feet flew high over my head. My back slammed against the frozen surface of the lake, and the breath was knocked from my lungs.

I tried to stand and, just as Harvey had, I slipped again and landed hard on my right knee.

Crunch.

Pain shot down my right shin and up my right thigh. I pushed myself into a seated position on the ice, teeth clenched as I examined my right knee, pressing on it and grunting in pain. Though I wore long johns, sweatpants, and a pair of jeans in thick layers, I still felt the unmistakably sickening way my patella was no longer a singular bone, but two distinct wedges that slid and popped in opposite directions.

My kneecap had split in half.

Shit.

Upon the wind, I heard my pup's desperate howls.

"Hang on, Harv!"

Harvey looked up and finally noticed me. He began scratching his long black nails at the ice, desperately attempting to scoot his way in my direction. A shift in the fog caught my eye, and suddenly, my blood froze over.

Skulking out of the fog, white fur whipped on the fierce wind.

A wolf.

The wolf.

Its enormous head sat low, broad shoulders hunched, bright yellow eyes fixed on Harvey. It bared its monstrous teeth, two-inch long canines gleaming in the twilight.

"Harvey!" I screamed. "Come on, bud! Come to Dad! Hurry!"

Harvey continued to scoot along the ice, oblivious to the approaching danger. The wolf was twice Harvey's size, and though the animal also appeared to be having a difficult time traversing the surface of the lake, the promise of an easy kill kept its splayed paws stepping ever closer to my dog. I knew Harvey would never make it without me, so I forced myself onto my hands and my good knee, stretched my injured right leg behind me, and began an awkward crawl across the ice.

I hauled myself farther and farther from shore, closing the distance between myself and Harvey while the wolf stalked him from behind. Had Harvey remained still, the wolf would have easily beaten me to its prey, clamped its jaws over Harvey's throat, and dragged him away into the fog. Harvey, however, kept scratching his way toward me, and with our combined effort, I was able to reach out and grip my hands over his rough and bleeding paws.

"That's a good boy," I grunted.

Warped, high-pitched thunder ricocheted in my eardrums, but it didn't come from the sky. It was an otherworldly noise, the chaotic fusion of whipcracks and laser beams. The noise came from below, and as I looked down, I noticed a man-sized spiderweb stretching twenty feet in seven separate directions beneath my belly.

Smaller lakes this far above the Arctic Circle were likely frozen solid this time of year, but Lake Adamant was a goliath. The cold hadn't penetrated nearly as deep as I had hoped.

The ice whined, boomed, and shifted beneath me.

Praying with everything I had, I gripped Harvey's armpits and swung him in an arc along the ice, in the direction of the shoreline. Had he been a true Labrador, his weight would have easily cracked the ice even further. I thanked God then and there that Harvey was born a mutt, that he had inherited his mother's border collie size.

I released my grip and watched as he slid in circles away from the cracked ice where I lie sprawled.

Now positioned between the dog and the wolf, I turned my attention to the predator and found its yellow eyes locked on mine.

"Don't do it," I warned.

It didn't listen.

Teeth bared and dripping with foam, the beast advanced. And it took one step too close.

The icy surface clapped and rumbled as the cracks beneath the wolf's paws extended and made contact with my own glacial web. I knew it was hopeless, and as he crouched to spring at me, I turned and met Harvey's big honey brown eyes one final time. I gave my big boy a smile, then I closed my eyes.

The wolf leapt, and when its fur touched my skin, the world gave out beneath us with a resounding crack. The wolf yelped as an astonishingly intense coldness engulfed us. Freezing water stung my flesh like a billion needles piercing my body in synchrony. My mouth flung open, lungs gasping for oxygen that didn't want to arrive. My muscles seized up. Gritty, metallic lake water flooded my mouth as Lake Adamant's chill sucked me under.

When I opened my eyes, it was to find cloudy blackness deep beneath my kicking feet. With all the strength I could muster, I looked up to find glassy ripples of green and indigo, faint wisps of the aurora warped behind a thick pane of frozen glass.

I kicked toward the surface and struck my head against the ice. I lifted my arms, hands gliding along the frozen underbelly of Adamant's surface, searching desperately for the hole I'd fallen through, but it was nowhere to be found. I stared up through the ice, and there, on the other side, I saw a distorted face smiling back at me.

Milky, lifeless eyes. Blackened, dripping flesh.

A fixed, ear-to-ear grin.

Smitty watched from above as I succumbed to the lake.

My vision began to fade. In my final moments beneath the ice, all I could think about was you, Ellie.

I closed my eyes and submitted to the frozen murk.

As I sank, I heard strange, loud, and distant knocks from above.

21

IN THE HOUSE OF THE DEVIL

What began as a quiet night at the Anchorage Fire Department has quickly erupted into a combustion of activity.

I shouldn't have snuck that fifth shot of Malamute.

Sirens blare as blue and red lights dance along the edges of my periphery. My head swims with that calming, familiar warmth of inebriation, a warmth that is slowly becoming icy with panic.

I forgot my helmet.

The buildings of Anchorage zip past the backseat window of Fire Engine No. 7 as I press my forehead to the glass, willing my vision to stabilize and my nerves to calm.

Isn't that what the whiskey is meant to do?

Life at home is becoming increasingly worse. I can feel the ties that bind my marriage quickly unraveling. Vanessa is colder and more distant every single day. I've spent the last year of my life watching my infant daughter succumb to a cancer that desperately wants to devour her. I failed my paramedics test for the third consecutive time. I drink more every single night.

And now, I have to feign sobriety to keep myself, and others on my engine, safe.

"You all right?" Smitty asks from the front passenger seat. I turn to him, seeing his blueberry eyes fixed on the road as we speed past the Ted Stevens Anchorage International Airport. I open my mouth to confess that, no, I am not all right, that I am drunk, that I need to go back to the station. I don't give a rip that Mullingar (the engineer driving us through sheets of ash) and Jones (the rookie riding in back with me) are present to witness my drunken announcement.

But before I am able to utter a word, I see Smitty's eyes widen, his clean-shaven face glowing with fiery reds and yellows. I look out the front windshield, and there it is.

Turnagain Home teeters against an inky black sky, spires of white-hot flame swirling upward from the windows. The inferno licks the underbelly of the moon, radiant heat bathing its silvery face in red so dense it appears to bleed from its craters. Thick, acrid smoke rolls and coils into the sky as Mullingar punches the brakes and skids the engine to a halt.

The four of us jump out, soot and smoke already flooding our lungs. The screaming sirens of other engines grow louder in the distance. Engine No. 7 is first at the scene, and though the building burns out of control, the lives of the old folks inside are our first priority.

Drunk or not, my instincts kick in.

I shoulder an air pack and pull a facemask over my head, sucking in fresh oxygen through the respirator.

249

"Brady, you're on ventilation," Smitty yells over the roar of the flames. "And where's your damn helmet?"

"Back at the station," I grunt. I unhinge a small steel box and press down on the switch hidden inside. A massive, L-shaped steel leg protrudes out the side of the truck and anchors the engine to the pavement.

"Fuckin' dumbass," Smitty says. He then takes off his Captain's helmet and thrusts it against my chest.

"I don't need it," I slur, then push the helmet back into his hands.

Through the clear acrylic of my facemask, I notice Smitty's silvery blueberries watching me very, very closely. He's seen me drunk on plenty of occasions, knows the way my left eyelid slouches a little too far down my cheek.

He shakes his head, grabs my jacket, shoves me up against the truck, and forces his helmet onto my head.

"Ain't riskin' your stupid ass up there. Sober the hell up and get on that damn ladder." And with that, he releases my jacket, pulls on his facemask, and steers Jones and Mullingar into the wreckage.

Say anything for John Smitson, say he is a stubborn old saint.

Securing Smitty's helmet a little more firmly to my skull, I unsheathe my axe from its holster, climb up onto the back of the truck, open the beveled steel lid of the control panel, and throw the switch. The large white ladder rises from its slumber and pivots upward at a sharpening angle as a man-sized basket swings into position at the end. I flip another switch and the ladder extends upward toward the flames, doubling and then tripling in length.

The Malamute makes my brain spin, but I shake my head and

force my eyes into focus.

I grip one of the ladder's rungs in my left hand and the axe in my right, and then I begin my ascent. Higher and higher I climb, and as I look down, I watch as three more engines whip into position behind No. 7. Six more guys, garbed in turnouts, rush into the hellfire, straight into the devil's house (or how I've always imagined it). Thirty feet below me, five others begin hosing the flames while another (I think it's Wharton) ascends No. 11's ladder.

I meet his gaze, he nods, and then he climbs into his own cherry picker, mere feet from a funnel of fire spinning out a second-floor window. Wharton swings his axe in a perfect spiral, splitting a hole into the blackened and burning roof. Smoke pours out of the hole he's made, and I suddenly recall that I should be doing the exact same thing.

The heat is unbearable.

Though it's meant to keep my body resistant to the flames, the layers of my turnout gear steam me from the inside like a potato wrapped in cotton, stuffed in a microwave, and spun on high. As I climb with the rising heat, sweat drips into my eyes, an annoying salty sting under my facemask that I'm unable to wipe away. I reach a third-floor window, peer through the glass and into a small bedroom. The tenant is long gone, either among those rushing out the front door with their canes and walkers, or burning alive in another part of the building. Inside the room, I see nothing but thick, black smoke. It's only a matter of time before the ceiling suddenly ignites in a carpet of flame. This room is a lost cause.

Wait.

I see movement inside. A pair of firefighter's boots sift through the smoke.

I need to get above the window. I need to ventilate. I need to help.

I bolt higher up the ladder, ignoring the whiskey-spins. I step into the basket at the end of my cherry picker, grip my axe in both hands, swing it back and then in a high arc over my head. The blade comes down in a swift blur of red-painted steel with a satisfying chop, and –

Whoosh!

A pillar of fire explodes out of the hole and into my face. The axe slips out of my fingers and plummets through the hole as I am thrown back against the railing of the cherry picker. Glass shatters as the window beneath my feet explodes outward from the force of the sudden flashover.

I can't see.

I can't think.

I forget where I am. I forget *why* I am.

When I come to, I see black smoke roiling out of the hole I've created. I descend down the ladder a few rungs to the blasted-out window, shards of teethlike glass stuck to the windowpane in a demonic grin. I can only hope the person I saw inside the room moments earlier had time to get out.

Suddenly, I see them. The same pair of firefighter's boots. This time, however, I only see the soles. This time, they're not moving. Whoever is in there is lying flat on their back, most likely unconscious.

Or dead.

I am the only one who knows. I am the only one who can help. But I can't get through the window. The ladder is too far from the wall. I could risk the jump, but if I miss, I will fall thirty feet into a burning dormer crumbling from the first floor.

I will fall to my death.

I think of my sick daughter at home. Of my wife. Of how badly I want to make it home tonight. To make things right.

So, I choose the safer route.

I take another step down, and a sudden shift in the wind momentarily clears the bottommost smoke inside the room. As I peer inside, my heart stops.

It's Smitty.

He's on the floor. His blueberries are open and they're staring right at me. The smoke rises a little higher, and I suddenly feel as though I'm in a dream.

The pick-end of my axe is lodged in his skull.

I slip on a rung and crack my chin against the ladder. Head spinning, I rush down the remaining twenty-five feet, jump down from the back of Engine No. 7, and allow my liquid courage to guide my sprinting feet across the asphalt, over the front lawn, and into the burning structure.

Even through my facemask, my eyes sting with ash. Tongues of white-hot flame lick their way up the walls, holding me hostage in a fiery hell. I try to scream Smitty's name, but my voice holds no tone against the raging inferno.

I have to find him.

I find the nearest stairwell and take the steps three at a time. Slabs of flaming roof crash down onto the floor, spitting embers into my face.

The place is coming down, and fast.

I have to find him.

I make my way to the third floor and leap over a burnt hole in the floor at the top of the stairs. I hold my breath and bolt down a scorched and blackened corridor. My legs feel like lead, my turnout gear heavier than I've ever known it to be. Exhaustion is settling in, and with it, tunnel vision clouds my senses. I am going to pass out.

I am going to die.

I have to find him.

Again, I yell his name into the flames. No response.

I swerve around a corner and narrowly avoid a flaming beam as it strikes the floor at my feet. I shield my face as a sheet of fire rises in front of me. Without thinking, I jump through the wall of flame, and there, at the end of the corridor, I see a doorway.

And in the doorway, I see his boots.

"Smitty!" I scream a third time. His boots remain motionless.

I sprint the length of the corridor and into the room with the fiery ceiling. His face is now partially melted. His skin is black with soot. The whites of his eyes swivel behind flickering lids, blueberries now a viscous foamy black. And there, protruding from the top of his skull and embedded into his brain, is my axe.

What have I done?

He wheezes as the life drains out of him. The flames rise higher around us, pressing in. But I feel nothing. I see nothing. All I can do is listen to the ragged wheezing of his lungs. Louder and louder they become, until the roar of the flames is but a whisper. My eardrums pound with the sound of his wheezing…

I fall to my knees, close my eyes, and beg the flames to take us both.

And then, I sink into blackness.

***

I awoke to the crackle, hiss, and heat of fire.

This fire, however, was quite tame. Not the living hell of my dream. It whipped, swirled, and popped on a stack of charred spruce and glowing embers, casting shadows inside an old, blackened hearth.

My gaze faded in and out, and I closed my eyes for just a few moments. When I opened them again, it was to find the fire almost entirely extinguished. It hadn't been moments, but hours. My arms were stuck to my sides, my cheek pressed against a cold, hard, wooden floor. I tried to flex my hands, yet all I accomplished was a weak curl of my fingers. For a moment, I was quite certain I was back at the apartment in Anchorage. That all of this had been a dream.

Ukippa. Horseshoe Hill. The Dilbrooks. Sophie.

And you.

But it couldn't be. Perhaps I was back at the Mansion. After all, Gloria had conveniently come to my aid on more than one occasion.

My foul-mouthed guardian angel.

No. The Mansion had reeked of cinnamon and cloves since the start of December. Gloria's infatuation with the Christmas season was almost toxic. I now smelled nothing but damp mildew and a foul odor reminiscent of spoiled meat.

I didn't know where I was, but at the same time, I knew *exactly* where I was.

I closed my eyes, willing myself to sink back into the dream I'd just relinquished. And though I'd tried for weeks to discover a way inside this place, now that I was here, I wished to be anywhere else in the entire world.

I was in the Shack. Trapped in a small basement, staring at a wall of stacked rock. This lower level was completely invisible from the outside, an underground hovel Moose most likely dug out himself. Aside from the gentle spit of the embers, there was nothing but silence. I slowly turned onto my back and took in my surroundings. Through the black of the den, I saw three more walls of stone. Above me was a ceiling of wooden slats, no doubt the floorboards of the Shack's main room above.

I'm not sure how I ended up in the house of the devil, but as I dozed in the darkness listening for him, I heard nothing and no one. I was weak, yes, but I needed to get out. I slowed my breathing until I hardly breathed at all. I rolled back over onto my side, pressed my hand into the floor, and pushed with all I had until I finally sat up.

And then, the hair on the back of my neck pricked up. My skin began to crawl. My muscles froze. I saw nothing, I heard nothing, but I knew.

He was in the room with me.

Tucked away in some shadowy corner.

Blood surged in my ears. My pupils dilated through the darkness, searching for him, searching for his hulking shadow, searching for a way out.

And there it was. Wooden steps leading up to a darkened doorway.

"You won't make it," croaked a deep, serrated voice from among the shadows.

"Please," I whispered. "I have a daughter."

There was silence. A seething, saturated silence that lasted decades. I wondered if I had actually heard anything at all, or if my fear had gotten the better of me, and all I heard was the fire's final embers snuffing out.

And then, he emerged from the darkness.

He stepped into the soft glow of the cinders, a monster made entirely of hair, shadows, and burning yellow eyes.

Just like the wolf.

"Quite the father," he said.

"What do you want?" I groaned.

"I've seen you watching me. Watching my house."

He bared large, brown and yellow teeth, and again, I thought of the wolf. It was a demon's grin, a sadistic smile that spoke only of the horrors I was about to endure.

"Please – "

"I've been watching you too."

"I won't – "

"Lucky I've been watching," he said. "Otherwise, you'd be blue and bloated on the bottom by now."

The lake.

I thought of my final moments in that glacial hell. I recalled the soft thuds and knocks that had echoed from above. I remembered Smitty's face grinning at me through the ice. But then, it hadn't been

257

Smitty at all.

It was Moose.

"Let me guess," he grunted. "She told you I was Satan."

I didn't say a word. I was too busy devising a desperate escape up the stairs.

And then, I smelled something. Something familiar. A rich, fishy musk. When I glanced to my right, I saw it, long and gray and ovular upon a bed of tarnished oak.

The clay *qulliq* sat front and center on the mantle, its thin sheet of flame dancing in miniature against the woodfire popping in the hearth below.

"Well?"

"'A devil,'" I corrected him. "That's what she said."

He tossed his head back and released what I assumed to be a chuckle, though it sounded more like shale crunching underfoot.

"The other guy said the same thing."

"The other guy?"

"Last guy that lived in the Cabin."

"Adam Kelsey," I said. My eyes darted from the *qulliq* to the ragged giant blocking the stairs, and then to the small shaft of light from above.

"That's the one," he said. "The snoopy shit-stain I killed."

There it was. Straight from the devil's mouth.

So, it's true.

"That's right, isn't it?" he asked.

It was an odd question, but I didn't have time to think about it. I needed to find a way past him.

He took one monstrous step toward me.

I grabbed the clay *qulliq* from the mantle and swung it with everything I had. An inch from making contact with his scarred face, his hand closed over my wrist and stopped my arm in midair.

"That's what she told you, isn't it?" he snarled, flecks of spittle splashing against my face. "She told you I killed him, didn't she?" With unimaginable strength, he twisted my wrist backward and sent my knees to the floor. Pain exploded up my split kneecap, and it was all I could do to keep from passing out.

"Yes," I finally conceded, dropping the *qulliq* to the floor with a clatter.

"'Course she did."

Without another word, he released my wrist. He turned his back on me, placed a hand against the wall, and grunted. And then, he took a seat on the large, creaky armchair beside the fire.

My path up the stairs was clear.

I bolted to the bottommost step, half-expecting the monster of a man to grab me from behind. But when I glanced over my shoulder, there he was, still seated in his chair.

He was *letting* me leave. But why?

The woodfire cast shadows upon his gnarled features, and when I looked at him, the shadows were no longer fearsome.

They were pitiful.

"You didn't do it," I said. "You didn't kill him."

"No, I didn't," he said. "Why would I?"

For many weeks now, I'd wondered the exact same thing. And for all my theories based around what I'd learned from Gloria Dilbrook,

Nicholas Holloway

from Denali Shaw, and from the photographs taken by Evie Brooks, I had only come up with one answer:

Adam Kelsey discovered the truth about what happened all those years ago at the Mainstay oil field, discovered the truth about a woman that had never been found. He confronted her killer, and then went missing.

"Prudence Gamble," I said.

I took my foot off the bottom step and turned to face Moose. Looked him square in the face. I wanted answers. He sat in silence for a moment, and I felt the air shift as he set his eyes upon me, his shadowy guise growing fearsome once again.

"The hell do you know about Prudence Gamble?" he asked.

"Only what I learned from Denali Shaw."

"Denali Shaw," he mused. "You've been doing your homework, haven't you? Just as snoopy as that Kelsey prick, you are. And what did the old Hermit of Mount Poe have to say about me, huh? That I killed Pru? That I smashed her head against her own desk and then disposed of her body?"

"Something like that."

"Big, scary fuck like me. Makes sense, doesn't it?" he grunted. "Denali Shaw is delusional. I loved Pru."

"But you couldn't have her, could you? Not with Don Dilbrook around."

Moose stood up and towered over me. I was treading dangerous water.

Stop talking, you stupid shit. Think of your daughter.

"You were jealous."

260

"I won't deny it," he growled and took a step closer, bear fists clenched. "But not enough to kill her."

"Don killed her, didn't he?" I finally said.

Moose stopped mid-stride, as though I had doused him in the same icy water he'd pulled me from.

"Don Dilbrook killed Prudence Gamble," I stated.

"And what makes you say that?"

"He got her pregnant. He told her to get rid of it, but she had Eldon anyway. And a guy like Don doesn't stand for that."

"That's your theory, is it?"

"It makes the most sense."

"Does it?"

"What do you mean?"

"Don Dilbrook has children all over Alaska," Moose said. "Kids Gloria doesn't even know about. One more would have meant nothing to him."

"Unless Pru started making demands."

Moose watched me for a moment. Then, he grinned, as though he knew something I didn't. As though he could see a tripwire I couldn't, a tripwire I straddled blindly. He nodded once, willing me to keep riding my own train of thought.

And then, a light switched on.

"Or maybe Pru went straight to Gloria," I whispered, more to myself than to Moose. "She told Gloria about Eldon behind Don's back. Gloria confronted Don about the baby, he got pissed, and *then* he killed Pru."

"Want to know what I think?" Moose grunted.

I certainly did.

"I think you need to pull off the rose-colored Gloria glasses," he said. "She calls me a devil, but have you ever considered maybe she's the hellhound?"

I thought about it for a moment, and then I understood.

"You think Gloria killed Prudence Gamble."

"I do."

"So then – "

"—the old groundskeeper might have uncovered the truth. And for some reason, he went and threw her son over a cliff. And then – "

I couldn't believe it, but it made more sense than any of my previous theories.

"Gloria murdered Adam Kelsey."

22

UNWELCOME GUESTS

"She had your mutt, y'know," Moose murmured, shoveling the ash out of the hearth and into a bin.

"Who?"

"The dead girl," he said. "Saw her out on the lake with a black dog, figured it must've been hers. You should'a said something."

"I thought maybe you had gotten hold of him," I confessed, red around the ears.

"And skinned him alive, eh? Scary ol' Moose," he grunted with a chuckle.

"He was with Evie the whole time?"

"At least until she ended up in that hut. Your pup must've been left to his own devices and found his own way out of the shanty."

I recalled the night I watched Evie Brooks' shadow stretch across the surface of Lake Adamant, a slender and haunting silhouette bathed in the orange light flooding from the shanty's open door.

And all this time, Harvey had been just on the other side.

I thought of that night often. How long after did Evie have her skull caved in?

"A couple nights after we moved in, Harvey heard something in the woods and ran off after it," I said. "It was Evie, snapping photographs. I found the pictures in her darkroom."

"Watching you, like you watched me."

"But why keep Harvey? She knew he was mine. She knew where I lived. Where I ate. Where my kid slept."

"Maybe she wanted a reason to talk to you."

"Then why not just knock on my door and return my lost dog? I'd have let her talk my ear off."

"Maybe she wanted you away from the hill," he said. "Away from Gloria."

My head was beginning to ache. My busted kneecap throbbed. I was ready to hike back to the Mansion, slurp down a bowl of caribou stew, and dive into the bed I'd been sleeping in for days (Sophie's old bed, actually, though Gloria made sure I knew it was off-limits until Christmas was over).

"What do you think of Evie Brooks?" I asked.

"What about her?" Moose said, stacking a fresh pile of logs.

"Do you think Gloria – "

"I'm not sure," he said. "Evie had a photograph of Kelsey pushing the Dilbrook boy over the cliff?"

"Right."

"Well," he said. "If Evie had the only proof Kelsey killed her son, what reason would Gloria have for killing her? You'd think she'd want to keep her around."

"Great minds think alike," I sighed. "Which is why I think Kelsey might still be alive."

Moose lit the fire and sank into his worn, leather chair. I let my hand descend to the floor, where my fingers stroked a small head of soft, black fur. I glanced down and Harvey stared back up at me, honey-brown eyes glowing like amber in the firelight.

"You're a good boy, Harv," I reminded him.

"Damn good boy," Moose agreed. "When you and that wolf fell through, he just kept sniffin' along the ice, followin' you the whole way. That's how I knew where to kick through."

"Not many folks in Ukippa would have stopped to help me. A lot of them seem to think – "

"— that you killed Evie Brooks," he said with a roll of his yellow eyes. "One of their own goes missing, and the first person they point fingers at is the outsider."

"Small towns," I mused.

He *hmph*ed, leaned over, and shot a snot rocket into the kindling.

"Why do you stay?" I asked.

"Eh?"

"Why stay here? What's in it for you? You don't like the Dilbrooks, and they call you a murderer. So, why stay on this hill?"

Moose stood up, walked across the small basement, and peered out the only window, three quarters of which was hidden under a layer of permafrost.

"I was born here," Moose said, his breath fogging the glass. "My dad worked for old Joe Dilbrook – Don's father – in Allakaket, where the Dilbrooks found their fortune. 'Bout a month before I was born,

265

the rig my dad worked on caught fire. Blew sky high. They only ever found his boots and a bit of his right shoulder. After the funeral, Margaret Dilbrook insisted my mother stay at Horseshoe Hill until she got back on her feet.

"I was born in the Mansion. In the library. Mom barely made it – I 'bout killed her on the way out. She got sick from the infection, and it wasn't too long after that, she went to sleep one night and didn't wake up the next mornin'.

"Don was a spoiled little shit from the get-go, so Margaret decided her son needed a friend. It wasn't the warmth in old Maggie's heart that kept me around. I was more of a convenient plaything for Don. Still, they gave me a place to sleep and put food in my belly, and Don and I eventually became inseparable. When I was 'bout eleven, Joe Dilbrook noticed how big I'd grown and decided it was time for me to earn my keep at the Mansion. They had a few maids, a groundskeeper, and a couple cooks who lived in servants' quarters on the west side of the hill. And that's right where they sent me."

"The west side," I interrupted. "You mean – "

"This Shack used to be one of six. The others are all gone now," he said, glancing around at the old, shambled walls. "They sent me over here, and this is where I stayed until Joe Dilbrook kicked the bucket and Don inherited it all."

"And then he hired you."

"And then he hired me," he answered.

"You mentioned you and Don were inseparable."

"Close as brothers, at one point. And that came with the fistfights," Moose promptly pointed out.

"Gloria said you were the first groundskeeper at the Mansion. The first one to live in the Cabin."

"They built the Cabin just before everything happened," he said. "No one else lived there before that. It always seemed strange, spending all that money on a Cabin they didn't even use."

"What happened?" I asked.

But I had a feeling I knew.

He was silent for a moment, then walked over to the hearth and used the steel toe of his boot to stoke the logs.

"Prudence Gamble happened," he said and confirmed my suspicion. "Drove a permanent wedge between us. He used her for all the things Gloria wouldn't give him. I didn't like it, and I made sure he knew it."

"And then Prudence was murdered."

"Disappeared. But yeah, she was murdered," he said. "At first, most people at the company thought Don killed her. He swore to me he was innocent. Said he couldn't lose the oil field. There were too many people relying on him. Said he didn't know who did it. He asked me to take the focus off of him, that if I did, he would have his best lawyers get me out of anything that came my way. So, I accepted. Problem was, I couldn't go back to Mainstay. 'Bad for business,' Don said. 'Bad press.' So, he quietly hired me on at the Mansion instead, and that's where I stayed for twenty-six years. Watched his kids grow up. Watched his wife grow cold. And as the years went on, I watched Don grow paranoid."

"Paranoid?"

"He kicked people out. Threatened them. Pointed a gun in a few of their faces. So, I asked him again..."

"You asked if he killed Pru."

"It started out a normal enough conversation," he grumbled. "Talked about replacing the Cabin's back deck and building a new one from scratch. And then, I just flat out asked him.

"Donny always wore a smile when I was around. Early on, I think he genuinely enjoyed my presence. Enjoyed the fact that, in his mother's eyes, I was less of a person than he was. Enjoyed having me around because, well, I'd always been agreeable and did what his parents told me to. And then after Joe died, after Don inherited the wells, I started doing everything *he* told me to do."

"But you stuck your hand in the fire."

"And he burned me the best way he knew how. That day, Don smiled like usual, but he also threatened to dredge the case back to the surface. To sway the public's view with evidence he said he had stashed away. He wouldn't tell me about the evidence, only that it linked me with Prudence Gamble on the night she disappeared. He told me to leave the hill, that if I ever tried to come back, he would kill me himself. I became an unwelcome guest in the only place I'd ever called home."

"But you didn't listen to him."

"I stuck around to keep an eye on him. We were both born on this hill. We grew up here together. And as fucked in the head as he was, I felt responsible for him. He gave me a job and a place to stay for so many years."

And then, something occurred to me.

"Adam Kelsey figured it out, didn't he?" I asked.

"He started coming around. Leaving shit on my doorstep like he was fuckin' Santa Claus. I finally got so sick and tired of sacks and sacks of potatoes that one night, I came outside, aimed my crossbow, and shot an arrow – *fhizz!* – right past his left ear."

Moose slapped his sap-stained jeans and hooted.

"But he didn't run. He just stood there with a stupid grin on his face. But the way he just stared. The way he grinned. It was strange. So, I stared back. And the more I stared, the more familiar he seemed. Almost like I'd seen him before. Almost like I knew him."

"What did you talk about?"

"About Pru, about Don's mental state, about if I knew how to get into the Mansion at night. He wanted something. Wanted to prove Don was the one who killed Pru. Wanted to threaten Don with what he knew."

"What was in it for him?"

"Blackmail, most likely. He got really close with Don's daughter, and even closer to the son. Probably tried turning them against their dad. And then, the son wound up at the bottom of a cliff, Kelsey disappeared, and the next time I saw Don, he was locked up in his room like a rotting vegetable."

"That's when the cancer came?" I asked.

And then, Moose started to laugh. Louder and louder he boomed, until Harvey awoke from his snooze and looked up at me, just as confused as I was.

"It wasn't the cancer," Moose said.

"What?"

"You want to know what really happened to Don Dilbrook? Take a look at his head."

***

I needed sleep. But more than that, I needed to get back to you, Ellie.

Moose helped me limp to the tree line that swung around back to the Mansion. I thanked him again not only for saving me from a watery grave, but also for looking out for Harvey, and together, Harvey and I began to push through the snow.

My knee objected to the hike and pulsed in protest. I found the top of a small outlook where the trees thinned out. There, on the other side of the hill, stood the Mansion, a black and toothy monolith set against the dark winter sky. Smoke billowed from the various chimneys. The grand oak front door stood wide open. Five figures stood on the snowy, sweeping front lawn. Parked in the circular stone driveway was Detective Weekes' shiny black SUV, and beside it –

I couldn't believe it. First Harvey, and now Betty. It was shaping up to be one hell of a day.

Betty stuck out like a sore thumb, neon orange against the pearly white snow. But something wasn't right. Betty's tires sat strapped to the flatbed of a large tow truck. The chipped decal on the passenger side door read:

S TKA SL M'S AUTO & TOW

I kept close to the tree line and followed the branches until I was able to make out the shadowy faces on the front lawn.

There was Gloria, arms waving in the air as she appeared to be arguing with Detective Weekes. Nukilik stood beside and just behind Weekes, the loyal dog. Walking up behind Gloria in her famous olive pea coat was Sophie. Tom Clark leaned casually against the garden wall, being very Tom, simply watching the argument unfold.

I couldn't hear what they were shouting, but I had a good idea of why Weekes and Nukilik had come. The entire town thought me a murderer. Weekes was certain of it. Nukilik wanted revenge for his slain deputy.

And I was nowhere to be found.

I was willing to bet my life savings (which wasn't much) to guess they'd found evidence inside the old orange Bronco. Evidence linking me to the crime. Evidence planted by the same person who stole Betty in the first place. The person who murdered Evie Brooks.

I hid in the trees and walked steadily closer until finally, I heard voices on the wind.

" – you deaf? He isn't even here!" Gloria yelled.

"We'll wait inside," Weekes replied calmly.

"Not without a warrant," said Sophie.

"Then we'll wait *outside*."

I heard Tom laugh.

"Stay out here and freeze, then," he said. "We'll call the chopper back and tell them we've got two popsicles in need of a morgue."

So, Sophie and Tom must have waited for me at the airport in Allakaket. But in the end, when I never showed up, Tom Clark must have done what Tom Clark always does. He called in a favor and flew Sophie into Ukippa on his own dime.

"He's been missing for three days," Sophie said. "If we find him, we will let you know."

"Like hell you will," Nukilik spat. I heard the cock of a pistol, and someone screamed.

"Put the gun down," Weekes barked. "Put it *down*, Nukilik."

There was a long, drawn out silence. I waited for the shot, waited for the screams, waited for the fight. Then, I heard metal swathe against leather as Nukilik angrily re-holstered his gun.

"I will find him," Nukilik snarled. "Count on it."

"Bravo, Detective Weekes," said Tom. "Do you let all your subordinates threaten witnesses like that?"

"Shut up, Tom," Sophie said quietly. "It's like I said, Detective. If we see him, we will let you know."

"You know I'm coming back with that warrant," Weekes stated with certainty.

"We'll see you then."

There was a grunt of disapproval before two pairs of boots crunched across the snow. The SUV's doors opened and shut, the engine turned over, and that was the end of the conversation. As I peeked around the spruce I hid behind, I watched Weekes and Nukilik drive away down the hill, the tow truck (with Betty strapped to it) following behind. Both vehicles disappeared down the switchback, and I was left to watch Gloria stomp past Tom and into the Mansion. Tom shrugged at Sophie, flicked aside a smoldering cigarette, and followed suit.

Sophie stayed behind, however, standing alone on the front lawn for a minute or more. I watched her sigh, her warm breath billowing in thick, ambient clouds. She turned and walked up the steps and onto the front porch, opened her arms, and out of the shadows came a sixth figure. Sophie wrapped her arms around the slender shadow, gave it a hug, and opened the front door.

And when the light flooded out to illuminate the shadowy figure, my heart stopped. My throat closed up. My ears rang. I fell to my knees, not caring about the pain shooting through my kneecap.

I couldn't believe my eyes.

It was your mother, Ellie. It was Vanessa.

Sophie ushered her inside, closed the door, and then traipsed back down the steps. She veered around the Mansion's east turret and walked to the tree line.

I watched as Sophie turned to face my direction. She knew I was there.

Looked right at me.

And then, she waited.

***

Harvey dozed at my heels, curled into a ball and tucked into the mossy roots of an overgrown poplar. Sophie and I sat on the ground with our backs against the stone monolith formerly known as Sam Dilbrook. Her eyes were fixed on the dark valley below, watching the nodding heads of the pumpjacks.

Up and down, and around we go. Grazing eternally on the blood of the earth.

"Please don't think I'm blowing you off," she said.

"Just think about it," I said. "Consider everything I've told you."

"I am. Really, I am. And Prudence Gamble, sure, that one might warrant a closer look," Sophie said with a prosecutor's indifference, as though we were discussing some convicted killer instead of her own mother. "But Evie Brooks?" she asked. "What about the photograph? Why would my mother resort to murdering Evie and setting her on fire for a photograph Evie would have happily handed over?"

"What do you mean?"

"When Evie lived here, she and my mother were closer than I have ever been with Gloria Dilbrook. Evie revered my mother, thought she was a saint for bringing up Sam as well as she did, given the circumstances. It's true that Evie and Adam Kelsey slept together when they both worked here, but if she witnessed Adam push my brother over that cliff, she wouldn't have given him any sort of head start. She would have run straight to my mother."

"But she didn't," I said. "That photograph was hidden away in Evie's house for three years, right? Why did she keep it?"

"I don't know, Laz."

"Eldon had the photograph when I caught him sneaking around Evie's. I think he took it from her house. Maybe he found the photo and wanted to hide it from Gloria, for whatever reason. And that's when I showed up."

"You think Eldon is capable of all that?" she asked.

"I think you underestimate him. All of you do."

And then, Sophie sighed. She stood up, rested her hand against the ghostly bark of a shimmering white aspen, and scuffed one of her shoes against the frosted grass around Sam's grave.

"He isn't dead, Laz," she finally whispered. She stood up and looked out at the vast expanse of woods stretching down the backside of Horseshoe Hill. "Adam Kelsey is alive."

"How do you know?"

She took a deep breath, held it in, and slowly let it roil like a cloud into the wind.

"How do you think I found you?" she said.

I did a double take, uncertain of what Sophie had said. But the longer I held her gaze, the more evident it became.

"You specifically wanted *me* for this job," I said, suddenly feeling very vulnerable. "You tracked me down."

"Yes."

"And – and Tom?"

"An amazing colleague. An incredible lawyer," she said with a shrug. "But too wild for my taste. We've recently reached an understanding. He will always be a great friend of mine. But he is your best friend, and he was the quickest way to make contact with you – "

"How the hell does Adam Kelsey even know who I am? Does Tom know him? I've never – "

For the first time ever, Sophie put her hands on me. But not like I'd longed for. She pressed her hands to my chest, and while it may have felt sensual for just a moment, she pressed more firmly and hardened her gaze. At that moment, she had never looked more beautiful.

"Please just trust me," she said.

And that was it. She turned on her heel and began walking back up the trail.

I'm not sure what made me do it, but I reached out and caught

Sophie's arm, spun her around, and crushed my lips against hers. The world stopped, a sudden pause in time that some people talk about and many people never experience. I deepened the kiss, pushed my fingers through her lush, chestnut hair, not knowing if this would be my only chance to express…

But wait.

She broke the kiss, lowered her face away from mine, then slowly pushed against my chest. I took two steps back, and she looked up at me.

"We can't," she said.

Vanessa was there at the Mansion, three hundred yards away, most likely warming herself by the magnificent black marble hearth in the Mansion's grand foyer. I wondered if that was the reason for Sophie's hesitation.

"Sophie – "

"Please don't think I'm blowing you off."

And with that, she turned back to the trail, took a few steps, and stopped. When I looked up, it was to find Gloria Dilbrook breaking through the trees.

"Sorry to interrupt," she said, her eyes shifting from me to Sophie and back again. "Your wife is asking for you."

***

The Mansion was eerily quiet. The towering stone archways and broad-shouldered oak staircase stood stark and frigid. A massive and ancient grandfather clock ticked as we crossed the foyer.

I was keen to find Tom Clark. To tell him everything. Beg him to help me, as he'd always done. But instead, Gloria led me down the dark, east corridor until we stood outside the double doors that led into the library.

"Gloria – "

"Later," she said, not meeting my eye. She turned on her heel, stalked away down the corridor, and disappeared into the shadows. I watched her go, and while most of me believed what Sophie said, that Adam Kelsey was indeed alive, that Gloria Dilbrook hadn't killed anyone (except maybe Prudence Gamble), I still had questions.

I took a deep breath, gripped the doorknob, half-considered leaving Vanessa in cold silence like she had done to me so many months earlier, then sighed and opened the double doors. My footsteps echoed like usual, from the old floorboards to the buttressed ceiling forty feet above my head. I noticed a soft snow falling outside the massive stained-glass windows, then allowed my eyes to sweep to the only occupied space in the enormity of the library.

Her lovely backside rested against the edge of Don Dilbrook's vast marble desk, her eyes fixed on the leather-bound copy of *The Girl in the Snow*. I released a fake cough to make myself known, and when she looked up at me, all I could do was stare.

None of this felt real.

My eyes and my brain became separate from my skull. I was completely aware of my surroundings, standing tall among thousands of books that cocooned me in a protective wall of leather bindings and old histories. But at the same time, I floated within a black vacuum, in danger and exposed, and there was nothing but me, Vanessa, and the viscous contempt that bubbled like tar between us.

"Who was she, Laz?" Vanessa whispered.

"Who was who?"

"Who was she to you?"

"Who was *who* to me?" I repeated.

"Why did you do it?" she yelled. "Why did you kill her?"

And then, I understood. The earlier incident with Weekes and Nukilik had evidently convinced Vanessa that I was indeed capable (and guilty) of murder.

"What are you doing here?" I asked, and though I spoke just above a whisper, my voice carried across the library, and it was firm.

"What the fuck are *you* doing here?" she hissed.

I took a few steps closer. She straightened up, her eyes darting back to *The Girl in the Snow*. But it wasn't the book she was interested in – her nervous stare was fixed on the diamond-shaped paperweight sitting atop its leathery face.

"I didn't kill her," I said, rubbing my eyes.

She didn't answer, just kept staring at that sharp, onyx paperweight.

"Whatever you heard, whatever you've been told, it's wrong, Ness. I didn't kill that woman. I didn't even know her."

Your mother locked her eyes with mine, and I suddenly felt very confused. I'd spent the last six years of my life admiring those sparkling chocolate jewels set within her face. Craving her. Wanting her. Lusting after her. Loving her with all I had. But now, they resembled the black and hardened shells of beetles.

Now, there was nothing.

Well, not *nothing*. A mutual indifference, maybe. In her eyes, I was nothing but the mistake she'd made far too many times. In mine, she was no longer even the mother of my child.

"I want Ellie," she said.

"You can't have her," I replied.

"I'm not leaving without her."

"You abandoned her, Ness. Do you realize that? You had her. You decided you didn't want her. You left her at the apartment. And then, you vanished. She's not yours anymore. You're not leaving with Ellie, and you're no longer welcome here."

Convinced that our conversation was pointless and content that it was over, I turned my back on her and walked back toward the library doors.

"I will tell them," she said. "I'll tell that woman. That detective."

I stopped with my hand on the doorknob, then turned and faced her.

"Tell her what?"

"About Anchorage. About Smitty."

Again, I was confused. Moreover, my psyche was confused. Here was a woman who had rocked me to sleep every single night after the Turnagain fire. Stroked my head while I sobbed. Kissed away my tears. Vowed to do whatever she could to help get my career (and my life) back on track. Pay the bills and the rent, if she had to. She promised to always stand beside me.

But promises never stuck.

"Don't you dare bring Smitty into this," I yelled. "He has nothing to do with it."

"I'll do what I have to, Laz. Ellie is mine."

And before I had time to realize what my feet were doing, I

walked toward her. I must have looked menacing… the look on her face was one I'd never seen before, one of sheer terror. She grabbed the onyx paperweight and raised it above her head.

"Stay the fuck away from me," she seethed. "You waste of fucking life."

I stopped and held up my hands.

"Ness – "

"I'm taking her home."

And with that, Vanessa stood up, keeping her eyes locked on mine and giving me a wide berth as she made her way to the door. She dropped the paperweight on the floor with a loud *thunk*, then stormed out of the library. But as she left, my eyes were drawn to the odd little object.

I heard Detective Weekes in my skull…

A really interesting wound, actually. Wide, shallow, and sharp. Something pointy punctured her brain, but it left a large, concave impression.

And then, I heard Moose…

You want to know what really happened to Don Dilbrook? Take a look at his head.

And as I stared at it just sitting there, sharp and black with those milky white striations, I knew I had stumbled upon the missing link in all of this.

***

I didn't have much time.

My encounter with your mother ended ten minutes prior, and I

280

knew that soon, someone would come looking for me in the library. And when they didn't find me there, all would fan out and search the Mansion high and low, and my mission would be for naught. So, when I made it to the third-floor landing, I tugged off my boots and tucked the paperweight into one of them, holding them at my side as I quietly padded my socks across the old wooden floor. I turned a corner and stared down a darkened hallway that ended with an arched, viridian door.

I stepped quietly down the hallway, taking a moment to admire my handiwork in the form of vibrant white baseboards.

Hard to believe that was nearly two months ago.

When I reached the door, I pressed my ear against the chipped and peeling wood. Behind it, I heard nothing but the steady *beep-beep* of a heart monitor and the occasional, telltale hiss of an oxygen tank. Deciding I needed to learn the truth, I grasped the doorknob, expecting to find it locked, but 'lo and behold, it turned and the door opened.

It was only my second time inside Don Dilbrook's bedroom, and my first time completely alone with the old oil tycoon. The room was vast and deep, more a chamber than a bedroom, with a sweeping, vaulted ceiling that rose almost as high as that of the library two floors beneath my feet. But for its enormity, the room lacked furniture, save for a magnificent black oak four-poster bed with its stark gray curtains drawn. The room was empty, cold, a wide expanse of space that echoed with the thin, rattling breath of its tenant.

I closed the door behind me, approached the colossal four-poster, and ripped back the curtain.

Don Dilbrook gazed up at the ceiling with mismatched, unfocused eyes. The right side of his face hung lower than the left, saliva dripping down his jowl. A feeding tube was lodged down his throat, a clear respirator fixed over his nose and mouth. It fogged with each of Don's rattling breaths and was followed by a hiss from the large oxygen tank standing beside the bed.

The old man needed a shave, but not much else. His face was full, his stomach rising into a large mound beneath the bedsheets. Even with his feeding tube, I'd expected him to be gaunt, hollow, transparent. Sucked dry of the life that cancer steals from many of those afflicted. I knew all too well what a cancer patient looked like. Had seen and met hundreds during the year and a half you fought for your life.

It was as Moose said – Don Dilbrook was no terminal cancer patient. At least, as far as his appearance was concerned. I examined his face. At his dazed, unfocused expression. The way his right cheek sagged.

A stroke, perhaps?

Most strokes affected the left side, though, not the right. And why would Gloria lie about a stroke?

No. That couldn't be it.

You want to know what really happened to Don Dilbrook? Take a look at his head.

The old man was definitely awake, but I had severe doubts that he was particularly aware. So, I began to examine his head more closely. And the more I looked at his sloping jaw, his gray eyes, the hardened shape of his face, the more I started to feel that uncomfortable familiarity. Like I'd seen him somewhere before.

I'm being paranoid, I thought. I'd seen pictures of Sam Dilbrook, after all, and Sam looked very much like his father.

I carefully and slowly tilted him onto one shoulder, hearing soft grunts escape his tube-plugged throat. And just as I was about to lie him back down, I noticed that his feathery white hair sunk inward at the base of his skull. I ran my fingertips slow and soft along the dip and found that his skull sank even deeper underneath his hair.

I yanked my hand away.

Reaching into my boot, I pulled out the onyx paperweight. I gripped my fingers around the flattened crown, then carefully fitted the sharp pavilion of its diamond shape into the dip in his skull.

A perfect fit.

While Don's injury hadn't killed him, it had affected his brain enough to render him almost fully vegetative. And I was willing to bet my entire existence that when it came to Evie Brooks' skull, Gloria's aim had been perfected.

"Tthh…"

The sudden noise made me jump.

"Ttthhh…" It was a little louder this time, and it was coming from Don. As I turned him over onto his back, his left eye remained foggy and drifting across the ceiling. His right eye, however, shifted and stared at me.

"Ttthhhaaa…"

"Shh. Be quiet – " I whispered, looking over my shoulder at the deep green door. I heard the unmistakable thump of boots on the third-floor landing beyond, knowing that if I stuck around much longer, Gloria would find me with her husband, the onyx paperweight, and the truth.

"Ttthhhaaa…" he gurgled, and as I looked back down at him, he clamped his lips around the clear feeding tube, and made a new noise. "…mmm."

"Mr. Dilbrook, what are you – "

"Ttthhhaaammm."

And just like that, the combination of the old man's seemingly random noises suddenly formed a word.

No, a name.

Sam.

***

That evening, we sat in the dining hall for Christmas Eve dinner. More than that, we sat in complete silence.

Vanessa ate nothing, just pushed her food around and watched me with glassy, hardened eyes. She rubbed her nose once, and I had the vague suspicion that she had snorted a line before the appetizer, much like she used to. Sophie and Tom Clark sipped quietly on their soup, exchanging small, uncomfortable glances. Gloria watched the enormous circular clock above the fireplace, and when I met her gaze, she quickly looked away.

She knew I knew.

The only ones who seemed to enjoy themselves were you, Eldon, and Harvey. As we finished up the main course, I watched Eldon sneak scraps of moose liver under the table, and heard the distant clinking of Harvey's dog tags as he gobbled them up. You clapped and giggled and, impressionable as you are, picked up a crust of bread and dropped it on the floor for Harvey's enjoyment. You and Eldon shared a laugh, and suddenly, it brought a smile out of everyone.

Everyone except your mother.

"Everything is going to be all right," Tom told me after dessert, alone beside the roaring hearth. "It will."

"Why did you bring her here?" I asked, but before Tom could answer, Vanessa interrupted us and demanded that Ellie sleep in the Mansion with her.

"Absolutely not."

We all turned and found that it was Gloria who had spoken up.

"Ellie is not a toy and will not be passed around as such," she said. "She will sleep in the Cabin with her father, as she has been for the last two months. Comfortably, I might add. Vanessa, you will sleep here and, if the fates align, you will be gone by morning."

"Excuse me?" Vanessa replied.

"You're not welcome here," Gloria stated firmly. "Any mother who abandons her child is not welcome in my home. Sleep well tonight, and tomorrow, I will make arrangements for a helicopter."

And that was that.

***

Though we had slept in the Mansion for the past couple weeks, I felt comfortable enough in the Cabin to spend a single night, at least until your mother was back in the air on her way to Fairbanks or Anchorage or even Mars, for all I cared. She no longer possessed any hold over my emotional well-being. I was a good man, I knew, and a good father. I loved you (and still do) more than anything on this earth, and I would have done (and still would do) anything to ensure you live a happy and healthy life, even if it meant keeping your mother at arm's length.

It's corny, I know, but I felt empowered in a way I never had before.

We sat together by the fireplace while Harvey dozed by the back door. My eyes alight with newfound hope, I watched you excitedly rip open an early Christmas present, a stuffed husky with shaggy white fur and blue button eyes I'd found in Sophie's old bedroom. When all this was over, when we escaped Ukippa, Detective Weekes, and the ridiculous suspicion that I had murdered anyone, I was going to take you to the Iditarod Museum, like I promised a lifetime ago.

At a quarter to midnight, I carried you up to your room, gently placed your sleeping body into the crib, changed out your oxygen tank, and kissed you goodnight. I slipped into my bedroom, changed into my pajamas, and decided to indulge in a nightcap. I walked downstairs, into the kitchen, and reached for the Malamute bottle on top of the fridge.

Suddenly, Harvey started to bark. I turned to the back door, and I froze.

A tall, dark shadow stood upon the back deck.

He wore all black, the hood of his jacket pulled over his head to conceal his face. With nothing between us but the sliding door's thin sheet of glass, we stared at one another. I instantly knew who it was. Had waited for this moment. This time, the figure stalking me was no ghost.

It was Adam Kelsey.

I heard a small shift in the darkness behind me, and as I turned, something hard slammed against my temple. White light exploded behind my eyelids. The world gave out beneath me.

I was long gone before I even hit the floor.

23

THE MISSING

awoke on the kitchen floor to a large, wet something slopping across my forehead.

One or two strokes would have sufficed to wake me, but as I lie there with an aching skull, a big slippery tongue continued to lap against my face and neck. I opened my eyes to find Harvey's upside-down face, his honey-brown hues staring curiously down at me, big floppy ears hanging over my chin.

And then, he resumed our morning smooch session.

"Off, Harv," I grumbled. I gently rolled onto my side, pressed the heel of my palm against the side of my head, and a sharp burst of pain erupted across an egg-sized knot in my scalp.

For a moment, I couldn't recall why I had fallen asleep on the kitchen floor. The world spun beneath me as I struggled to recall just how much whiskey I'd drunk. I remembered walking downstairs, remembered the cold kitchen tile on the balls and heels of my feet, remembered reaching up to grab the whiskey atop the fridge.

Remembered Harvey barking, and –

I swung my face around to peer out the sliding glass door. The back deck was covered in fresh white powder, but it was entirely vacant.

Adam Kelsey was gone.

My mind desperately wanted to convince itself that it had all been a hallucination. After all, I had been seeing ghosts (or what I assumed were ghosts) for months. It had been a trick of the darkness. Everything was all right, I tried to tell myself.

But everything wasn't all right.

I recalled the sound of footsteps behind me. The sudden burst of painful white light. Someone snuck into the Cabin. Someone knocked me out. Dizzy as I was, I jumped to my feet, steadied myself against the concrete countertop, and stumbled to the stairs.

"Ellie!" I yelled.

My legs fought me the whole way up, and when I reached your door, I twisted the handle and collapsed into your bedroom. I crawled to the edge of the crib, head spinning, guts threatening to expel last night's moose liver, then pulled myself up and peered through the railing.

The crib was empty.

In my ear, I heard Smitty's raspy voice whisper a single name –

Vanessa.

Anger, panic, fear, and hatred saturated my being and consumed my core. Adrenaline flooded my system, dulling the pain in my skull and in my knee, slowing the spinning world back into its fixed equilibrium. I checked the upstairs bedrooms and closets, found nothing, and then limped down the stairs. I swept the entire bottom floor, the dining room, the office, the kitchen, and threw open the sliding glass door.

On the back deck, under a fresh layer of powder, I saw the grooves of large boot prints etched in the snow. They led down the steps and into the woods.

Not a hallucination, after all.

I pulled on my Wolverines, bolted down the steps, and hobbled off into the dark woods. I followed the boot prints deeper into the trees, the snow growing shallow under the dense canopy of black spruce. Branches scratched at my cheeks, brush and brambles clawed at my legs, ripping my long johns. In my haste, I'd forgotten to put on proper clothing, the intense cold already making my skin sting and my bones rattle, but I didn't care.

"Ellie!" I yelled, my voice carrying through the trees.

I came to the clearing where the trail broke into a fork, and it was here that I noticed two more sets of boot prints join Kelsey's. One set, I assumed, belonged to Vanessa.

But who did the third set of prints belong to?

I looked to the larger and more open western path. The snow was undisturbed. I then looked at the eastern path that led to the cliff. The canopy and overhanging brambles had grown so thick that the path itself was nothing but hard-packed dirt. The boot prints vanished on this spot.

But I had to be certain.

I ducked my head under the brambles and dashed down the eastern path, leaping over overgrown aspen roots, swerving around thorny thatches of devil's club. The path opened up and I found myself atop the snowy cliff. And then, I saw something very strange.

Two snow angels. One large. One small.

Apparently, Kelsey led your mother here, and the two of you made snow angels.

It was strange.

At the edge of the cliff, I noticed a jumble of boot prints. And that was it. The trail ended here. My eyes drifted back to the edge of the cliff, and a sudden and horrible nausea flooded my senses.

I stepped up to the precipice, got down on my hands and knees, and looked over the edge.

"Ellie!"

But as I squinted my eyes through the darkness, a brilliant band of green and purple light shimmered in the sky, illuminating the ground seventy feet below.

At the bottom, there was nothing but snow.

***

I emerged from the woods less of a man than when I entered. A very large part of me was missing, and I knew I might never see it again.

Vanessa had won.

Regardless of wanting to convince myself otherwise, your mother stole you from under my nose with the help of Adam Kelsey. But where were you now? Where would she ultimately take you? And how did your mother know the previous groundskeeper?

Unable to think straight, I stumbled from the tree line and

climbed the steep, snowy grade that led to the Mansion's lofty back porch.

And then, I heard a shriek.

"Laz!"

When I looked up, it was to find Sophie sprinting down the snowy slope, chestnut hair whipping violently on the wind. She threw her arms around my neck and held me tight, gripping the hair on the back of my head as though afraid to let go.

"Oh my god, what happened to you?"

"Vanessa, she – "

But I couldn't continue. I broke down, right then and there. Collapsed to my knees and buried my face into Sophie's stomach.

"Ellie's gone," I moaned into her bathrobe.

"Laz – "

"Vanessa took her. Kelsey, he – "

"Laz," she said again. She took hold of my face, tilted my head upward, and wiped the wetness from my cheeks. It was strange to see her smiling.

"What?"

"Ellie is fine. She's inside. A little blue in the cheeks, but we fixed her with a new oxygen tank and wrapped her up next to the fire."

Without bothering to respond, I stood up and looked at the towering turrets of the Mansion. I looked back at Sophie, and she smiled.

"Go on," she said. "She's in the front parlor."

I took off at a full sprint. I didn't care that my long johns were soaked through and torn down the sides, that my scratched legs left streaks of blood in the snow. I bounded up the steps of the back porch, threw open the double doors, and ran down the southern hall, across the foyer, past the library, and into the front parlor.

You sat on the floor between Eldon's legs, giggling like a mad woman as he guffawed and mindlessly *boop*-ed your nose with your new stuffed husky.

"Laz!" I heard Tom Clark yell behind me, then turned to find him running down the hall. He pulled me in for a bear hug, nearly squeezing the life out of me. "Jesus, man, we were worried sick."

"What happened? Where – "

"Gloria found her just past the tree line. She was all alone without her oxygen."

Gloria found her…

Of course. That explained the third set of boot prints.

"Merry Christmas, Laz," said a smoky voice.

Gloria sat just beside the door, looking up at me with a rehearsed and vacant smile. Behind those dark brown eyes (or were they black?), I saw nothing.

I wanted to rip you away from Eldon, hold you tightly to my chest, and leave this place forever. But I just stood there, watching you laugh beside the ornamented pine tree.

"Where's Vanessa?" I yelled at Gloria.

"Not here," Tom interjected. "We checked her room when we found Ellie. I ran down to the Cabin to see if she was with you, but nobody answered."

"I was in the woods. I was looking for her."

"Did you find anything?" he asked.

"I found boot prints," I said, my eyes landing on Gloria again.

Sophie entered the parlor, draped a blanket over my shoulders, and pressed a steaming cup of coffee into my hands. The warmth seeped through me immediately, from my palms to my fingers, up my arms, and into my shoulders. Whether the warmth came from the mug or from Sophie's touch, I couldn't say.

I told them about the previous evening, about how I tucked Ellie in, how I went downstairs for a nightcap, how Adam Kelsey stood upon the back deck, staring through the glass from under his hood until Vanessa knocked me unconscious.

"Jesus," Tom whispered, pressing a palm to his forehead. "And you're sure it was Kelsey?"

"Who else would it be?"

"Any number of people from town," Sophie answered. She rubbed her eyes, pulled her hair back into a tight ponytail, and sat down beside her mother.

"I know what I saw."

"I believe you," Sophie said. "But if it *was* Adam, you think he and Vanessa – "

"I don't know what to think," I said. "I don't know how they could have known each other. But he helped her. He distracted me so she could sneak in and conk me over the head. She stole Ellie, escaped out the front, they met up in the clearing in the woods, and – "

"You said there was another set of prints."

Again, my gaze swept across the room and landed on Gloria. Her dark eyes remained fixed on the roaring hearth. Tom and Sophie must have noticed, for they glanced at each other nervously. Tom placed a hand on my shoulder.

"Laz," he said. "There's no way Gloria could have – "

"It's all right, Tom," Gloria interrupted. She leaned down, tucked her hands under your armpits, and pulled you into her lap. "What is it you think I've done, Lazalier?"

The room went silent, all eyes fixed on me. Eldon flinched and began whispering nonsense, scratching at his arms. He stood up and moved to the window, staring out into the cold, eager to avoid the impending confrontation.

"I think you helped Vanessa," I said. "I think you introduced her to Kelsey. I think you gave her a spare key to the Cabin. Encouraged her to get rid of me, like she's always wanted to."

Sophie cut in. "Laz, please just – "

"Hush," her mother snapped. "Let him finish."

"Once Vanessa took Ellie from her crib, she met you out front, and you both joined Kelsey in the woods. You led her down the path to the cliff. And while you and Ellie were making snow angels, you had Kelsey throw her over the edge."

"Kelsey killed my son," Gloria replied softly. "You said it yourself. Why would I want his help? Why not just throw him over the cliff?"

"I think that's exactly what you did," I replied. "After he got rid of Ness, I think you got rid of him."

"What a monster I've become," she sighed, with a hint of sarcasm.

"Tell them," I addressed Gloria. "Tell them about Prudence Gamble. Tell them about what Kelsey did to Sam. Tell them about Evie. Tell them about *this*."

I reached into my jacket pocket and withdrew the onyx

paperweight, its black and white striations glittering in the firelight.

"What is that?" Tom asked.

"Laz, this is crazy," Sophie said.

"There's no reason for it," Tom added. "Why would Gloria go through all that trouble? Where's the motive?"

And then, as I looked at you in Gloria's lap, noticed the way she stroked your hair even amid all the accusations, I knew.

"For Ellie," I said.

"Ellie?"

"One of her own children is dead, the other barely visits. Her husband isn't going to be around much longer. She'll be all alone up here."

"I have Lizanne," Gloria spoke.

"Do you?" I shot back. "Where is Lizanne, Gloria? Gone home for winter, just like Evie Brooks? Evie never made it, did she? Did Lizanne ever make it home? Or is there another hut somewhere in the woods, burned to hell with Lizanne inside?"

Gloria kept her eyes fixed on mine. She sighed and shook her head.

"You really don't know anything, do you?"

"Then tell me!" I yelled. "Tell us all what the hell is going on!"

The fire in the hearth emitted three sudden, muffled pops. At least, I thought it came from the hearth. I heard the tinkle of glass hitting the floor, and then, Sophie screamed. Gloria clapped her hands to her mouth. Tom gripped my arm and yanked me to the floor. When I looked up, I saw Eldon beside the window, but the window was no longer intact.

Sharp cracks webbed outward from three small holes in the glass.

Eldon turned and stared at us with wide, confused eyes. He looked down at two small holes in his chest, thick and dense scarlet spreading outward through his white and green Christmas sweater. He opened his mouth to speak, but through a third hole in his throat, all I heard was a gurgle.

His knees hit the floor. Blood spurted from his mouth. He fell forward.

And then, the Mansion's front parlor exploded in gunfire.

24

UNDER FIRE

There was nothing but noise, smoke, and debris.

And then, a sudden and ear-splitting silence.

I was on my stomach, hands clasped behind my head, nose buried into the old and mildewy shag rug. When I glanced up, it was to find Tom mouthing at me, his face red and the veins bulging in his neck. He was screaming something, but all I could hear was the muted, underwater version of his voice. His handsome face was streaked in red cuts where glass had flown and sliced his cheeks to ribbons.

I was confused, but at the same time, I knew precisely what had happened.

I spun around and saw you curled up in a ball beside the fireplace, little hands cupped to your ears, eyes round and glassy as the ornaments that had, until moments ago, hung like jewels from the Christmas tree. You must have read the confusion and the fear on my own face because, in that moment, you started to sob and scream, tears rolling down your face, wet trails of peach and pink descending the gray film of dust upon your cheeks.

Holding myself flat against the floor, I crawled across the rug and pulled you under my body just as another firestorm of gunfire echoed from outside, peppering the front parlor's ancient, flowery wallpaper. Plaster exploded outward with each blast, exposing the lath hidden behind the walls while dust and old paint swirled among the snowflakes drifting in through the glassless windows.

I'm not an expert on guns, but judging by the sheer number of bullets and the speed with which they freckled the walls, I knew enough to recognize that the shooter was firing a fully automatic something-or-other.

The second onslaught ended, and again, there was silence.

"We have to get out of here," Tom mouthed at me, and this time, he had no voice at all. He kept completely silent, leading a panic-stricken Sophie across the floor and out into the hall. The ringing in my ears began to subside, and in its place, I heard the telltale crunch of boots on snow.

The shooter was approaching.

Tom beckoned me into the hall from beyond the doorway, but I knew I didn't have time to crawl. I had the entire parlor to cross, and I had a terrified toddler clinging to my waist.

I had to risk it.

Without giving myself a moment to change my own mind, I grabbed you and your oxygen, jumped to my feet, and sprinted toward the doorway. Just as we cleared the jamb, more gunfire erupted, bullets whizzing past my ear and blasting through the opposing wall. And just before I turned the corner into the hall, I glanced over my shoulder to find the shooter climbing through the window. In the soft glow of the winter moonlight, I saw his face.

But before I could tell the others what I'd seen, Sophie led us sprinting down the hallway and into the library. Once we were all inside, she threw the doors closed and locked them.

"We have to get below," she said, running the length of the library to the wall of books behind her father's desk.

"What are you talking about?" Tom gasped, holding his side. A trickle of blood seeped through his fingers. "Below where?"

And straight out of *The Addams Family*, Sophie pulled down on a thick, weathered, leather-bound volume. There echoed a resounding *click!*, and then she pushed against the wall with everything she had.

"Help me!" she screamed.

Tom and I rushed across the library, our feet echoing on the floorboards with your arms wrapped tightly around my neck. Tom, Sophie, and I pressed our shoulders against the wall of books, and felt it begin to cave inward.

Whump! Whump! Whump! echoed across the library.

"He's trying to kick down the door!" Tom panted. "Push!"

The three of us planted our heels into the floor, pressed our backs against the wall of books, and finally, the wall budged as a dark and secret tunnel opened up behind us. Sophie ushered us into the pitch-black cavern, and once inside, we began to push the wall back into place, the final sliver of light from the library beyond fading away.

A loud crash erupted as the shooter finally kicked down the door. He must have seen the wall of books closing up, his boots thumping hard and fast, growing louder and louder until...

Siiippph!

The edges of the wall sucked back into place with an airtight seal. For a moment, silence and darkness pressed in on us. I heard nothing but my own thudding pulse and a deafening ringing in my ears. I held your head against my chest, caressed your soft, dusty curls, and quietly shushed your panicked whimpers. Sophie switched on the flashlight of her phone, revealing all of our faces in a circle, sweaty and white as bone, our blackened pupils constricting at the sudden illumination.

And then, we heard the metallic grind-and-click of a new magazine being shoved into the gun.

"Get down!" I yelled.

We dropped to the floor just as a third wave of bullets battered loudly against the wall of books. As heavy as the faux wall had been to force open, I assumed it had been constructed of tougher material than the plaster and drywall of the front parlor. I expected small shafts of light to pierce through the wall, but none came. The wall had done its job, and the shooter must have known it, because he stopped firing.

We were lying on the floor of, for all intents and purposes, a sort of panic room. And for good reason.

"He'll find the switch," Sophie whispered. She shined her flashlight in the opposite direction and revealed a long, dark, and narrow passageway. "We have to go."

Tom grunted as he stumbled to his feet, clutching his bloody hip.

"Tom – "

"I'm fine," he whispered. "Let's go."

Holding you with one arm, I wrapped the other around Tom's waist, letting him drape his arm over my shoulders. We followed

Sophie and her tiny beam of light down the dark, cold, brick-lined tunnel, sinking deeper into what I imagined to be the throat of the Dilbrook Mansion, the large house swallowing us into its bowels.

"Bit cliché, Soph, don't you think?" Tom chuckled. "The old 'book and the secret passageway' gag?"

"Dad insisted we have one," she replied with a roll of her eyes.

"Where does it lead?" I asked.

"Into the old wine cellar," she said. "At least, it used to be a wine cellar."

"What is it now?"

"We call it the Breathing Room. It's full of Dad's oxygen tanks. It connects up into the kitchen, so we can run out the back."

"Who the hell is shooting at us?" Tom grumbled.

"I didn't see him," Sophie said. "Laz?"

When I didn't answer, Sophie stopped and shined the light in my face.

"Laz, did you see who it was?"

I nodded.

"Nukilik."

"Holy shit," Tom whispered. "Makes sense, the way he waved his gun at us yesterday when he and Weekes were looking for – "

Both of their eyes fell on me.

"Where's Gloria?" I interrupted, doing my damnedest to diffuse the awkward tension.

"She ran out of the parlor as soon as she saw Eldon fall down," Tom said.

"Oh my god. Eldon," Sophie whispered, her eyes becoming

glassy.

"What do we do?" Tom asked.

"We need to get to the ridge where my brother is buried. It's the only place where there's any signal on this goddamn hill."

"And then what?"

"We call in a chopper. We need to get you to a hospital, Tom."

"Are there any guns in the house, Sophie?" I asked.

"I'm sure there are," she said. "But I have no idea where they're hidden. I know Dad used to always keep the shotgun in his bedroom."

"Maybe that's where Gloria went," Tom suggested. "Straight to Don."

"I think you're right. I think maybe she – "

Siiippph –

Sophie went silent. Her eyes grew wide. All three of us looked back and forth at each other, and then we heard it. Soft, scuffling boots on cement, growing steadily louder from the direction we'd come.

"Fuck," Tom grunted.

"Come on," Sophie whispered. "Hurry."

We followed Sophie quickly down the brick passage and through a large archway until finally, our path opened up into a long, dimly lit, underground room with high, trellised ceilings.

The old wine cellar was half the size of the library but still large in its own right, larger than any wine cellar I'd ever seen (which, admittedly, wasn't very many). Dim winter moonlight glowed softly through small round windows near the ceiling, windows that were right at ground level. We hurried down a black spiral staircase, 'round and 'round until we made it to the bottom, following behind Sophie as she weaved between old wine barrels interspersed among dozens of large aluminum oxygen tanks.

"We have to get to the other side!" Sophie pointed to a large steel door at the other end of the room but in her haste, she clipped her shin on an overturned wine barrel, twisted her ankle, and tumbled to the floor, knocking over a number of large metal tanks and causing the cellar to erupt in a loud, clanging cacophony.

Even though he was bleeding from his hip, Tom attempted to lift Sophie to her feet, but to no avail.

"Take Ellie and go," I yelled, pressing you into Tom's chest. You screamed in protest, but I shushed you softly and kissed your head. "Go! We'll meet you in the woods."

"Laz – "

"Ellie comes first, Tom! Please!"

With fierce reluctance, Tom looked down at Sophie clutching her ankle.

"Go!" Sophie yelled.

With a grunt of frustration that only ever came when Tom Clark was unable to help his friends, he turned, ran toward the steel door, and flung it open. And then, you both disappeared up the darkened stairwell.

"Come on. Up you go," I whispered to Sophie as I crouched down and helped her up onto her uninjured foot. "Put your weight on me. That's it. We have to – "

Gunfire thundered from high and behind. To my right, a wine barrel exploded in a mess of wood chips and a spray of Sangiovese.

Sophie screamed and we ducked as more bullets sliced through a row of aluminum tanks just ahead of us, releasing an angry hiss of compressed oxygen.

The gunfire ceased, and as I carried Sophie toward the steel door, I looked over my shoulder to find Nukilik twisting down the spiral staircase to get a better shot.

"Why are you doing this?!" I yelled, my voice echoing off the cavernous ceiling.

"You kill her!" he screamed in a manic Inuit accent, making his way to the cellar floor as he fumbled with a fresh magazine. "We find her blood in your Bronco! You kill my daughter!"

And suddenly, it clicked.

The day we found Evie Brooks' charred corpse, the day Detective Weekes and the other state troopers investigated the burned hut in the woods, Nukilik had been there, looking somber and concerned. He knew Evie had stayed behind in Ukippa instead of visiting her mother for the winter in Texas, like she'd always done before. Evie had made the sudden career shift from the Dilbrooks' live-in nurse to a career in law enforcement, not due to a change of heart, but because she wanted the chance to be around Nukilik.

Her father.

"It wasn't me. I swear I didn't – "

But Nukilik didn't want to hear it. He snapped the new magazine into his rifle and began firing. More and more wine barrels exploded while more and more oxygen tanks clanged and violently hissed their contempt.

"Laz!" Sophie screamed. "The door!"

305

With every ounce of strength I had left, I carried Sophie to the other side of the cellar and through the doorway into velvety darkness. I set Sophie on the bottom step of the stairwell leading up to the kitchen, then began pushing the massive steel door on its squealing hinges.

I looked up to find Nukilik charging toward us. He raised his rifle and began firing off more rounds. A single bullet struck the rugged steel door, sparked, and –

BOOM!

The hissing oxygen ignited and combusted into a roaring bloom of hellfire. The last thing I saw was Nukilik's horrified eyes as he was blown backward by the blast. The Breathing Room took its final breath and was suddenly engulfed in flame.

And then, I slammed the door shut.

***

By the time we made it outside, the bottom floor of the Mansion was roiling in smoke. I held Sophie by her waist and helped her to the tree line, where Tom stood behind the thick trunk of a large black spruce, holding you tightly in his arms.

"Nukilik wasn't alone," Tom said, nodding his head to the east. I turned, and like a torch in the night, the Cabin was already fully engulfed in flames. I could see the shadows of various Ukippans scoping the woods behind the Cabin, no doubt looking for me. I turned to the west and noticed a bright glow on the western ridge of Horseshoe Hill.

They'd also ignited the Shack.

"Jesus," I said.

I wondered where Moose was, if he was alive, fighting for the fate of the only hill he'd ever called home. And though I never killed anyone, I felt responsible for all of this. I should have taken Gloria's advice from the beginning. I should have left it alone.

All of it.

"Have you seen my parents?" Sophie asked, her panicked eyes glowing in the firelight as she searched the woods for any sign of Gloria and Don. "Did they make it out?"

"I've been watching, Soph," Tom sighed. "I haven't seen anyone."

She pushed away from me and began to limp out of the trees.

"Sophie, get back here!"

"I'm not leaving them."

"Sophie!"

"I'll go," I interrupted. "Sophie, I'll go. You're hurt. You both are. Besides, Harvey is still in there."

"Laz, no," she said. "Ellie needs you."

"Which gives me all the more reason to get out of there alive. Go to Sam's Lookout. Call the helicopter."

"No. None of this would have happened – you never would have been here if it weren't for me," she whispered, her eyes glistening in the fiery glow.

"You gave me an amazing opportunity, Sophie," I said, wiping a tear from her cheek. "I'll be fine. I'm the best damn firefighter Anchorage has ever seen, remember?" I winked at Tom and offered them both a smile. "Watch Ellie for me."

And without giving either of them another chance to talk me

307

out of it, I turned and bolted up the snowy hill. Just as I reached the property line, I noticed the glint of the axe I used for chopping firewood, one sharpened corner lodged into the splitting block.

I gripped the wooden handle, pulled it free, and for the first time since Turnagain Home, I rushed into the inferno.

***

Without a respirator, helmet, and full turnout gear, I became fully aware (and all too quickly) that this was most certainly a suicide mission.

I'd forgotten how intensely hot a burning building can be. How devastatingly unbearable it is to breathe in the boiling air. How quickly the ash and soot coats the back of the throat in a slimy, acrid film. How the combination of searing light and pyrexia sizzles the corneas.

How easily, little by little, it chokes the focus and the sanity right out of you.

Even with the sleeves of my sweater tied around the back of my head in the form of a makeshift facemask, black smoke poured into my lungs, slowly suffocating me from the inside out. I was only at the library, and already, I felt dizzy. I peered inside, finding the secret entrance to the panic room sealed, the wall of books now a wall of blackened ash and bullet holes. All of the walls, the curtains, and the ceiling were aflame, everything except Don's marble desk. And now that I wasn't hurriedly escaping a deranged gunman, I noticed something I hadn't noticed before.

Don Dilbrook's only copy of *The Girl in the Snow* was gone.

I abandoned the library and rushed down the east hallway to the front parlor, hoping I might find a terrified Harvey curled up in a corner. But he wasn't there. I spun and glanced all around the grand foyer, but I saw no sign of him. I rushed past a tall and roiling column of flame and into the dining hall, but again, Harvey was nowhere to be found.

I'd spent so many weeks searching for him, only to find him... and then lose him again.

Ellie needs you, I heard Sophie in my head.

And for the second time in two months, I was forced to abandon my dog.

"I'm sorry, Harv," I choked behind my sweater. My throat felt like sandpaper and my eyes burned, but not from the flames whipping and roaring all around me. This time, my eyes burned with tears. I gulped down the golf ball lodged in my throat, wiped the wetness from my blackened, soot-streaked cheeks, and ascended the broad, main staircase.

Straight to Don, Tom had said. I had to get to Gloria.

The flames rose higher, brighter, and hotter as I took the stairs three at a time. The skin of my legs began to blister beneath the shredded cotton of my long johns. I finally made it to the third floor, took the first corner, sprinted down the main corridor, and kicked open the arched, viridian door.

The walls of Don's bedroom were engulfed in flame, the ceiling alight with roiling heat, soot, and smoke. Gloria sat beside Don's four-poster, her back to me, her hands resting within one of Don's palms.

It appeared as if she was praying beside him.

The curtains of the four-poster suddenly caught fire, and I knew it was time to go. I rushed across the room and narrowly dodged a burning oak beam as it plunged from the ceiling and crashed to the floor.

"Gloria!" I yelled. I reached out, grabbed her shoulder, and —

Her head fell back, milky eyes wide open and staring intently at the ceiling. Her chin, lips, and eyelids were blackened with soot, much of the skin of her cheeks already burned away to reveal the raw, red flesh beneath. Pink and gray foam bubbled from the corners of her blackened, open mouth.

And then, I understood.

Gloria died of smoke asphyxiation, seated at her husband's bedside.

I couldn't believe it. Everything I had uncovered, every bit of evidence that had Gloria Dilbrook written all over it, it all meant nothing now. She was dead, and there would be no confession. No way to tie up all the loose ends. No way to reveal all the secrets of Horseshoe Hill.

The truth had died with her.

I looked down at Don, alone in his bed, hooked up to all his expensive equipment. One eye was fixed on the ceiling. The other, however, stared directly at me, wide and horrified. Behind his oxygen mask, I saw his lips quiver as he breathed in the untainted air. I noticed the occasional clench of his neck muscles. Watched his fingers twitch as the flames inched ever closer to his bed.

He was very much alive.

I needed to get him out.

***

My knee still throbbed, and Don's weight didn't help. The old man was dead weight over my shoulders as I carried him as quickly as I could down the burning staircase and into the foyer, his large oxygen tank clunking behind us with each step I took. My eyes stung with ash and heat, my vision beginning to fade as I choked on the burning air, even through the sweater tied around my head. I felt my lungs struggling to keep up, my muscles cramping and losing strength.

We crossed the foyer and passed through the scorched doorway that led into the kitchen. Relief washed over me at the sight of the open French doors that led out onto the porch, where I saw the snowy hill that led down into the trees beyond. An invigorating cold drifted in through the French doors, my lungs burning but my mind focused on getting back to you. I took a couple steps past the steel door that led down to the Breathing Room –

Behind me, the door squealed on its hinges and swung open.

A pair of charred hands enclosed over my face, blackened fingernails digging into my skin, raking at my eyes. They tugged my head backward, ripping the sweater from my face as the full blast of heat and smoke enveloped my senses. I couldn't see. I couldn't breathe. I lost my footing and toppled backward, sending Don rolling to the floor and out of my reach. My attacker climbed on top of me, singed fleshy fingers enclosing over my throat, the pressure of his palms pressing down on my windpipe.

I opened my eyes and through the smoke, I saw Nukilik's face burned almost beyond recognition, skin black and melted and dangling from his cheeks, hair singed clean to the scalp, eyes blood-red from hypoxia. His lips were burned away, large yellow teeth bared in anger and hate and murderous intent. I grabbed at his hands and tried to wrench them from my throat, but he only pressed down harder. My eyes bulged, my body burned, my legs kicked in desperation. As I struggled, I felt something hard dig into my side…

And then I remembered.

I released Nukilik's hands, reached into my jacket pocket, gripped the hard edges of my savior, and swung it upward.

The sharpened pavilion of the onyx paperweight crunched into Nukilik's skull. His bloodshot eyes widened for a moment. Then, they rolled back into his head as he fell backward onto the floor.

Suddenly free of his grip, I gasped for breath, but all I tasted was smoke and soot and desiccation. But what could I do? So, I gulped in the poisonous air. I choked. I gagged. And as I looked up, I saw Don lying on the floor, oxygen mask askew, his good eye still staring desperately at me. With every ounce of strength I had left, I crawled across the scorched floorboards, fixed his mask, and tugged him through the kitchen.

I felt a blast of cold air on my back. Felt a snowflake melt on my forehead. Heard the *chuf-chuf-chuf* of helicopter blades.

I pushed Don over the edge of the porch and into the snow. Unable to move another muscle, I collapsed on the hard, damp wood of the porch, and gazed out into the trees. And right as I blacked out, I saw Smitty there, just beyond the tree line.

But tonight, he looked very different.

***

I don't remember much after that.

I recalled the deafening roar of wind in my ears. Sophie's voice yelling above me, begging someone to help. Your distant, panicked cries. Felt the ground disappear beneath me, my body jostling atop a leather gurney. Heard the hiss of oxygen and felt a pair of strong hands pressing down on my chest, again and again and again.

At one point, I opened my eyes. I turned my head, and I saw it.

As we flew high above Ukippa, icy Lake Adamant glowed with oranges, yellows, and reds as three houses on a hill burned to the ground under fire and smoke.

25

PRISON

On the first page of this manuscript, Ellie, I mentioned that I lie here alone in this prison, typing these pages on an old laptop.

I should probably clarify that, in fact, I will never actually make it to prison in the literal sense. Though Detective Weekes likely has a lot of evidence stacked against me, I can feel what is happening to my body, inside my lungs, within my heart, and I know I will never make it to a trial.

After that final night on Horseshoe Hill, I recall my eyes slowly drifting open to find myself enclosed within four bright, white walls. At first, I assumed I drifted into some sort of purgatory, at least until I noticed small blue anchors dotted along the walls.

Surely, purgatory didn't have wallpaper.

Then, I heard the beeps and the whirrs and the hisses of all the hoses and wires and machines I was hooked up to. And though one of the countless needles in my hands was certainly a morphine drip, I still felt the burning pain in my lungs and the slight tracheal sting of the intubation tube forced down my throat. I was stuck in a bed I didn't want to be in.

I couldn't speak. I couldn't move.

This was my prison.

"Two heart attacks," I remembered hearing the doctor say, his voice muffled as though he spoke through a thick pane of glass. "But he's far from out of the woods, Ms. Dilbrook."

Sophie.

And though I tried to speak her name, all I felt was a grunt escape my throat, followed by the slightest brush of a hand on my shoulder, and I was out again.

When I came out of the darkness a second time, the walls were no longer bright white. They were gray and yellow with inky green anchors, a cloudless moonlight casting shadows through a window I hadn't seen prior. My throat felt raw, but it felt somewhat normal. I noticed that the intubation tube had been removed, and I wore an oxygen mask over my nose and mouth instead. Yet still, I was attached to my machines and wires like a puppet to its strings and found it very difficult to move without the help of the nurses, my marionettes.

I looked around at the four walls of my prison, at nothing but the tacky wallpaper and a small TV mounted in one corner. It was a single ward, likely due to the fact that my heart couldn't handle any unexpected stimulation from another patient. I glanced at the full moon outside the window, at the first cloudless night I'd seen in weeks. I didn't know how many days or nights had transpired since the Mansion, the Cabin, and the Shack had burned to rubble, and I didn't care.

What I did care about was where you were, Ellie, where you had ended up after our ride in the helicopter. I had no doubt in my mind that Sophie or Tom had you in their care, and that simple fact warmed my heart. But I knew that, in the very likely event of my death here in this hospital bed, social workers were bound to eventually show up. And so, when Tom visited me next, I made sure he showed up with a laptop and a copy of my Last Will and Testament.

I turned my attention to the small table beside my bed, and suddenly, I was transported to the burning library of the Dilbrook Mansion. For there, upon the table sat the only copy of D.J. Dilbrook's *The Girl in the Snow*.

Atop the leather-bound book sat an envelope with *Lazalier* scrawled in beautiful cursive on the front.

With all the strength I could muster, I ripped open the envelope, unfolded the letter inside, and began to read.

26

WITH LOVE

Hey you,

Let me begin by saying that you are one of the greatest men I've ever met. More than that, you are an incredible father. Ellie is very lucky. I am praying for your swift recovery and hope the two of you are reunited soon.

I knew who you were long before we met in that pub in Anchorage. Please know that in all I've done, you were the key. I am bound by my profession, a profession that dictates evil must be made to atone for its crimes.

It pains me to say that this evil has hit far too close to home, for far too long.

I love my father, but I discovered long ago that he loves women and power far more than he ever loved me, my brother, or my mother. He has many children in Alaska, maybe even elsewhere. Children that he never cared for. Children that he abandoned. And though it kills me greatly to know how terribly he suffered in his final days after the fire, I find solace in the knowledge that his death has brought an end to his suffering, his selfishness, his lies, and his greatest secret.

It was my father, not my mother, who killed Prudence Gamble.

When I was very young, I overheard my father confess his secret to my mother. She sat idly by and simply listened as he confessed to his years of betrayal. His infidelity. His having a son with Prudence. Hidden in the shadows, I listened as he confessed to crushing the poor woman's skull with an onyx paperweight. The same paperweight that once sat on his desk in the library. The same paperweight that the state troopers will never find when they search the wreckage.

My father confessed to my mother that he hid Prudence Gamble's body where no one would ever find it. He allowed the world to try and pin the disappearance on his old friend, Moose, but there was never enough evidence to convict him.

I was horrified at what I overheard, yes. But in a sad, sick way, I understood why he did what he did.

My father killed that woman, but he did it for our family.

A few years ago, I found Eldon Gamble in Fairbanks. Alone, homeless, hungry, and mentally handicapped, I fed him the necessary breadcrumbs that led him back to Ukippa. Back to my father. His father. Dad was incredibly disturbed and tried to get rid of Eldon, but Mom was more reasonable. Smarter. She suggested that we take Eldon in. Get him out of the cold. Keep him close. I suppose she thought if we treated Eldon like family, he would never need to learn the awful truth...

That his own father murdered his mother.

And then, I made another shameful discovery.

A year before Sam and I were born, my father traveled to Juneau on business. He met a young prostitute down on her luck, waved his money in her face, and took her to bed. When she awoke the next morning, he was gone, but he had left a sizable tip on the bedside dresser.

Her pimp kicked open the door, stole my father's money, beat her, and left her to her fate.

That fate involved a police deputy who took the prostitute, bruised and battered, to his home. He fed her, clothed her, tended her wounds… and then assaulted her. Nine months later, the prostitute gave birth to a son. She disappeared when the boy was six years old, and it was then that the boy named Adam was re-introduced to the deputy, his father.

At least, to the man he assumed was his father.

Many years later, when Deputy Amos Kelsey died in Bettles, Adam Kelsey discovered his true heritage. He discovered that the oil tycoon who had taken his mother to bed all those years ago was his true father.

He found out about our family on his own, but how he found out about us remains a mystery, even to me.

And then, he waited.

The summer I took the bar exam, my father learned he had developed an early stage of multiple myeloma from all his years in the oil industry, and he asked me to visit. I flew into Bettles, had to beg for a ride to Horseshoe Hill, and Adam Kelsey was the only one who stood up. I took a bit of a liking to him, and then won him the groundskeeper position at the Mansion.

I flirted, but Adam kept his distance, and I couldn't understand why.

319

At least, not until my brother, Sam, got involved.

Sam didn't have many friends. In fact, he didn't have any friends. He was very easily swayed by powerful personalities. And even though he hated my father, he did anything my father told him to do.

And like my father, Adam Kelsey was also extremely manipulative.

Sam idolized Adam. Helped him around the Mansion. Fixing fences. Re-shingling the roof. Chopping firewood. It was the first time in his life that Sam did chores without having to be told. I'd never seen my father prouder of my brother. Dad was finally beginning to see the man beneath the troubled boy. He attributed my brother's newfound work ethic to Adam Kelsey, and started treating Adam like he was more than just a groundskeeper.

Like he was part of the family.

Which, in truth, he was, though none of us knew it.

Adam, in turn, began treating Sam like the younger brother he'd never had. Invited him down to the Cabin for midnight whiskeys. Took him out into the woods and taught my brother everything he knew.

I watched them from afar, subtly jealous of my brother. Jealous of all the time he'd been spending with Adam. I liked Adam first, after all. Brought him to Horseshoe Hill. Got him the job as groundskeeper. But it was a crush, pure and simple.

Nothing but a crush.

But with Sam, it became much, much more. Sam's simple idolization of Adam Kelsey became fixation. Fixation became adoration.

Adoration became obsession.

My brother fell in love with Adam Kelsey. And this was the weapon that Adam had waited so long to use.

Adam quickly made friends with just about everyone in Ukippa. Sat in Galoshes and listened to each of their stories. Heard how cruel my father was to his workers in the oil field, and to their families. Because of how his mother had been treated, Adam Kelsey had grown up with a burning hatred of wealthy and powerful men. Had learned that one of these men was his biological father, and his hatred burned even hotter.

Adam began to quietly convince Sam that my father was a monster. He was too wealthy. Too high on his perch, up on a hill overlooking the peasants. Too ignorant of the fact that the citizens of Ukippa were either starving or close to it. Too quick to turn his eyes away from the extreme poverty and suffering happening across Lake Adamant.

To put it simply, Adam Kelsey used Sam. Used my brother's obsession with him. Molded his mind. Secretly turned him against my father. And once Adam had wriggled his way deep enough into my brother's fragile psyche, Sam began to loathe my father. When I looked at Sam, I no longer saw the innocent kid I'd grown up with. I saw nothing behind his eyes. Adam had flipped my brother's head upside down. He became unhinged.

Adam Kelsey was a wolf, and Sam was the sheep.

Too often that summer, I listened to my brother and my father, alone in the library, screaming at one another until the walls rattled with mutual hate. One day, I heard my father ranting and raving about how useless my brother was, how he wished my mother never had twins, wished that she'd only had me, wished that Sam had been stillborn.

Then, I heard a thump, and everything went quiet.

I opened the door and saw my father on the floor, bleeding from the back of his head. Sam stood over him, holding the onyx paperweight in his fist. He didn't say anything. Just looked at me, and then dropped the paperweight and walked out the door. That was the last time I ever heard my father speak. The brain damage that followed turned him into a vegetable.

So, you see, it wasn't the cancer. It was never the cancer. My brother made my father that way.

And Adam Kelsey was behind it all.

My mother cradled my father's head and told me to go after my brother. To find Sam and bring him back to the Mansion. I wasn't in the best state of mind, but I remember begging her to call the helicopter. She told me she'd take care of it, that the important thing was to find Sam and to bring him home.

My first instinct was to sprint to the Cabin.

I banged on the door, crying out for Adam to come and help. But he never came, so I grabbed the spare key from under the mat. Inside, the Cabin was dry and stale, and I noticed the back door was open. The smell of honey lingered in the air as I called out to Adam again, but he wasn't home. I went out onto the back deck and noticed footprints in the dirt, leading into the woods.

Twinstincts. Twin telepathy. Call it what you want, but I knew immediately where Sam had gone.

I found the clearing and followed the fork down the eastern path. I heard a voice in the distance, and then I slowed down to listen. It was Sam. He was crying. Incoherent. Moaning. It was the most terrible sound I'd ever heard. I assumed he'd come out of his blind rage and maybe thought he'd killed Dad, then sought the refuge he knew only the woods could provide.

I was about to call out to Sam, but then I heard another voice.

It was Adam Kelsey. And he was laughing.

Harsh, loud, and triumphant.

Maniacal.

I listened to my brother beg Adam to help him. To take him away. Take him far, far away from Ukippa, where they could start fresh. Together. Just the two of them.

He told Adam he loved him.

Adam stopped laughing. Then, I heard a loud smack. I heard Sam whimper, heard him fall, heard his body slide against the gravel.

"Don't you get it?" Adam yelled. "I'm your brother, you faggot."

The twinstincts hit me hard again, and I knew that the final piece had clicked into place, in both my mind and in Sam's.

Adam Kelsey was our brother, and that meant Sam could never, ever have him.

I heard Sam start to cry again, but it wasn't sadness. It was confusion. It was heartbreak. It was rage. I knew that Sam needed me in that moment, so I sprinted down the trail. As I broke through the trees, Adam looked up in surprise.

But it was too late.

Sam launched himself at Adam. Caught him around the waist. They struggled, Adam grabbed Sam around the neck, Sam slipped... and together, they disappeared over the cliff.

Time stopped then. The world became fuzzy, hot, and fluid all at once. I don't know how long it took for my mind to catch up, but when *it did, I was screaming. I heard a pair of feet rushing toward me. It was Sam. It had to be. It had all been a mistake. A trick of my mind.*

A pair of soft arms wrapped around me, and I heard a distant voice whispering in my ear that everything was going to be okay.

But it wasn't Sam.

It was Evie Brooks.

She pressed her body tenderly against mine, holding my shoulders as I screamed like a banshee into the summer evening. Had I been smarter, or perhaps in a sharper mindset, I might have realized then that she, too, had been in the woods that day. She had seen everything I had seen. I know now that she witnessed it all, because tears were flooding down her cheeks.

But she wasn't grieving for Sam.

Adam and Evie (as my mother liked to call them) had developed a sort of relationship that only comes from two outsiders hired to serve the same family. Apart, they were alone. But together, they shared a secret bond. A bond that blossomed into something I had hoped for early on with Adam. A bond that my brother obsessed over, but eventually lost his life trying to obtain.

But for Evie, it hadn't been a crush, and it hadn't been an obsession. She had truly loved Adam, and I would bet my life that if Adam Kelsey had even the slightest ability to love another human being, he would have found it in Evie.

As Evie and I stood there sobbing, I felt something hard wedged between us. I looked down to find her camera pressed between our ribs, the strap hanging loosely around her neck.

I smelled the sweetness of her honey-scented perfume.

I met her eyes then, and I knew.

Adam and Evie had been together that day, alone in the Cabin. Sam had rushed in, calling out for Adam. Evie stayed in the bedroom while Adam went to investigate. Sam somehow convinced Adam to go out into the woods with him. Not wanting to make her presence known, Evie followed, but not before grabbing her camera. She followed them into the trees, most likely following the sound of their voices, as I had.

And just as I broke through the trees, she saw Sam stand and lunge. She raised her camera, and —

Click.

She took a single, damning picture.

When Evie looked into my eyes, she knew that I knew.

Sam was flawed, of course, but I couldn't let it become public knowledge that he had lost control and murdered our groundskeeper. I couldn't. I wouldn't. Adam Kelsey used my brother to hurt my father, and then tossed him aside like an old rag. My brother's memory deserved more dignity than that.

"Evie," I whispered.

She must have known I was about to ask for the camera. Instead, she clutched it to her chest, stood up, and disappeared into the trees.

I gave chase, zigzagging through the woods, following her as she made a break toward the Cabin. I followed her past the tree line and watched her run up the wooden stairs to the back deck and into the Cabin, closing the sliding glass door behind her with a click of the lock.

We stood there, both of us weeping, staring at one another through the glass. I knew she was hurting, and she knew I was hurting.

Neither of us could compartmentalize what we'd both just witnessed.

Evie and I had been great friends ever since she'd first taken the job as my father's live-in nurse. We shared so much with each other. Learned each other in and out. Trusted each other fully and completely. And as we watched each other sob through the glass, I noticed her hand falter.

Her fingertips slid down the glass, and she unlocked the door.

I'm not entirely sure how long we stood out on that back deck, holding each other, crying into each other's shoulders. She began to question why Sam would do such a thing, why he would send both himself and Adam to their deaths.

I hate to say it, but this was the moment I decided to exercise the trait I'd inherited from my father. As I mentioned earlier, Dad was incredibly manipulative, incredibly convincing.

As was Adam.

As am I.

I told Evie my version of the story. Told her that Sam was the softest person I'd ever known. That he loved life too much to end it for anyone, most of all himself. From my vantage point, Adam provoked Sam, Sam launched himself at Adam, they struggled, got too close to the edge, and had fallen.

"It was an accident, Evie," I whispered into her ear.

I pulled back to stare into her eyes, and she stared back into mine. Reading me. Looking for any trace of the lie I'd just told. I kept eye contact and willed her to believe me. Her eyes softened, and she started to cry once more.

I knew then that my lie held steady.

We walked hand in hand back into the woods and to the cliff. We peered over the edge, but the drop was too steep, and neither of us could see the bottom.

And then, something strange happened.

I believe there is good in everyone, Laz.

I also believe there is evil in everyone. I'm not proud of it, but right then and there, standing beside Evie on the edge of that cliff, I wanted to give her a gentle nudge. My body trembled. My mind screamed at me to end it, once and for all. In that moment, I heard the evil inside me, and I was so close to acting on it. I wanted to end her life in order to preserve my brother's innocence. And if I wasn't so certain that my lie had convinced her that all of it had indeed been an accident, I would have pushed her over the edge.

But I held back.

Together, Evie and I descended the cliff, and when we made it to the bottom, we couldn't believe our eyes.

There sat my mother, alone beside Sam's body, staring down into his bloody face. Her eyes were puffy, her jaw was set. And as we looked around, we noticed something was missing.

Adam Kelsey had disappeared.

For a long time after that day, Evie and I never spoke of what we had seen in those woods. We never spoke of Adam Kelsey. I never asked to see the picture she had taken. She stood beside me on the day we buried my brother, and while I understood she was sad for me, sad for my mother, sad for my family, I knew her mind was still on Adam.

Where he had run off to.

How he had survived.

What he was doing.

Why he hadn't come back for her.

Evie moved out of the Mansion some weeks after Sam's funeral and found a place of her own on Ricketts Knob. I flew down south to interview for an opening with the Anchorage Prosecutors Office. We didn't see each other much after that.

That winter, I called up Mom, just to talk. She mentioned that Evie Brooks had abandoned her efforts of being a nurse. She had taken up a spot at the Ukippa Peace Office, oddly enough, and was working closely with Nukilik on tracking down Adam Kelsey.

But I knew she would never find him.

What you need to understand, Laz, is that a mother will do anything to protect her child. What you must also understand is that Dilbrooks are very good at covering their tracks.

Quite literally, in fact.

A few days after Sam's funeral, I found Mom in the library. She was just sitting there at Dad's desk, staring down at his book. I asked if she was okay, if she needed anything, and she told me to sit down.

For the next hour, I sat in silence as she told me everything. She told me things I had already uncovered for myself, like my father's countless bouts of infidelity, the fact that he had children all over Alaska, and that he had killed Prudence Gamble after she had threatened our family.

Then, Mom told me things I didn't know.

She told me that Prudence Gamble had never been found. And the reason she'd never been found is because Dad had wrapped her body in burlap, dug a hole to the east of the Mansion, and buried her in lime and soil.

And then, he built a structure on top of her grave. A small side house...

A Cabin.

Mom went on and said she knew, early on, that my brother had developed an unhealthy obsession with Adam Kelsey. She'd seen it in the way he looked at the groundskeeper. How Sam watched him at work. "Like a hungry, feral cat," were her words. She said she warned my brother not to get too attached, that it wasn't going to end well for either of them.

She told me that, on the day Sam died, she heard my screams and came running. When she got to the cliff, I wasn't there, and she feared something had happened not only to Sam, but to me as well. She made her way down the cliff and found Sam and Adam at the bottom, both of them dead. And just like she warned him would happen, she knew Sam finally went too far.

Much like me, my mother didn't want it to be known that my brother was a murderer.

So, she dragged Adam's body away from the base of the cliff and stashed it deep in the woods, covering her tracks as she went. She came back to my brother's body to grieve, and that's when she noticed Adam Kelsey's necklace in the snow. She pondered what to do with it, but then Evie and I showed up, and she quickly stuffed it in her pocket. Evie and I both assumed Adam had survived and run off, and my mother didn't dispute it.

When she went back a few days later, she found Adam's body in pieces, ripped to shreds by the same wolves he'd idolized his entire life. She wrapped up what remained of Adam's carcass in a trash bag, loaded it with heavy stones, and sank it in the depths of Lake Adamant.

Mom finished her story by telling me that, for better or for worse, we had done everything right. And that was that.

At least, until Evie Brooks met Lizanne.

A month or so before you and I met in Anchorage, Mom hired Lizanne to make Dad's remaining time on earth as enjoyable as possible. Lizanne and my mother got on famously, and Mom discovered something of a kindred spirit in the new live-in nurse.

Mom doesn't have many friends in Ukippa, Dad's a vegetable, and I live in Anchorage. Three years and hardly any civilized conversation finally got the better of my mother.

One night, she invited Lizanne to have dinner with her. They talked, they laughed, and they finished an entire bottle of Malamute. Lizanne mentioned that she had seen a photograph of me and Sam in a bedroom upstairs, and she asked about us.

And then, Mom started to cry.

I know it must be hard to imagine stone-faced Gloria Dilbrook having a mental breakdown, but that's exactly what happened. She told Lizanne about me, about how much she missed me, that she never felt so alone in her entire life.

She talked about Sam, about his unhealthy obsession with the former groundskeeper. And then, she skirted the conversation along the edges of her darkest secret.

To her own horror, my mother woke up the next morning with a terrible hangover and the foggiest memory of telling Lizanne she knew what had become of Adam Kelsey. She begged Lizanne not to say a word to anyone. Tripled her pay. Offered her unlimited vacation time.

Lizanne just smiled, hugged my mom, and swore that she would never tell a soul.

Little did we know that Lizanne is a habitual liar.

Lizanne and Evie became acquainted in Galoshes a few days before Lizanne started working for my parents. The two sparked an instant connection when Evie mentioned she had been our previous live-in nurse. Lizanne asked Evie why she quit, and Evie told her about the mysterious disappearance of Adam Kelsey. Mentioned that she had never stopped looking for Adam, and never would.

After Mom's drunken little confession, Lizanne met Evie for a beer and told her that my mother knew exactly where Adam could be found.

To say that Evie Brooks became a bloodhound after that conversation would be an immense understatement. She focused all of her attention on Horseshoe Hill. On my mother.

On our family.

Evie began to search harder than ever, and her search ended shortly after your arrival...

Laz, I imagine you remember one of your first days in Ukippa, the day you picked me up from the airport in Allakaket. We parked outside of Galoshes, I told you to go on ahead, to grab me a glass of zin while I took care of something. I felt your eyes on me as I walked across the square and into the Peace Office.

What you don't know is that Evie Brooks asked me to meet her in her office, and when I walked in, it wasn't to find the Evie I had grown so close to over the years.

In her place sat a bitter and distrusting woman I barely recognized.

She told me she knew my mother was somehow involved in Adam's disappearance. She didn't believe Adam would just run off and not give her any indication of where he'd gone.

I calmly reminded her that she and I had scaled the cliff together, that we both noticed Adam was gone. How dare she even suggest my mother was in any way involved with Adam's disappearance?

Mom was at the bottom of the cliff, grieving for her son, and nothing more.

Evie started to laugh. She asked me if I remembered how high the snow had been that day. If I remembered that there were no shoeprints leading away from the bottom of the cliff.

"Did he just flap his arms and fly away?" she laughed.

I said I didn't know, and she screamed at me, saying I knew more than I was letting on. I shook my head, told her it was nice to see her, and I turned to leave. Evie warned me to get out of Ukippa, to stay far away, that she planned on shaking the truth out of my mother and that, if I stayed, she would have my entire family under a microscope.

I told her goodbye for the last time. Then, I met you in Galoshes, sipped my zin, and told you the story of Adam Kelsey. It wasn't his full story, no.

Merely the beginning.

You mentioned during one of your first nights in the Cabin that you saw Lizanne out in the snow. You saw her talking to the trees. You saw her hand something to someone hiding in the woods.

From what I can gather, on that night, Lizanne slipped Evie a key to the Mansion.

For every year she spent in Ukippa, Evie Brooks flew south to Texas each winter to be with her mother. This winter would have been the same, had it not been for Lizanne spilling my mother's secret, and Evie's sudden obsession with finally dismantling my family.

One night, Evie used the key Lizanne had given her to sneak into the Mansion. I don't think she knew exactly what she was looking for, or even if she was looking for anything in particular. Anything linked to Adam, I expect. Anything that would condemn my family. Eventually, she searched the library and finally discovered something that would take my family down…

Adam Kelsey's jade necklace stuck out from the pages of Dad's leather-bound book.

But what Evie didn't notice was my mother, hidden in the shadows.

My mother is, and always has been, a firm believer in the idea that if you're in her house and you're not supposed to be, she has every right to shoot you dead. Or, in this case, take a diamond-shaped paperweight to your head. She didn't mean to hit Evie as hard as she did. At least, that's what she says.

My mother killed Evie Brooks, and she did it for our family.

When she figured out Evie was dead, she decided to dispose of her body, just like she had disposed of Adam Kelsey, and just like my father had disposed of Prudence Gamble all those years ago.

Old habits die hard, I suppose.

The permafrost was too thick, so digging a hole was out of the question. The lake was frozen solid, so that idea was also nixed.

Mom knew that Moose kept a few barrels of Mainstay oil in his shed. She also knew of an old hut in the woods.

And so, as cold as it was, the answer was fire.

She staged the hut to tie Adam and Evie together. She bound Evie's lifeless body in handcuffs, wrapped Adam's jade necklace around her neck, stashed her in the hut, upended a barrel of oil, and set it ablaze.

Adam was still missing but presumed alive, and it was no secret to anyone in Ukippa that he and Evie had been romantically linked in the past.

"A crime of passion," my mother said to anyone who would listen. "The wolf killed the poor girl. We loved her so much."

Say one thing for my mother, say she's a good liar.

There's a final chapter to this story that I hope brings you some clarity, if not a little bit of comfort. The only thing I've ever wanted is to bring about some good in someone else's life. This is the main reason I became a lawyer.

Sometimes, however, the law doesn't work the way it should. During custody battles, more often than not, a mother wins sole custody of her child. This is the case even if she is the terrible parent. Even if she doesn't deserve her child.

Even if the father is a great man.

Tom Clark and I planned to spend Christmas with you and Ellie for weeks before we made the trip to Horseshoe Hill. And just as we were in the process of finalizing the details, Tom called me one afternoon from his *office. He told me that there was an issue. That a woman named Vanessa Brady stormed into his office and demanded to know where you had taken her daughter.*

I immediately rushed over.

It was all a bit confusing, to be honest. Tom tried calming her down, but she was beside herself, crying and screaming that she had made a mistake in abandoning Ellie in your apartment. Said that it was so difficult caring for such a sick child, that she lost control and decided to just be rid of all the pain and discomfort that came with caring for Ellie. That she had chosen herself, had chosen cocaine and men over her own daughter. That it had been many, many moments of weakness.

That she wanted Ellie back.

And then, she threatened to go to the state troopers if you didn't agree to hand her over.

I took her hand and assured her that wasn't necessary, that she could fly to Ukippa with us and see that Ellie was safe and well taken care of. And after buying her three glasses of white wine at Anchors, I was able to convince her to pack a bag, and to pack warm.

I still find it incredible how easily people place their trust in me.

I must confess I was nervous when I saw how you reacted when you saw Vanessa on our front porch. I hoped that she would arrive, see how happy and healthy Ellie was while in your care, and that her heart would soften. I hoped that she would spend Christmas with us, that the two of you would find some sort of middle ground, and decide how you wanted to split custody.

The moment I saw Ellie in her arms, however, I knew that Vanessa had other plans. She confessed to me how badly she wanted Ellie back. I suppose she assumed that I liked her enough to ask if I Tom and I would help her take Ellie away from you.

So, Tom and I agreed.

I gave her a spare key to the Cabin and told her that if she planned on knocking you out, to make sure one hit would do it. Tom's job was to distract you, and so, he pulled on his black jacket, lifted his hood over his head, and waited on the back porch.

But unbeknownst to Vanessa, Tom and I had other intentions.

After the deed was done, the four of us walked through the trees, me and Vanessa in front, Tom behind us with Ellie in his arms. We had an admittedly lovely conversation about the aurora and how she had never seen it before, about what it was like growing up on Horseshoe Hill, and then I asked her what she had planned when she made it back to Anchorage.

"I plan to never see that city again," Vanessa said. But under those words, I knew she wanted to add, "Or Lazalier."

We continued to chat as we hiked past a beautiful clearing, down an old eastern pathway shrouded in brambles, and arrived at a stunning overlook. Suddenly, the world glowed within a kaleidoscope of dancing purples and greens.

And like a moth to a flame, Vanessa became entranced by her first glimpse of the aurora. Her feet carried her closer to the shimmering lights.

I quietly took Ellie from Tom's arms. Together, she and I made snow angels in the freshly fallen snow. I remember Ellie giggling beside me as I looked up and watched Tom move into position behind Vanessa. He sighed, placed his hands on her shoulders, and gave her a push.

She vanished over the edge.

As soon as Tom, Ellie, and I made it back to the Mansion, Mom was awake. She asked where Vanessa had gone off to, and all it took was a look into my eyes to know exactly what had transpired.

"I'll take care of it," she said.

When you awoke, it was to find Vanessa and Ellie gone. They simply disappeared, and you feared the worst. Feared that Vanessa succeeded in stealing your daughter while you slept. When you made it to the Mansion to find Ellie untouched and Vanessa missing, you assumed it was my mother's fault, and she decided not to contradict you.

Laz, I know you loved Vanessa dearly. I know that, at one point, you couldn't live without her. But you need to understand that you never needed her. You are a great father, Lazalier Brady, and an even greater man.

You deserve nothing but the truth, Laz. Tom Clark and I killed Vanessa. And we did it for your family.

With love,
Me.

PS.

Before Dad died, he made me the warden of his estate. I have complete control over his will and his assets, and I plan to use this new title to atone for the sins of my family…

I have given four million dollars to the Laura-Jean Duntz Women's Facility in Juneau to assist in what I assume Adam Kelsey might have done with his life, had he chosen forgiveness over revenge.

I have paid all the funeral costs for poor Eldon Gamble and Evelyn Brooks, and have planned a visit to Evie's mother in Lubbock, Texas, so that we may grieve Evie together.

For you, Laz, I plan to cover all hospital fees associated with your injuries, and have allocated an additional eight million into an account for one Elizabeth Nicole Brady, should she ever need to take care of her father, just as he has so selflessly and courageously taken care of her.

27

IF YOU ARE READING THIS

I can barely breathe.

With each inhale, my lungs sear from within. I can feel the crusty blackness inside my chest, and now I fully realize the agony you have suffered since leaving your mother's womb. The oxygen mask sits snugly on my face, each hiss drawing ragged breath from my lips.

It's true what they say. Suffocation is the worst way to die.

"You're going to be all right," Tom Clark lies.

He sits beside my hospital bed, his hair singed, his handsome face streaked with small scars and healing burns.

I cannot speak. My vocal cords have been so terribly damaged. I squeeze his hand and I feel another golf ball in my throat. It has nothing to do with the smoke I have inhaled, and as a single hot tear rolls down my cheek, he squeezes my hand in return.

"You're going to be all right," he repeats, and I can hear the unstable crack in his voice. "You're going to get through this." Whether he says these things to reassure me or to reassure himself,

I'm not entirely certain.

I'm not mad at the contents of Sophie's letter. I'm not mad at Tom for what he did to Vanessa. Because even though Tom had always hated your mother, he didn't push her over that cliff in hatred. Tom and Sophie knew that your mother would have won full custody, and that the only way for me to have you was for your mother to just – well, to just disappear. I'm not mad at either of them for leaving you without a mother who would have never properly cared for you. A mother who, I'm certain of it, would have abandoned you again.

They did it for us.

For *you*, Ellie.

I turn my eyes to meet Tom's, and though I cannot speak, he knows what I am asking of him.

"I will," he says.

Tom Clark is my best friend, Ellie. If you are reading this, you will have grown up calling him Dad, or some variation of it. Or perhaps he will have insisted that you call him Tom all these years, that your real Dad is gone. Gone, but never forgotten. If I know Tom as well as I think I do, you will have grown up living the life every young girl, every young woman, deserves. He never wanted a child of his own, but perhaps that is why fate (or God, or whoever) led the two of us to become such great friends in college. Perhaps he was always destined to raise you the way I will never be able to.

So, please don't grieve for me, Ellie, because Tom Clark is more than a viable substitute for ol' Dad. In truth, Tom is one of only two great men I have ever met in my life.

The other is John Smitson.

That night, after I ran back into the Mansion to save the Dilbrooks from the burning wreckage, after I carried Don onto the back porch and pushed him into the snow, I collapsed. And as I choked on the smoke still roiling in my lungs, my eyes were fixed on the trees.

There, between two white aspens, stood Smitty.

But this time, his skin wasn't melted away, but firm and freshly shaven. His eyes weren't milky white, but that stark and piercing silvery blue that had earned him the nickname "Blueberries." His turnouts were cleanly pressed, not a streak of soot on the Kevlar. He had a buzz cut of slightly balding black hair, but now, there was no axe jutting from his skull. Instead, he held it against his shoulder, the blade sharp and gleaming in the light of the aurora. And when he smiled at me, he didn't leer like the ghost I had grown accustomed to. He just smiled that Smitty smile.

And then, he turned and disappeared into the ferns and brambles.

I never saw Smitty again after that.

I like to imagine he got what he was haunting me for. To remind me not to beat myself up. That accidents happen. That it is human nature to let fear for your own life keep you from saving another. And in saving Don Dilbrook, I suppose some part of me forgave myself for not being able to save Smitty.

Smitty haunted me to help me forget. To remind me to forgive myself. To encourage me to push on through the flames.

The same in death as he was in life.

I squeeze Tom's hand again, and as I glance over at him, I notice that his face is pressed into his other hand. His shoulders tremble, and I hear the faint sound of weeping through his palm.

He never intended any of this to happen. I know that. I want to tell him that it's okay. To let him know that he will never be able to move on with his life if he cannot learn to forgive himself for what has happened to me. But, as I am unable to speak, I know it is a lesson he will have to learn for himself. Perhaps I'll come to him in some ghostly form, my skin black and my eyes milky white.

Perhaps I'll haunt him until he learns to forgive himself.

In all he did, Tom Clark just wanted to help me out. He saw me struggling in my life, and he found an opportunity that seemed like it would get me back on my feet, an opportunity that would take my mind off all the things I'd lost. He genuinely wanted to help me, and so he introduced me to Sophie.

The funny thing is, even if Tom had never introduced us, I still would have eventually crossed paths with Sophie Dilbrook.

She planned it that way, after all.

As Sophie mentioned in her letter, she knew who I was long before we ever traded glances across the smoky bar in Anchorage. It took me a long while to understand what she meant by that confession.

The final secret came to light when I picked up the book she left behind and began flipping through the pages.

The Girl in the Snow tells the story of Dale Sanbrooke, a young and lazy Alaskan wildcatter who inherits two of his father's oil wells. At first, the wells are nothing but a nuisance. The deeper he drills, the drier the wells become. He wants desperately to fill the useless wells, move to Australia, and pursue a life that many young men born into wealthy families aspire to.

A life full of travel, a life full of adventure, and a life full of women.

One night, Sanbrooke finds himself in Ketchikan, in a last-ditch effort to confront his father and tell him that he plans to fill the wells. Sanbrooke's father beats him to a pulp, threatens to disown him, and demands he work the wells until they produce the richest oil in Alaska.

Bruised and bloody, Sanbrooke leaves his father's hillside chateau, buys a bottle of Alpine Lake (now renamed Malamute, thank you very much), and takes a walk along the docks of Ketchikan's Inner Passage.

A heavy snow begins to fall as he drunkenly stumbles along a ferry terminal, where he notices a woman perched on the railing of a high berth, her legs dangling over the edge. Forty feet below, deep black water froths and swirls. She looks on the verge of jumping, and Sanbrooke knows that if the plunge doesn't kill her, the freezing water will. As he approaches, the moon breaks through the clouds and illuminates the woman's face.

She is young, like him, and though he notices a wedding ring glinting on her left hand, he also notices cuts and bruises around her eyes, throat, and shoulders. He tries to talk her down from her suicidal perch, but it only prompts her to slide further off the edge of the railing.

And just as she is about to jump, she looks at Sanbrooke.

She notices his own cuts and bruises, and her face softens. In that moment, she realizes he needs her as much as she needs him. He reaches his hand out to her, she takes it, and she is about to climb back onto the berth when her shoe slips on the icy railing.

Almost ripped from a tacky Hollywood romance, Sanbrooke catches the woman's wrist at the last moment. He holds her as she dangles above the water, crying and screaming that she doesn't want to die, that it was all a mistake coming to the berth. Almost miraculously, Sanbrooke pulls the young woman over the railing and to safety. They slip in the snow and she falls against his chest.

And there, they share a look. A look that defines a man's path when he finally finds the right woman.

And though they indulge in a beautiful few weeks in Ketchikan together, tangled in hotel bedsheets and confessing their sins and hopes and dreams to one another, the young woman eventually goes back to her abusive husband, and Sanbrooke never sees her again.

Alone and heartbroken, he returns home to his two wells.

Upon his arrival, however, Sanbrooke discovers that finally, the wells are producing rich, black oil.

In all the books I've read in all my years, I've garnered a sort of respect for authors who can hold my attention from the first page until the very end. And while the tale that old Don Dilbrook penned was something of a novice masterpiece, I can understand why no publisher ever wanted it.

It was a cliché, and as I mentioned, it was a piece of fiction that was similar in scope and drama to the silver screen films of the time, but less effective.

After all, who in the lower 48 cares about a love story set in Alaska?

While I immensely enjoyed reading *The Girl in the Snow*, it wasn't the story itself, nor the protagonist, that had caught my attention. It was the character of the young woman, abused by her husband and on the verge of suicide. Had it not been for Dale Sanbrooke, she would have died on impact, or froze, or drowned to death. He'd saved her, loved her, and then lost her.

The woman's name, in particular, set a fire in my throat and a tingle in my belly.

Her name was Samantha Lassleer.

All of my friends growing up knew my mother simply as Mrs. Brady. As I mentioned before, my first name is my mother's maiden name. Before my father, my mother was Amanda Lazalier.

Samantha Lassleer.

Amanda Lazalier.

I swirl the two names on my tongue like two fine whiskeys. They are so strikingly similar, and though my voice box doesn't work, I can taste the nearly identical syllables, sharp and crisp in my mouth.

My name is a tough one to remember, and an even tougher one for the average Joe to spell out. And though Don Dilbrook was far from the average Joe, one could forgive a man for misspelling a surname as difficult as Lazalier.

In the book, Dale Sanbrooke and Samantha Lassleer meet in Ketchikan, the same town where I grew up. Sanbrooke notices bruises on Lassleer's body, and it was no secret to me or to any of our neighbors that my father liked to hit my mother. Sanbrooke saves Lassleer by pulling her back over the railing of an old shipping berth, and now that I think back on it, my mother loved to take me to the docks when I was a kid. She would sit me up on the railing and encourage me to wave at the wealthy Southies aboard their massive cruise ships coasting through the Inner Passage.

I've heard it said that authors write what they know. They use experiences from their lives as fodder for their fiction. They set their stories in towns, cities, and landscapes they are familiar with and are comfortable writing about. They base their characters off of people they've known for years, or strangers they've met only once.

Beautiful strangers who dangle their feet over black, roiling water.

And while "suicidal" is the last word I would ever use to describe my mother, who's to say there was never a time when my father beat her up so bad that she considered the only way out of her hopeless marriage and her battered life was to end it altogether?

I think back on Christmas Eve, when Sophie and I stood alone at Sam's Overlook. There had been a moment between us, the moment I grabbed her wrist, pulled her against me, and kissed her.

And then, she pushed me away.

At the time, I thought maybe she wasn't ready to move on from Tom just yet, or perhaps that she just didn't like me in that way. But as I lie here, I consider the possibility that Sophie pushed me away for an entirely different reason.

I lift my scorched hand and pull out her letter out from beneath my pillow. I scan the folded pages and find the sentence I am looking for:

I found Eldon Gamble in Fairbanks… I fed him the necessary breadcrumbs that led him back to Ukippa.

I scan further down and read snippets of Sophie's encounters with Adam Kelsey:

Adam discovered his true heritage on his own. How he found out about us remains a mystery, even to me.

And then:

I flirted, but he kept his distance. I couldn't understand why.

Suddenly, it clicks.

Sophie knew that Eldon Gamble was her father's son, and so, she guided him back home. What she didn't realize was that Adam Kelsey was also her half-brother. Adam, however, had discovered this truth on his own and kept it a secret until he could use it to collapse the Dilbrook family.

When Sophie tried to act on her feelings toward him, he pushed her away...

Just like she pushed me away.

I knew who you were long before we met in that pub in Anchorage.

I believe Sophie Dilbrook read *The Girl in the Snow*, understood the reality interlaced in the fiction, tracked down the real-life Samantha Lassleer, and then found me. She researched my life. Learned about the problems in my marriage. Threw herself into Tom Clark's life as a means to interact with me. Deliberately sat herself across the bar from me in Anchors and recognized the similarities in my face.

The same similarities I saw in Don Dilbrook's face. The same similarities I noticed in the pictures of Adam Kelsey and Sam Dilbrook.

Behind the viridian door, a weary Don Dilbrook mistakenly called me *Sam*.

I am left on my deathbed with a sudden shock to my identity –

I am the third illegitimate son of Don Dilbrook.

***

I have three final visitors today, and all are visitors I wasn't expecting.

My first visitor is all shoulders and shadows.

Moose sits at the foot of my bed with a sad smile behind his burly beard. He doesn't say anything. He just watches me type away behind this old laptop. I am nearly finished writing our story, and when I am done, I will type him a note, telling him to keep these pages hidden away, until such a time when he thinks you are old enough to read them.

And if, by chance, I survive my surgery tomorrow, I will burn these pages and tell you the story myself.

My second visitor snoozes at Moose's feet. And though they don't normally allow dogs in this particular hospital in Allakaket, they have given Moose permission to let me see Harvey. To let me feel his tongue on my hand. To let me look into his honey-brown eyes. I think the nurses and doctors know what I know, that to survive my surgery will be nothing short of a miracle. I think they know my candle is reaching the end of its wick. Harvey is well-behaved enough to come into my ward and offer me a last goodbye.

Whatever has happened to his Shack, I know Moose will take good care of my pup, and I know he will take good care of this manuscript.

My third visitor stands in the corner beside the window.

Her cheeks, lips, and eyebrows are black. Her long salt-and-pepper hair is singed. Her eyes are wide open, and they are milky white. And as she stares at me, she offers me an eerie grin.

Apparently, I've traded in ol' Smitty for a newer ghost. And while I'm still not entirely certain how I feel about Gloria Dilbrook, it appears that, if nothing else, I feel responsible for what has happened to her.

Oh, well.

If all doesn't go to plan, I will be joining her soon enough.

***

They are about to take me into surgery.

The plan is to replace my lungs with a donor pair. It's a risky operation, they tell me, but it's the only way I can hope to come out of this.

I have never been more scared in my life.

I'm not afraid of being put to sleep, but I *am* afraid I will never wake up. I am afraid of the after, if there is one. I am afraid of never being able to see your face again.

But more than anything, I am afraid of what you will think of me when you are older. When you are able to make your own decisions about people. When you are able to properly judge who I was as a man, and as a father.

I have spent the past two weeks in this hospital bed, feverishly typing this manuscript on Tom's laptop to tell you exactly what happened in those three houses on that lonely hill.

I only ever wanted to do right by you, El.

I only ever wanted to help you understand.

I can only pray that I have been successful.

And if you are reading this, I didn't make it.

I love you, Ellie. I will always love you. And Heaven or not, I will wait for you on the other side.

Love always,

Dad.

ABOUT THE AUTHOR

Nicholas Holloway is a mystery author based in Texas. An avid traveler and nature enthusiast, Nick garners a love of dynamic landscapes and believes a story's terrain is just as important as its characters. Holloway's debut novel, *The Loop*, won the 2020 Book Excellence Award for Suspense Fiction. He is currently writing the sequel, *That Which Was Golden*.

He lives in Austin with his wife, Nichole, and their dog, Harvey.

THREE HOUSES ON A HILL

NICHOLAS HOLLOWAY

CPSIA information can be obtained
at www.ICGtesting.com
Printed in the USA
LVHW030010240421
685383LV00003B/707

9 781733 229173